CW00862746

The GOLDILOCKS VENTURE

HÉLÈNE HANNAN

ARCHWAY
PUBLISHING

Copyright © 2019 Hélène Hannan.

All rights reserved. No part of this book may be used or reproduced by any means, graphic, electronic, or mechanical, including photocopying, recording, taping or by any information storage retrieval system without the written permission of the author except in the case of brief quotations embodied in critical articles and reviews.

This is a work of fiction. All of the characters, names, incidents, organizations, and dialogue in this novel are either the products of the author's imagination or are used fictitiously.

Archway Publishing books may be ordered through booksellers or by contacting:

Archway Publishing
1663 Liberty Drive
Bloomington, IN 47403
www.archwaypublishing.com
1 (888) 242-5904

Because of the dynamic nature of the Internet, any web addresses or links contained in this book may have changed since publication and may no longer be valid. The views expressed in this work are solely those of the author and do not necessarily reflect the views of the publisher, and the publisher hereby disclaims any responsibility for them.

Any people depicted in stock imagery provided by Getty Images are models, and such images are being used for illustrative purposes only. Certain stock imagery © Getty Images.

Scripture taken from the King James Version of the Bible.

ISBN: 978-1-4808-8244-7 (sc)
ISBN: 978-1-4808-8243-0 (hc)
ISBN: 978-1-4808-8245-4 (e)

Library of Congress Control Number: 2019915795

Print information available on the last page.

Archway Publishing rev. date: 10/31/2019

Words of Appreciation

I would like to thank the space agencies of the United States, Canada, France and India for their mission, resources and the wonder they instill. I thank my sister Nancy Hannan for her support and "Friendship" poem used in Bella's song. I would also like to thank my sons and stepson for their inspiration and my stepdaughter Clara Magner for her assistance with proofreading. I would especially like to thank my husband Mike Magner, a member of the U.S. Army Medical Corps, for his assistance in editing the science portions and his steadfast encouragement.

Dedication

I dedicate this book to the brave members of the American and Canadian armed services.

List of Athena Crew Members

2am – 2pm EST

1. Microbiologist and Captain – CAMILLE TREMBLAY, Canadian army captain medical corps, French-speaker
    Hobbies: Chess, running, yoga, martial arts

2pm – 2am EST

2. Medical doctor and psychiatrist – AVA CAMPBELL, Canadian-west coast
    Hobby: Knitting/crochet, missionary work

Night Crew 8am-8pm EST

3. Pilot and mechanic – EMMA KELLY, U.S. air force
    Hobbies: Electric guitar, martial arts champion

4. Nuclear fusion engine and external systems engineer – ZOË DIMITROPOULOS, chief engineer
    Hobby: Darts

5. Computer Systems and videographer – LILIAN JONES
    Hobbies: Video games, electronic sounds for music

6. Astrophysicist –HELEN "AURORA" YAZZIE, Native American from Alaska
    Hobby: Drums

7. Animal biologist – HARPER ANDERSON, Mid-western.
   Hobbies: Shooting and other outdoor activities, wrestling

8. Biochemist and herbalist – VIVIAN LI, understands Chinese
   Hobbies: Flute, reading

Day Crew 8pm-8am EST

9. Solar specialist – LUCY KARLSSON, Peace Corps
   Hobby: Piano keyboard

10. Life Support engineer – RIYA PATEL
    Hobby: Card games

11. Botanist – ISABELLA "BELLA" GARCIA
    Hobbies: Classical guitar, songwriting

12. Marine scientist, meteorologist and communications expert – ARLA JOHNSON, U.S. Navy, second in command
    Hobbies: Drawing, martial artist

13. Geologist – KIARA WILLIAMS, Southerner
    Hobbies: Painting, hairdressing

14. Soil specialist and waste management expert – EVELYN MILLER
    Hobby: Clay art

Contents

Prologue

I am aware that there are many stories out there about us, the fourteen women who travelled to outer space on their own. Maybe we are even legendary. Most of the stories are unbelievable, and some are also untrue. I want to set the record straight. Therefore, I'm writing this account of our unique adventures. I hope my readers have the desire and patience to learn the truth from someone who was there from the beginning. I am Camille Tremblay, Astronaut from Quebec, and this is our story of lasting friendships and discoveries.

Part I — Journey to Ross

one

It's Time

"Can't believe today's the day!" says Arla, my closest colleague during our training. We had an instant affinity, maybe because we are the same age and both former military.

"I know and it's almost time!" I answer excitedly in a French Quebec accent.

"Tempting to stay here."

"Do not back out on me now," I say, knowing she wouldn't. Because of her leadership training, I had chosen her to be my second and would be very disappointed if she didn't go.

"That's not what I meant. It's too awesome an opportunity."

"For sure, it can change life as we know it."

I can see the portentous NASA minibus arriving as planned, at noon, in the sandy parking lot of Cocoa Beach, Florida. We, the fourteen female astronauts, have been staying here the past year. Our anxious extended families have visited intermittently, and most are here for our last day before launch.

Gazing out over the vast ocean, I take in the beauty of the picturesque cotton ball clouds hanging above the glistening ocean water, an impressionist's dream of turquoise blue by the shore with streaks of the darkest blue and navy blue at the horizon. A few fast-moving sailboats and wind surfers quicken by, leaving white streaks, like comets, behind them. I feel the gentle wind and note, high above, thin wispy clouds—perfect for our flight.

Arla and I decide to take a last plunge in the waves. I dip my feet in the soft, wet sand and admire the cheerful sound of the undulating waters. We can't resist running in with our boogie boards. We thoroughly enjoy the warm saltwater all over our athletic bodies. We stand up and feel the pounding force of the crashing waves in front of us as it pushes our tumbling bodies. For fun, we turn around, catch a wave and race to shore on our boards, not caring that we are now covered in sand. We laugh.

Arla declares, "I win." Then, she sighs. "I love the oceans, everything about them."

"This is fun. You are right, it is hard to leave all this, especially them," I say, nodding toward our families on the beach.

"I guess we need to hurry though."

"Yes, we better."

We jog onto the private beach to join the others. The astronauts and families have been enjoying the morning, sunbathing. A few young nieces and nephews are building sandcastles, and other children are burying new friends in the sand. Teenagers are flirting and sharing secrets or playing volleyball. My father, and other parents, siblings, and spouses, are sitting and chatting under colorful umbrellas in comfortable beach chairs. Many are well acquainted with each other and trying not to talk about their very real concerns.

Then, I have this brief thought that I may never be here again; never feel the soft, wet, wonderful sand; never see the tall, pretty palm trees and bold greenery; never smell the tangy salt air; never hear the loud, sharp cries of the seagulls. I walk to my dear, patient father who is standing on the beach. I look him tenderly in the eyes, not knowing what to say while taking in a deep breath with sniffles and watery eyes. I hug him and whisper in French, "I love you, Dad."

Sensing my sadness, he responds in French, "Love you always and see you here in two years," and in English, "Same bat time, same bat channel."

Remembering the childish Batman shows he had me watch as a kid, I smile back and embarrassingly say in English, "You are so corny."

"It's time!" I yell. I know time for our relaxing visit is up for my thirteen colleagues who are pre occupied with their families on the beach. I signal by waving my hand that we need to go. The astronauts know they must leave and put on their beach covers. I dry myself and comb out my long, straight, dark-brown hair, which I tie into its usual French braid. I bronze easily and have a nice Malibu tan from our too few sojourns at this beach.

The astronauts hug their families tightly, uttering sometimes tearful goodbyes for at least thirty minutes. I don't want to intrude on these final face-to-face conversations. Some parents give their daughters their final bits of advice. A few siblings plead to their sisters for them not to go. One young niece asks for a pet alien. All hug each other tightly. Finally, family members offer to help us with our beach items.

Arla, a former navy officer, and her newlywed husband are in a tight embrace. They start French kissing and stroking each other's attractive bodies. In a couple minutes, it's obvious he's all go. Arla suddenly realizes there are children around—she stops cold. She tries re-assuring her husband saying, "This will be great for our future— just a couple years and we're set for life."

The minibus fretfully honks its loud horn, signaling that it really is time to go. I walk slowly with the thirteen to the minibus, where I press a code and the doors open. I see their sadness at leaving their families. To encourage them, and myself, I announce, "This is the most exciting day of our lives!"

"I know," says one astronaut despondently.

Another murmurs something inaudibly.

After Arla confirms that all astronauts are assembled by the door, she says half-heartedly, "Yes ma'am, we're ready."

After years of preparation, the U.S. and Canada are now on the verge of launching a historic space mission—today! Our youngest astronaut, Emma, a bold red head, gets in first and sits in the front driver's seat. The minibus is driverless, though Emma watches, ready to override any errors. As the astronauts travel to the Cape Canaveral Space Center, numerous reporters and private citizens drive by taking pictures. Other Americans honk their horns, wave, and blow kisses. The more gregarious astronauts happily indulge them by returning waves and kisses.

"This is going to be awesome!" exclaims Emma.

"Yep," agrees another.

two

Preparation

I sit in the front of the minibus and think about the upcoming voyage and what we did to get here. We are part of the "Goldilocks Voyage" project, a joint U.S.-Canada space mission to Ross 128 b, a Goldilocks planet eleven light-years away. After significant scientific discoveries, the project was initiated and carefully planned about ten years ago. Harp's spectrometry had found Ross 128 b, a rocky exoplanet, in orbit around an eight-billion-year-old class M4 star, Ross 128. This red dwarf was found to be stable, emitting very few violent solar flares. Ross 128 b was calculated to be thirty-five percent more massive than Earth with a corresponding higher gravity. It was also expected to be cooler, on average, though receiving more sunlight than Earth. Just over fifteen years ago, the newly launched infrared *James Webb Space Telescope* provided direct imaging with strong indications of a significant atmosphere on Ross 128 b. Improved spectrometry indicated that earthlings could quite possibly breathe the exoplanet's atmosphere and that abundant water was present. In addition, other physicists used quantum metrology and string theory to find a small traversable wormhole near the Kuiper Belt. They were convinced that the wormhole linked to a location near Ross 128 b. NASA and the Canadian Space Agency received approval to develop a space mission to prove these theories and to develop sustainable environments in space.

They planned a unique aspect to this project. For political and practical reasons, it was decided that the mission would have an all-female crew. Activists had staged numerous protest marches against NASA, alleging it favored male astronauts—all too obvious from the one token female astronaut consistently on its roster. It also made practical sense to include only women because women are generally smaller, needing less space and food. An average man needs two thousand five hundred calories a day to maintain his weight, whereas an average woman only needs two thousand calories a day. It was also argued that a single gender crew eliminated complications due to pregnancy. In my opinion, most women were easier to manage and cooperate better. Therefore, two years ago, the space agencies commenced a search to find ethnically or politically representative, willing, and qualified female scientists and engineers in top physical health.

Several events in my personal life led to my applying to the project. At age twenty-nine, I was contemplating changes to my life. I had just ended yet another disappointing relationship. He was a hockey player. I had even taken up massage to impress him. He then decided one woman wasn't enough and obnoxiously proceeded to blatantly fraternize with other, younger, wilder women. I was unwilling to share my body with whatever diseases he'd bring home, and terminated the relationship. I couldn't understand what was wrong with men. I had a friendly, pretty face and a slender, yet curvy, figure. I was successful in my career and had no weird habits or addictions. However, no romance ever seemed to work out. I adamantly decided to forgo romantic relationships altogether, loosening my ties to Earth.

Moreover, I was nearing the end of my mandatory army service. When I learned of the NASA search, I wondered, why not apply to the NASA astronaut job posting? I knew that I would miss my army "family", but I was looking at other options. This posting was the most intriguing. I fulfilled the minimum requirements. I had assiduously achieved the rank of Captain in the Royal Canadian Army Medical Corps and had earned a doctorate in epidemiology. I had always wanted to help others. I had joined the medical corps because I knew that diseases killed more soldiers than bullets; I had seen the application of epidemiology as a way of being of service to my country. The NASA posting prompted my interest in finding an accessible habitable world for human settlement and desire to be of service to our entire overcrowded planet.

For the space agency application, I designed a few experiments to study how microbes multiply and infect organisms in space in order to prevent harmful infections and maintain healthy bacteria. I filled out the mounds of paperwork—résumé, references, psychological tests, criminal report, proof of health, credit rating, and identification papers. I didn't mind as I had extra time and it stopped me from moping.

I called my dad for help and said in French, "Hi, Dad. I have a question."

"Hello. What is it?"

"Where was Mom born?" My mother had died almost twenty years ago. Even though I couldn't imagine why this question was relevant, I needed to answer it.

"Why do you want to know?"

"I'm filling out forms," I explained vaguely. I didn't want him to try to dissuade me from applying.

Dad struggled to recall, but finally, it came to him. "Windsor, Quebec."

"Thanks, Dad."

I considered the opportunity a longshot and scoffed to myself as I submitted the voluminous application. Then, several silent months later, I received an unexpected online interview. After hours of questioning, not only was I chosen to go, I was chosen as team leader for the mission due to the leadership skills I had developed while in the army. I jumped for joy. This was amazing! I could hardly believe it. Politics may have played a part in my selection too. Though fluent in English and educated at McGill University, I was born in Quebec and served as the representative French *québécoise*. This may have been to appease the people; I thanked politicians for calling for yet another vote for Quebec separation.

I was giddy. I had to call my dad to tell him the exciting news. I said (in French), "Hi, Dad. Guess what?"

"Hi, sweetie. Guess what about what?" he asked (in French).

"I made it!"

"Made what?"

"I was accepted to the space program as an astronaut!"

"Ha, ha. What?"

"Really!" I applied, "and I'm even going to lead the next main mission."

"Seriously?"

"Yes! It's a dream, huh?"

"It's astounding."

"I'll be in space for two whole years."

"Oh, that's a long time."

"We're going to another star system through a wormhole!"

"That far out?"

"It's so cool! We might find an inhabitable planet! Humans would have room to expand. This could be the answer we've all been hoping for. We can go now with an experimental superfast fusion engine."

"Seems dangerous." Then he asked a lot of questions, mostly regarding safety precautions.

"We'll be fine. If we find life on another planet, what do you think it'd be like?"

"Hopefully kinder and fairer than here." Then he voiced his socialist opinion on economic policies that favor the elite class. I respectfully, but barely, listened, knowing there was no point interrupting, until he concluded with, "They're only getting greedier and more corrupt. Tonight, I'm meeting with the party on a vote to even out the playing field."

"Right. Good for you, Dad. I'll need to close down my apartment and move my good furniture and stuff to your garage. I'll give you access to my bank account. Can you take care of my car?"

"Yes, of course I will. I'll miss you, kiddo."

"I'll miss you too, Dad. I love you. Bye. Got lots to do. I need to go to Saint-Hubert in a month."

"See you soon."

"Yes, this Sunday."

The following month, I arrived at the Centre Spatial John-H.-Chapman, in Saint-Hubert, Quebec. I soon learned that another Canadian was also selected for the journey. I first met Dr. Ava Campbell at the Canadian Space Agency. Ava, an attractive blonde in her mid-thirties, was a general practitioner and psychiatrist from British Columbia. She had a pleasant demeanor and I instantly knew we'd be friends. She told me that she and her husband had done missionary medical work for the Presbyterian Church in Cameroon, where he was killed by robbers. I assumed she was looking for a change too. We started our in-depth training together. For two months, we studied emotional and medical concerns unique to space travel. These included the importance of constant activity, muscular dystrophy and the need for weight-bearing exercise, prevention of decompression, and exposure to radiation.

After the two months, Ava and I traveled together to Cape Canaveral to meet the others and to begin our year-long astronaut training. We met Dr. Zoë Dimitropoulos, Lucy Karlsson, MSE, and Riya Patel, MSE, who had been NASA engineers for several years and were selected for the mission. The most experienced, Zoë, was named chief engineer. At almost forty, she was our oldest trainee. She was familiar with just about every aspect of the structure of the ship. Zoë was strict, no nonsense; she looked like a stereotypical drill sergeant, though she hadn't served.

The engineers discussed every aspect of the ship's design with the astronauts-in-training. Zoë started at 0700 hours, and you didn't dare come in late. During an introductory presentation, she provided us with her background and life's work. She lectured, "While working on my postgraduate degree in nuclear science and engineering at MIT and for years at NASA, I'm proud to have helped design and build most of the main engine and exterior structure. The spacecraft, named the *Athena,* is the first of its kind. It was built in pieces while in orbit and looks like a huge bicycle wheel." She showed us photos of the construction. While switching slides, she continued, "The main living and working sections are in the narrow four hundred fifty-meter diameter ring. This ring rotates around a central tube to simulate gravity by centrifugal force. The *Athena* is designed to remain in low orbit around Ross 128 b. We will send down a three-person reusable shuttle for surface explorations. To prevent descent from orbit, there are rocket-powered boosters with highly flammable fuel storage containers under the ring. As a temporary and emergency energy source, solar arrays were installed throughout the top side of the ring. Twelve long spokes connect the ring to a central tube. The widest spoke contains a passageway from the bridge of the ring to the center of the tube."

Zoë's eyes lit up most when she discussed this central tube and the engine. She continued, "At the lower end of the round stationary tube, which is about the size of a single-wide trailer home, is a slightly smaller cylinder attached with a ball joint, much like a shoulder joint. Inside the smaller cylinder is a prototype fusion reactor, theoretically capable of generating power to push the engine at speeds over eighty-eight million kilometers per hour. In theory, in less than two hours, we could reach the Sun. Unfortunately, at this theoretical speed, if we hit even a tiny speck of dust, the *Athena* would break apart from the impact. We'll be travelling a fraction of that speed. At NASA, we nicknamed this powerful reactor cylinder 'Superman'. At the other end of the central tube is a clear glass dome about seven meters in diameter, nicknamed the 'Bubble'. The Bubble was designed for stationary space observations. In the entire central tube, we'd be weightless." After this summary introduction, she discussed the fusion reactor in much greater detail.

After a short break, Zoë summarized the assistance provided by other nations. "Due to its size and complexity, the Goldilocks Project was actually a huge multi-national endeavor. Superman was developed with the advice and assistance of the Chinese and the Russians. They're both advanced in the development of fusion reactors, but the U.S. was the first to assemble a working model for space travel. Competition in this area has been fierce, vicious at times. Though relations with China and Russia are usually strained with trade wars and armament debates, the Chinese and Russians were willing to provide a modicum of financial assistance and advice. The Chinese even flew a few nuclear engineers to space to work on the reactor. In return for their assistance, we shared our know-how with them hoping to improve relations. Personally, I don't find that their technical assistance was necessary."

Finally, she concluded this presentation on the assistance provided by other nations. "Other nations helped immensely with the expenses and sophisticated technologies. NASA's partner, the Canadian Space Agency, provided medical technologies, safety protocols and equipment, a weather tracking satellite, a probe, the small-space garden with supplies, and much needed funding. Our ally France built the Bubble observatory, including its far infrared and sub-millimeter telescopes and other detection equipment. France and India designed, built and tested the *Athena*'s shuttle, named the *Chidiya*, which means 'bird' in Hindi. It is designed to travel back and forth from a spacecraft to any planetary body. The *Chidiya* is also designed for amphibious use because the surface of Ross 128 b is likely covered with water. The Japanese designed and provided the compact living space and long-term life-support systems. The U.S. shares technology and research with these countries too. In addition to national governments, private companies contributed computers, food and other products in exchange for publicity. All tremendously helpful and needed to reduce the enormous cost and pacify public objections. I'm now open to questions." We asked many. Though Zoë seemed gruff at first, I grew to appreciate her true passion for the *Athena*.

This was the start of our training. The other NASA engineers also presented topics. The second NASA engineer, Lucy, specialized in electrical engineering and, particularly, solar panels for the emergency back-up power system. The opposite of Zoë, Lucy was gentle and personable; she had served in the Peace Corps, developing solar power for remote communities. She had a constant smile and always seemed concerned about our well-being. However, I didn't understand much of her technical jargon.

The third NASA engineer, Riya Patel, helped design the life support systems. To outshine her fellow engineers, she had the most colorful presentations and was a livelier, more understandable, presenter. She stressed the essential need to provide air, food and water. She had us simulate monitoring atmospheric pressure, oxygen levels, waste management, and water supply; troubleshooting life-threatening issues; and suppressing potential fires.

Early in our training, the other astronauts-in-training introduced themselves and described their areas of expertise. First to follow the NASA engineers was trainee, Lilian Jones, MCS, a lively IT expert. She explained the computer and video systems. She could reprogram navigation if necessary. She showed us how we could access nearly countless research papers and, for entertainment, read novels or watch videos.

After her, First Lieutenant Emma Kelly, BSE described her positive experiences as a U.S. Air Force mechanic and test pilot. She expertly explained ascent and descent procedures and showed us how to manipulate the thrusters and our shuttle in a simulator. She would remain an officer while on the voyage, as the Air Force, which also provided funding, was keenly interested in this project's aviation technology.

After the engineers, the crew's scientists described their projects and the ways we could all assist in their experiments.

The first scientist to present was astrophysicist, Dr. Helen "Aurora" Yazzie, a Native American from Alaska, who first became interested in astronomy while studying the *aurora borealis*. She appeared shy and was barely audible, while she explained that she would chart our course and conduct astronomical studies. She seemed brilliant but scattered. As team leader, I was informed of Aurora's disability, an inattentive-type attention deficit disorder resembling a mild autism. To accommodate her, Lilian was tasked with assisting Aurora in organizing her reports to NASA.

The second scientist to present was an accomplished and extroverted botanist, Dr. Isabella "Bella" Garcia, who would oversee our sustainability studies on vegetarian food production in space. She described her project to grow a vast number of edible plants.

The third scientist was former U.S. Navy Lieutenant Dr. Arla Johnson, tasked to study the exoplanet's watery surface and weather patterns. She had studied marine science and meteorology and made professional presentations in these areas. Because she was familiar with our communications equipment, she also explained the radio and our hand-held communication devices.

The fourth scientist was congenial geologist Dr. Kiara Williams, a Black Southerner, who would be studying the rocky features of the exoplanet. She presented briefly on the theoretical composition of its crust and core. She spoke in a pleasant Southern accent and wore noticeable amount of make-up and flowery perfume. I wondered about her science skills and suspected that she was chosen for her diversity.

The fifth scientist was calm biochemist Dr. Vivian Li, who would be testing for organic compounds. She also minored in eastern studies and was familiar with Asian medicines. In additional to her impressive biochemistry experiments, she explained her interest in medicinal plants and her project to grow them in space.

The sixth scientist was soil specialist Dr. Evelyn Miller, who described her sustainability studies including plans to study the viability of worms in space for gardening and waste management. She was the most light-hearted of the presenters, adding silly cartoons to her presentations.

The seventh scientist was our medical doctor, Ava Campbell, MD, responsible for our overall physical and emotional health. She discussed medical concerns in space and met privately with each of us. She explained health issues due to zero gravity, even differences in brain scans.

The eighth scientist was animal biologist Harper Anderson, MS, a tomboy with a pronounced Minnesota accent, who would oversee space studies on animal husbandry with rabbits, chickens and honeybees. She was an understudy, as the first choice could not handle the flight simulations without getting nauseated.

Lastly, I, Captain Camille Tremblay, presented my fascinating microbiology experiments and taught first aid. As team leader, I liaised with the space agencies and coordinated daily schedules.

After our initial presentations, we went to other lecture-type training every morning, had a quick, nutritious lunch, and afterwards practiced weightlessness and many other simulations until evening. Our year of training to prepare for this space voyage was intensive and exhaustive. Hence, now, I feel ready.

three

Blast off

I stop reminiscing as we approach the back gate to Cape Canaveral. There are numerous reporters and photographers. We oblige them with waves and a few prepared statements. The photogenic Emma and comical Evelyn enjoy posing for the cameras, briefly. We need to move quickly to prepare for our flight from the ground to the *Athena*.

We are greeted by the impatient NASA commander, who announces, "Welcome ladies, glad you managed to get here in the nick of time."

I start, "Sir, I apologize—"

"OK, first do any of you still need any help getting your affairs in order, just as a precaution?" The astronauts shake their heads.

"Good," he says, "You know the risks." We had been well-informed that there are many life-threatening dangers inherent in this mission: Explosive fuels, airless space, radiation, technological failures, to name a few. "You have a half hour to disinfect and put on your g-force suits. You know where the locker room is."

"Yessir," I say. To my crew, I say, "Not much time. Let's go."

We rush to the showers and scurry to get ready. There are seven showers and seven sinks. While half of us brush our teeth, the other half shower. Quickly the locker room becomes warm and misty. We are provided with brand-new sterile toothbrushes and antiseptic mouthwash. At the farthest sink is Evelyn, who is the tallest of the astronauts, exaggerating each step of mouth-cleaning in jest. She is lanky, awkwardly tall like a growing teenage boy, with oversized feet and a plain, but ever smiling, face. Her mousy, shoulder-length, khaki hair had likely been styled once but has now grown out like weeds and is constantly disheveled.

Next to Evelyn is Emma. Though Emma is just two centimeters shorter, she is Evelyn's opposite. Emma is strikingly beautiful, looks like model, and is the cameraman's favorite. She has short, well-cropped auburn hair with shiny carrot highlights and curls. She's wearing a skimpy bikini. I see her body is freckled and has a few small tattoos of planes she has piloted or repaired. She is athletic but round in the right places and walks with an air of confidence.

Next to Emma are me and Arla. We could almost be body doubles, same body type as Emma, though not as tall, and our features not as striking. Arla has a standing dolphin tattoo on her calf, and under it, a ring of coral resembling an anklet.

Next are the other three, shorter triplets, the voluptuous, pretty, and friendly Bella, Lucy and Kiara. Perky Bella has full-bodied wavy black hair and tanned skin. She has a colorful 1960's style peace sign tattoo on her lower back. Lucy has very pale pink skin and blond hair. At the beach, she wore a big white sunhat, long sleeve shirt and long skirt because she gets bad sunburns. Kiara has long curly black hair and perfectly manicured finger and toenails.

After we finish brushing and scrubbing our hands, we wait for the showers. We will need to soap our bodies for at least five minutes with antimicrobial soap and shampoo our hair. "All y'all, I have my favorite magnolia blossom conditioner and moonflower perfume—plenty to share," offers Kiara.

"Give me some conditioner!" shouts Riya from a shower.

"Thanks, NASA doesn't understand long hair," sighs Arla.

"Yah thanks, I would need a half hour just to comb out my hair," shouts Harper.

"Love this moonflower," says Bella.

"I can't wait to shower to get all this sand off me," I sigh, and then shout to the ladies in the showers, "Are you almost done in there?"

After a few minutes, Lilian and Vivian step out first. They are both of average height and twiggy, with perfectly straight, colorful, bob styled hair. The next ladies out of the showers are the muscular, square and olive-skinned Zoë, with short peppery black hair, and the muscular, curvy and comely Harper, with her long, wavy, light-brown hair. I envy her curvy hair because mine is bland—fine and straight. Zoë shows off the large, unique, triangle-shaped tattoo across the back of her shoulders with its apex at the small of her back. It consists of interwoven physics and engineering symbols. Next out of the showers are Ava and plainer, round-faced Aurora, both in their mid-thirties, soft-spoken and of average size and height. Aurora combs and braids her hip-length black hair as the last of the initial seven, the attractive tiny dark-skinned Riya, comes out of the shower.

"You're last Riya," I complain.

"It takes time to properly wash my long hair."

"Mine too."

The groups of seven hurriedly switch from brushing teeth to showering and vice versa. After our showers, we put on comfortable, disinfected undergarments and the orange g-force suits. Exactly one-half hour after we entered the locker room, a female NASA employee comes in to label our personal clothes for our families and to move us quickly to the next phase.

We step out of the locker room and pass by the deep training pool. We see two astronauts in space suits submerged and training as we did. We watch briefly as they tether their support lines. Now, there is a simple model satellite in the pool. One astronaut begins using a pistol-grip hand drill and the other a power saw as they learn to work together making mock repairs. We wave as we walk past them, picking up our pace as we hasten toward NASA's medical center.

We prepare for the final loading process. The NASA medical team and Ava make their final checks, and all the crew members check out fine. They attach heart and other monitors to us —in case of heart attack. A NASA physician injects us with nanobots that spread throughout our bodies to allow NASA and Ava to monitor vital signs. He also takes a DNA sample for body part recognition—not a comforting thought. The crew members eye each other nervously and take a deep breath.

After this ordeal is done, we take a slow transport outside toward the massive rocket. We are greeted by a cheering crowd. We smile and wave again. The excitement mounts. It seems surreal.

We start to board. Our few pre-selected personal clothes and one personal hobby have been disinfected and are already loaded. I chose to bring a chess set. The animals for the experiments—four sedated bunnies, incubated chicken eggs, a thirty-centimeter cube containing a honeybee hive, and a similar-looking box of worms— are loaded and secured. One by one, we leave the shuttle and take a small elevator up the highly flammable, methane-fueled, French-built Ariane III rocket launcher to its capsule.

We hear an announcement, "All guests stay back from the rocket. You must be behind the yellow lines."

Harper comments, "Yah, but we'll be strapped to that."

"Any stray spark could set it off," adds Lucy.

"Last chance to back down," quips Evelyn.

"What, and miss all the fun?" I say.

I take the lead, open the hatch, and enter the capsule first. Everyone piles in, with a self-assured Emma at the main flight controls. A NASA specialist follows us, makes sure we are all fastened properly, and then ominously shuts the hatch.

Locked in the hatch, we sit anxiously for the last fifteen minutes to lift-off. All specialists quickly clear the site and give their OK. It is a long few minutes as we listen quietly for all final reports to come in. Finally, we receive the "All systems go."

Perspiring, Lucy stammers, "This is really it!"

"You OK?" asks Ava.

"I guess so. Maybe. No. My mouth feels so dry."

"Your life signs look fine—just a bit short of breath. You nervous?"

"Definitely."

Bella adds, "Me too. Seems to be taking forever."

Evelyn blurts, "I know!"

Then NASA announces, "Three minutes to launch. All systems go."

I suggest, "Everyone take several deep breaths."

All breathe deeply. Evelyn, who is sitting beside me, takes exaggerated breaths. After a few, she breathes out in my face. She laughs and asks, "How long before I get dizzy doing this?"

I smile and shake my head.

NASA announces, "Two minutes to launch. All systems go."

Evelyn quips, "Any last requests?"

Emma replies, "How about an order of hot Mexican tacos?"

"With extra sauce," adds Kiara.

Arla radios, "NASA, we'd like a double order of tacos with extra sauce."

"Not funny," grunts Zoë.

NASA radios, "What was that?"

Arla radios, "Nothing, Out."

"Copy."

"Double check your seat belts," I suggest. We perform last minute checks.

"One minute to launch. All systems go."

Emma shouts, "Yo, let's go!"

We are all equally excited as we listen to the radio messages until the final count-down, the "10-9-8-7-6-5-4-3-2-1." We blast off in a deafening roar and soon feel the intense g-forces. In less than a minute, the g-forces subside as we enter the cold vast vacuum of space.

four

Welcome to the *Athena*

In a few minutes, the floating capsule docks securely on the side of the ring. I unlock the hatch and meet the latest of the teams of technicians and scientists. Teams have been inside readying the *Athena* in three-month shifts for the past several years. We grab our personal items and step up onto a three-meter wide corridor. The technicians assist us and carry in the animal cases. New to weightlessness, we find it hard to maneuver, even with the assistance of the experienced crew. The area becomes snug with all of us. We see the long bridge, open to the engineering or control room, both containing computers and instruments. The ceiling, barely above our heads, has lights and instruments hanging from it. The area is dimly lit with dull gray floors, reflective white walls and various lights, some blinking and flashing. It looks functional but the metal seems hard and cold.

"The bridge is remarkable," says Zoë.

"For sure," agrees Riya.

"It seems so narrow, enclosed," sighs Harper.

"I had pictured something more spacious, too, like a cruise ship, but looks more like a submarine," I whisper to Arla.

"Not exactly," Arla whispers back.

Taking unusually large steps down the corridor, Evelyn says, "This is fun."

Doing the same, Bella says, "I can fly." She and Evelyn laugh.

Then Evelyn bumps her head on an instrument. "Ow! That hurt."

"Careful, hold on to something," advises a tall scientist, "I still do that a lot."

"Me too," says another.

We are so absorbed with the new place and sensation of weightlessness that we forget to introduce ourselves. Their genteel leader holds out his hand, "Welcome aboard ladies. I'm Dr. Bradley Meyers. Are we glad to see you!"

I shake his hand saying, "Thank you, Dr. Meyers. I'm Dr. Camille Tremblay. Please call me Camille. And this is my crew. May I introduce Dr. Arla Johnson, my second in command, and Dr. Zoë Dimitropoulos, our chief engineer?"

"Call me Arla."

"Yes, though I've met Zoë, Lucy, and Riya," answers Meyers.

The new female and departing male crew introduce themselves and shake hands.

Meyers offers, "Let me show you around before we descend. These three technicians and I will act as your guides. We have a few more hours before we go. It's been quite a remarkable experience, but we're looking forward to getting back."

"We would appreciate the tour. I'm surprised that I feel lighter. We have the artificial gravity?" I ask.

"Only partial, not yet fully operational. You'll need to initiate the fusion reactor for that, just the solar arrays on for now. Here strap these on." He and the technicians hand us magnetic soles to strap under our shoes.

"Great, thanks!"

"This here is the bridge with navigation, engineering, astral lab. Other labs are to the far left. Life support to the right. This is the brain and heart of the ship."

"Nice! Show me everything," says Lilian.

Meyers obliges her. "There are cameras and audio all over the ship. You can monitor all the ship from here on this large screen.

This is part of your IT workstation." He shows us how to turn the screen on. An image of the *Athena* appears. He enlarges any section with a touch screen. The sound in the section simultaneously gets louder as he enlarges the screen. He continues, "You can control all portals and air locks here too."

In her excitement to inspect the electronics, Lilian almost steps on a small, round robot. A technician warns, "Look out for the automated cleaners, our little vacuum-sweeper-moppers. They're smaller than the usual household ones. There are two in here operating all the time, cleaning floors, walls, workstations, ceilings. They are magnetic, designed to work in zero gravity and in small spaces."

"I like these. They can detect which surfaces to avoid too. They know when to re-charge and fill themselves. They empty their own waste into the ship's system," adds Riya.

"Cool," I comment.

"Here's your chair, Captain, with radio communications built in."

"I like it! It's pretty big, comfortable. I can get used to this," I say as I sit on the swivel chair in the center of the bridge.

"This workstation controls astral—for you Dr. Yazzie." Meyers points to an instrumented station under a tube.

Aurora checks it out intensely. "I see two clocks at atomic time."

"We want to test Einstein's theory of relativity. There should be a thirteen second difference when you return. It's a critical study, as I'm sure you know. The second clock is a back-up," explains Meyers.

Pointing to the long, slender tube with a ladder that is barely wide enough for one person to climb, he says "This leads to the stationary central cylinder, which connects us to the special observation dome. Beside astral are the controls for your pilot... Ms. Kelly, right?"

"That's me. Call me Emma."

Meyers turns to a handsome technician. "Please show Emma the controls."

"Sure," the technician readily agrees. "Here, have a seat." He smiles at Emma. He stands closely, quietly discussing the controls with her.

"Over to the right are workstations for sensors for the reactor and structure, next to the gauges for the electrical and life support systems." Zoë, Lucy and Riya move to the right to examine their workstations. "Any questions? If your chairs aren't comfortable you can adjust them. You can strap yourselves in to not float away too."

"I can see outside." Evelyn looks out a porthole the size of her head.

Aurora joins her. "Beautiful, there's the Moon."

Meyers explains, "That's nothing. There're only a few small portholes in the ring. It was thought that when the wheel is at full spin, looking out would make you dizzy. You should see the Bubble though. I'll take you there later.

Everyone ready. Soles on?" asks Meyers. We nod. "Let's continue on our tour. Follow me to the left. We'll be following the track that winds 1.4 kilometers around the ring." We can see the floor tipping upward slightly on both sides. We walk slowly as we adjust to walking with the slight centrifugal force as we develop our "sea" legs.

We follow him to the left to an area also open to the bridge. Meyers explains, "This cubical is a second communications station for personal radio messages and news broadcasts. Your families can transmit from any NASA or Canada base."

"Can I try?" asks Lucy, sitting in one of three seats near the radio.

"Not right now. We need to continue on."

I ask, "Arla, can you help her with it later?"

"Of course."

"These next workstations are open labs. This first lab is for marine science and weather. The second is a geology lab." He offers, "Your chair, Arla. There's an extra seat in each lab for an assistant."

"Nice! It's *everything* I asked for!" Arla examines the two aquariums, one with salt-water and one fresh water, containing edible seaweed, and her weather monitoring station.

"And here is the station for your geologist—sorry forgot, which one is the geologist?"

"Thanks, that's me, Kiara Williams. "Mine has everything too! I feel like a little kid in a candy store."

"You can check it out as we move forward," says Meyers, "This next section has sealed labs. The first is the biochemistry lab."

"That's mine," exclaims Vivian as she peers into the anteroom. "I guess I'd need to suit up to go in the actual lab."

"Yes, that is recommended," advises Meyers.

"Oh, I have to wait to see it later then," laments Vivian.

"Next are labs for medical and microbiology—believe this includes you Captain."

"Yes, me and Dr. Ava Campbell. We'll check it out later too."

"I assure you that they are state-of-art and ready for use. NASA spared no expense here: Chromatography and mass spectrometry equipment, gel electrophoresis and emission spectroscopy instruments in biochemistry; Electron microscopes, culture units, and medical testing kits in the medical lab. Next is an enclosed medical unit with three beds. It's been sterilized but you can enter."

"Good to have this enclosed isolation bed in case of infectious disease," I comment.

Ava looks around. "I appreciate the multi-task medical scanner, surgical lights, emergency medical devices." She opens a locked cabinet and smiles. "And full pharmacy."

"We seem to have all we need for any possible medical situation," says Harper.

"All great, really, but it would be nice to get a change in color from these drab gray floors and white walls—a little *feng shui*," complains Vivian Li.

"The next section is a little better on the *feng shui*," offers Meyers. "Let's head into your living area, starting with your private sleeping quarters."

Vivian walks ahead and assents, "You're right. This is easier on the eyes." She sees a row of fourteen private quarters, like boxcars, each with translucent-paper wall. Inside each of the boxcars, we can see walls with a solid, pastel-color on the other three sides. Each of the quarters has a different color but is otherwise the same, with a foldable twin bed, linen to match the wall color, a storage unit, and a water closet. In the corner is an antique white desk, with portable computer and seat, perpendicular to a vanity.

"These really are nice!" agrees Arla.

"Pick any one and put your stuff inside," says Meyers.

I choose the first one because I like the color of lilacs, which remind me of the bushes in my childhood home. When choosing, there are some minor conflicts and discussions, but everyone comes to an agreement.

"The bed is actually comfortable," notes Harper. The technicians leave the animals with Harper and the worms with Evelyn.

The handsome technician walks in with Emma and offers, "Let me know if you need any help with anything."

"Aren't you sweet. I'm good for now."

"What's the screen on the wall for?" asks Ava.

Lilian answers, "Remember from training—oh right, you missed that talk. We can send and receive personal visual broadcasts from home or just use it as a larger monitor. I can help you with it."

"That would be nice, thanks."

After settling in, we change out of our g-force suits and into comfortable clothes.

"Glad you like your quarters. On each end and in the middle, there's a shower and a laundry station with washer and dryer. They're self-explanatory. Let's move on. It's a long trek," says Meyers.

"OK, let's move on!" I repeat more loudly, and the ladies exit their new quarters.

"Next is the sound-proof chapel designed for quiet personal time or small group discussions."

"It looks like a Japanese teahouse, serene," says Kiara.

"I like it," says Vivian.

"I do too. We could have private conversations here," says Ava.

"And being sound-proof, musicians could practice there without bothering anyone," suggests Emma, "I get complaints about my guitar."

"There's room for our instruments to the side," says Lucy.

I nod. "Fine with me."

We walk to the next section. It's an exercise area with treadmills, stationary bikes, weight-simulating equipment and open exercise floor with mirrors.

"It's cheerful. I like the light canary," says Evelyn smiling.

One of the technicians explains, "You can play video games and watch any kind of instructional video for various exercise routines."

"Do you have any yoga?" I ask.

"For sure, look at the list. Is there anything in particular you want?" asks the technician.

There are dozens of selections. "No, thanks that should be enough."

"What video games do you have?" asks Emma.

"Mostly NASA simulations. NASA provided the hardware, but I believe one of you brought some popular games," Meyers answers.

"Yes, I did," says Lilian.

"Nice!" says Emma.

"Do you play these?" asks Lilian showing her collection to Emma.

"For sure, whenever I have time," says Emma.

"Me too."

We walk through a portal to the last area of the living space, a dining hall for fourteen persons, with brightly colored furniture. It includes a kitchen with various experimental appliances and kitchen devices.

"Place looks like a 1950's diner," comments Bella.

"And, we can cook!" says Kiara.

"*You* can. Some of us, maybe not so much," says Lilian looking at Evelyn.

"I'm still working out the kinks."

We shake our heads, remembering some of her trials.

We walk through another portal. "This is the start of the 'farm'," says Meyers, "To conserve power, the next part has been heated only to just above freezing. The next space is five meters high, causing a protrusion in the ring." Here the men fully stretch out. "Then, there's the water and waste treatment systems. Also, you have storage for about two thousand kilograms of farm supplies."

"Good. We'll need those," says Bella. "Oh, I see they planted my trees!"

"There's just spindly twigs," comments Harper.

Bella bends one. "No, look they're flexible."

"Won't they grow too high?" asks Lilian.

"No, all are dwarfs. I can't wait. It'll be *amazing*."

"I can imagine it," agrees Evelyn.

At the end of the arboretum, I note an airlock with window. A technician explains, "See out the porthole. You'll be able to zipline outside along a spoke to the lower part of the central tube."

Evelyn says, "Oh fun! I love ziplining."

"Yep, it'll be like flying," agrees Emma.

"Seems creepy. I'll pass," says Lucy.

Meyers explains, "It's not meant for fun. This may be different from the ziplining you're used to. There's another spoke like this a third of the way through—Canadians big on precautions."

"Precautions are good," I comment.

Meyers advices, "You'll want to move quickly through this cold half of the ring."

"Let's jog," I suggest.

"Good idea."

Here the track is in the center, with parallel areas just over a meter wide on both sides. We jog past the "barn" area, with rabbit pens on one side and chicken-roosting boxes on the other. Next to the barn are three more workstations for our animal biologist, botanist and soil specialist. After the barn are the "fields". The fields consist of two narrow strips almost half the circumference of the ring. The track is in the middle to allow access to either side. These strips hold planting bins with adjustable shelves. There are grow lights affixed to the ceiling and under the shelves. For now, only the emergency lights are on.

Meyers opens the door to the shuttle bay. We walk inside though it is also very cold in here. Like the arboretum, the bay area has an extra high ceiling causing a bulge opposite the arboretum.

"Nice!" exclaims Arla "This must be the satellite that we will launch around the exoplanet to monitor weather and other information."

"Yes, it is," confirms Zoë.

Though the satellite is remarkable, we are agape by the sight of the shuttle *Chidiya*.

"Yep, she's mine!" Emma raves, "Look at her. I've studied her. She's a three-person, aerodynamic, amphibious floatplane. There's one set of stationary tail wings and a second larger set of expandable wings for flying through a planetary body with an atmosphere. These wings are the first of a kind! She's an engineering masterpiece. See the airlock in the back to allow us to exit to repair satellites and other spacecraft. Her main engine is rocket-powered, using the same fuel as the *Athena* thruster engines. For land use, she has a secondary electric engine."

"Infatuated much?" quips Zoë.

"Definitely."

"I get it, really," says Zoë, "Superman's my true love."

"The *Chidiya*'s certainly impressive. But it's freezing in here, let's go. Or, I can leave you lovebirds," I tease.

Next Meyers informs us, "This is the storage area for food, about fourteen thousand kilograms of it."

"We won't starve," says Riya.

A technician says, "This is your grocery store, without a payment counter."

Another says, "Yep, with all the MREs you can stomach. By the way, part of the packaging is reusable for food storage—for after you harvest your garden."

The first technician adds, "There are also bulk, non-perishable foods for experimental cooking and hypo-allergenic toiletries—no scents." Then he demonstrates how to select meals and supplies. "Get something for dinner and tomorrow if you want."

We do our "shopping", choosing tasty sounding MREs (Meals, Ready to Eat). Bella and Riya choose vegetarian options. Next, we walk through the units consisting of the remaining life-support systems. The technicians thoroughly explain the function and robotic diagnostic system of each unit. Then we arrive back to engineering and bridge, where we started.

Meyers takes Aurora and me through the long gray tunnel in the ceiling, the spoke leading to the central tube. We climb the ladder in the tunnel, becoming completely weightless as we near the central tube. We pass quickly onto the padded wider tube leading to an observation dome made almost entirely of glass, the Bubble.

Aurora arrives first and is wide-eyed. "This is nice."

I exclaim, "More like this is really awesome! I can see the Earth, the Moon, and the Milky Way! Look at all the stars."

"Yes, the French were really showing off with this," says Meyers.

"Definitely! It's like floating in space!" Aurora and I stare at the Earth as we encircle the equator. "It's so beautiful." I'm in awe. "Pictures do not do it justice!" We can see the entire wheel, the innumerable bright stars all around us except those directly below us.

"Takes my breathe away every time."

As we are freely floating, I'm about to hit the glass. I gasp. "Will it break?"

Meyers assures us, "Don't worry. The combination of the exterior low-thermal expansion pane with the internal triple pane alumino-silicate glass can handle your bumping into it. But you can use a tether for your safety."

Aurora checks out the telescopes and other observation devices. "I could stay here always, even fall asleep here," says Aurora.

Meyers warns, "Due to solar winds and galactic cosmic radiation, no one should stay in the Bubble for more than six hours at a time."

"Good point."

He continues, "At the other end of the central tube is the dormant Superman. We cannot view the fusion engine directly because the mechanisms that cause the wheel's circular motion are between this shaft and Superman." After a few minutes, we reluctantly head back and let the others explore this marvel.

After all visit and return from the Bubble, a technician says, "We've explored all the accessible areas of the *Athena*. Well that's it, ladies, hope you enjoy."

Meyers suggests, "Let's eat—last time here for us. I can't wait for real food." We walk to the dining hall. It was designed for only fourteen people; some need to stand to eat. Zoë, Arla, and I squeeze around a table with Meyers, another scientist and an engineer.

Zoë complains, "I see what you mean about the food. I hadn't tried this freeze-dried artificial food before. Not much smell to it."

"True, but sometimes MREs are OK," I say and then ask Meyers, "What are your plans when you get back?"

"I'll be going to my daughter's birthday party tomorrow," says Meyers smiling.

"Sweet! How old is she?" I ask.

"She'll be five. Here's her picture."

"She's so adorable. Look at her!" I hand the picture to Arla and Zoë. We talk about our families but mostly about technical aspects of the *Athena*, along with some issues and solutions.

The other astronauts sit or stand crowded with the other nine men, exchanging funny anecdotes. Evelyn decides to play "Space Girl" by The Imagined Village and comically dances, which makes us laugh. Then she plays more dance music. The other members of the space crews start to get comfortable with each other. Some begin to flirt and dance. When a seductive song plays, Emma, brashly feigns a sultry strip tease, slowly swaying her hips, snaking her arms, shaking her top, as the others cheer her on. She dances suggestively around a central support pole. Returning to dancing with her partner, the handsome, all-too-eager technician, she presses her body against him as she kisses him passionately on the lips. At the same time, knowing Zoë is a lesbian, Emma touches Zoë 's hair, teasing, "Want a threesome?"

Many in the hall laugh and chant, "Go Emma!"

I can see Zoë's obvious discomfort. I sigh knowing I'll have to confidentially discuss this sexual harassment with Emma later.

Meyers sighs and shakes his head, "NASA is watching."

I decide to stop this before it goes any further. "Is it not time for the maintenance crew to return to the capsule?"

Emma whines, "Aw, you're no fun."

I respond in a low, but stern, voice, "You and I need to talk, privately."

Emma smiles and says, "I was just kidding around. You don't really think . . ."

The technician stares angrily at me. I respond, "May I suggest a cold shower?"

NASA radios a warning that it is time for the men to depart. They assemble their personal items and start walking toward the capsule. We thank them and express our goodbyes. Emma and some of the women pout—the last men they will see for a long, long time.

My crew members check out different parts of the *Athena* on their own. I meet with Emma in the chapel. "Thanks for coming. I need to talk to you about your behavior at dinner."

"Yes, Ma'am."

"You realize NASA watches everything we do."

"I know."

"You know also that fraternizing among NASA employees is generally against policy."

"Yes, but I'm not employed by NASA. I'm still Air Force."

"It is not about NASA or Air Force. We are all part of the same project."

"Of course, you're right. But *he* didn't mind."

No, *he* did not, it was unbecoming, but we were not on public television—even so, I assume NASA will edit it out. *He* is not my concern. My concern is my crew. *Zoë* was clearly upset. She has a wife."

"Oh?"

"Unwanted touching is sexual harassment in any organization," I remind her.

"I'm really sorry. I didn't think—"

"I assume this means it will not happen again?" I ask.

"No, of course not."

"And . . . ?"

"and I'll apologize to her."

"Good idea. I have other work I need to do. You can go. Dismissed."

"Thank you, Ma'am."

After that meeting, I go to my quarters to work on the detailed schedule and duty rosters. As instructed by NASA, I prepare a twelve-hour work–exercise schedule, outside the four hours of free time and eight hours of sleep time. Six astronauts will be on a new day shift and six on night. Except for the grow lights, there is no longer any real difference between night and day. I need to consider work teams and to be certain that someone is always watching the essential systems, while others are awake to provide support if needed. I schedule constant activities to keep everyone busy to prevent boredom and homesickness. I struggle to make the schedule fair and to incorporate the crew members' requests.

It's been an extraordinary and long day. While I'm working, most astronauts are unpacking. Most have not slept the previous night, or nights, and are worn-out.

I hear our botanist Bella, who is vegetarian, ask our animal biologist, Harper, "How can you possibly think of raising and slaughtering those cute little fuzzy bunnies for food?"

Harper, whose family business is cattle ranching, snaps, "Uff-da! Humans *need* protein and vegetarianism is unhuman and pretty stupid."

Bella argues, "Eish, you can get enough protein from legumes and nuts."

"That's right. I do," agrees Riya.

"Legumes, really! There's no taste. Yuck," counters Emma.

"Seaweeds have protein." Arla says, then walks away, not really wanting to be part of a deteriorating debate.

"Double Yuck," retorts Harper.

Kiara interjects, "Harper, how can you say Bella's stupid? That ain't right."

Harper smirks and says, "Just give me a dripping quarter pounder with cheese. Ooh...."

"Sounds great," adds Zoë.

Simultaneously, Riya says, "Real mature."

"Gross!" says Bella. "Meats have harmful bacteria."

"Every living thing has harmful bacteria. It's normal to eat meat! You don't know what you're talking about," argues Harper.

"It's not! And raising meat's not practical," counters Bella.

Harper shouts, "Course it is! Humans have been raising meat for thousands of years! You're just wrong!"

"A lot has gone on for thousands of years—not an excuse!" shouts Bella.

"Irrelevant propaganda!" shouts Harper even louder.

"No, it's not! It's—"

I step out of my quarters and interrupt her, "Stop! Debates are not won by the loudest screamer. And I am trying to work here." I shift to a gentler tone and say, "You obviously are all exhausted. It has been a long day. Please get some rest."

Harper acquiesces. Sheepishly, they settle down. I ask myself, why do I feel like I'm babysitting?

I decide to reduce conflict by scheduling Harper on a different shift than Bella and Riya. Lucy, Riya, and Evelyn seem wide awake, so I ask them to monitor our life support and maintain communication with NASA, and suggest they contact their families if they wish. When I finish the schedule and duty roster, I announce to everyone, "Listen. For shifts, the term "day" refers to our plants' artificial sunlight hours, not Earth time, and "night" refers to our dark hours. The night team, starting at 0800 hours Eastern Standard Time, comprises of Aurora, Lilian, Vivian, Harper, Emma and Zoë. The day team, starting at 2000 hours, includes Bella, Riya, Evelyn, Kiara, Lucy, and Arla. You have four hours of free time each day to socialize with everyone. Because all will need to check in medically with Ava, her schedule, starting at 1400 hours, straddles six hours day shift and six hours night. I am scheduled opposite Ava, starting at 0200 hours, to cover her and maintain contact with everyone. I'm not a medic, but I do have the CPR and first aid training. Any questions?" They have none or are too tired to care. I remind them,

"Please check with Arla to arrange some radio calls to your families. Good night, everyone."

I fall into an uneasy sleep. Six hours later, at 0200 hours EST, I wake up. Ava says, "I heard you twice. Are you OK?"

"Yes, just had one nightmare about a giant rabbit eating my schedule and then wanting to eat me. Then another about floating aimlessly in the Bubble in space and finding myself about to be burned up by the Sun."

Ava sighs in sympathy. "Not hard to interpret those dreams."

"Pretty obvious."

She goes to her quarters as I walk toward the bridge to radio the schedule to NASA. I brush up against a cheerful Evelyn carrying her worms.

"Good morning," Evelyn and I say simultaneously.

Noticing her box, I back away and beg, "Please keep those away from me."

She jokes, "Why?" Wouldn't you like a nice high protein breakfast?"

I grimace. "Oh, worms are so slimy. Not sure why, but I always hated seeing those squirmy worms after a rain."

"They're full of calcium and minerals and in some parts of the world, they're a delicacy. We'll have chickens and they devour them. Worms increase the amount of air and water in the soil, break down organic matter and leave behind fertilizer—"

"You win but keep them in the soil."

Mimicking a snobby waiter, Evelyn concludes, "You're not worthy."

"I guess not. My MRE is fine."

We join Lucy and Riya on the bridge. We chat pleasantly while watching the monitors and answering NASA calls until the 0800 hours EST shift change. It was an exciting first trip in space for all the crew. In the upcoming day, we will have an exciting first trial for the space program.

five

Superman Awakens

My overly tired bridge crew leaves for their quarters, and the night shift enters as I contently start an audio log and radio transmission, "December 17, 2046, 0800 hours Eastern Standard Time, the fourteen-member crew, including myself, of the *Athena* have been aboard in low-Earth orbit for sixteen hours adjusting to the ship. All reviews are completed. All systems and personnel still a go. We are preparing to initiate Superman."

"You're enjoying that chair," comments Zoë.

"Yes, I am." I grin while connecting us to NASA and then command, "Zoë, do your stuff! Light this baby up."

After a deep breath, Zoë enters the proper sequence in the controls to initiate the very first fusion reactor in space for the very first time. Everyone on the bridge watches her intently.

After a few minutes, Zoë mutters disappointingly, "Nothing, frickin' nothing, why?" She grabs my radio controls, "NASA, Superman didn't fire as expected. Do you have an explanation? Over."

NASA radios back, "No, all systems appear to be functioning as expected. Over."

She complains, "Matt, this should have started. Look for the unexpected." She runs a diagnostic too. After a half hour, bright lights come on. The ring starts to spin faster at its optimal two rotations per minute. It even starts to feel warmer.

Zoë shouts, "Success!" We all cheer. She radios NASA, "It fired!"

NASA responds, "Just need a little patience, Zoë. Out."

Zoë tells us, "This is only the beginning. In about thirteen hours, Superman should be completely warmed up and ready to leave orbit."

A half hour later, NASA radios to remind me that we have a show to do at 0930 hours EST and to be sure to display our private sponsors' logo. We will be online with a fourth-grade classroom in Florida for a nationally televised "Question & Answer" session. I have done these before, and have earned the popular title, Captain Camille. I really like the kids and their endless curiosity. This show features me and the night crew.

At 0930 hours, I start the live session by saying, "Hi students. I am Captain Camille Tremblay and here are six members of my crew."

The class shouts, "Hi, Captain Camille!"

I introduce each astronaut in turn, with Emma last. "You may remember Ms. Emma Kelly. She was a U.S. women's mixed martial arts champion."

One child asks, "Wow, are you *all* fighters?"

I answer, "No, but Ms. Harper Anderson here wrestles and shoots well, and Dr. Arla Johnson and I have black belts."

Another child asks, "Do you ever fight? Who wins?"

I answer, "We spar sometimes. Emma would definitely win."

One asks, "Do you have a gun?" To give the others air time, I motion for Harper to answer.

Harper answers, "Not on board. It would be too dangerous if I made a hole in the wrong place. We only have tasers and tranquilizers, but I doubt we'll need them."

One student asks, "Miss Kelly, what do you like to do in your free time?"

Emma answers, "Play electric guitar. I plan to start a band called 'Hyper-Space' with Dr. Aurora Yazzie here, who plays drums; Ms.

Lucy Karlsson, who's not here now but who plays keyboard; and Ms. Lilian Jones over there does electronic sounds."

One boy blurts out, "I think Miss Kelly's the coolest! Are you going to fight an alien?"

Emma answers quickly, "Sure hope so—only kidding. This is a peace mission."

One student asks, "Aren't there fourteen? Where are the other crew members?"

I answer, "Sleeping. We like to have some awake and watching at all times, so we switch out."

One boy asks, "Where are you going? Is it far?" I motion for Aurora to answer.

Aurora answers softly, "No, we'll be staying in the Orion-Cygnus Arm of the Milky Way to visit the Ross 128 system, or more precisely to the exoplanet Ross 128 b. Because it's confusing, we call the star Ra, for the Egyptian sun god, and the exoplanet is just 'Ross' to us."

Another student blurts, "Huh? I thought you were going out farther than anyone else."

Aurora says, "We are."

Another asks, "Are you bringing back any aliens?" I motion to Arla.

Arla answers confidently, "It's not part of the plan. We don't know the effects another life form might have on Earth's environment. We plan to bring back inorganic matter, like rocks."

I add, "Even a rock might be dangerous if there is life on it like tiny, harmful, unseen viruses."

A student recommends, "Don't bring back any rocks, just aliens, OK?"

The questions continue for almost an hour on everything from how we brush our teeth to how we eat, pee and poop—the usual. Finally, a girl asks how she can be an astronaut. Bingo! N.O.W. contributed to these broadcasts to encourage girls to join male-dominated fields. Throughout the broadcast, the *Athena*'s many cameras zoom in on various sponsors' products. We all say goodbye to the students, and they wish us well.

Later, as the farm warms up, Harper and Vivian inspect it and set up Harper's animal pens and beehive. The four soft, plump bunnies seem happy for more space, sniffing the air and hopping around. Vivian prepares her space nearby to grow several healing herbs and spices. She also sets the timing of the main lights on the computer, dimming them to simulate night at 0900 hours EST. The rest of the night team stay on the bridge/engineering, with Arla close-by in her marine lab. Zoë checks and re-checks all systems with Aurora, Lilian and Emma. Then Aurora works in the Bubble for a few hours. I check out my microbiology lab and set up one of my experiments. I'm testing the effects of space travel on probiotic stomach bacteria. The lab is very quiet, but I like solitude sometimes. When done, I talk to my dad, then exercise, eat and go to sleep at 1400 hours EST.

I only sleep a few hours. I feel somewhat rested for the next show with similar students in Hawaii at 1300 hours local time. This time we feature our day crew, doctor and animals. The children ask many questions and enjoy the bunnies. Everything goes well per our sponsors and the students, and viewers, are encouraged to learn more about space.

Three hours after this show, we all put on our g-force suits and strap ourselves in our seats. This is a big moment. I make a log entry, "December 17, 2046, 2100 hours Eastern Standard Time, all systems go. Superman performing as expected. Main propulsion engine is primed to go. We are ready to leave Earth orbit and accelerate to seven hundred thousand kilometers per hour. First stop, Mars." Currently, Mars is the closest it has been in years. Zoë, Emma, Lilian and Aurora are busy with last minute communications with NASA.

Lilian announces, "The course is programmed and we're ready. It's exciting. No one has ever travelled this fast."

"I'm so nervous," says Lucy. "Why do we need the g-force suits?"

To reassure her, I say, "Just a precaution. We are only accelerating at one g. It will take about five and a half hours to reach full speed. They'll be a jolt, but it should be like riding on an airplane."

"You're right. I know that. Went over it in training," says Lucy.

"All passengers, please fasten your seat belts," orders Emma mimicking a flight attendant.

"Are you going to show us the emergency exits?" asks Evelyn.

"Seriously, everyone, try to remain strapped in, if possible, for the duration. It may be disorienting to walk with the spin."

Then, I radio NASA, "Are we a go? Over."

"All good from here. Over." radios NASA.

"How does it look from engineering?" I ask

"All good here," says Emma, "I live for moments like this!"

"All good here too," says Zoë.

I radio NASA, "Continue with count-down at five minutes. Over."

Bella as she grabs Evelyn's arm. "Some say that Superman won't remain attached. Or, what if it does and we fall apart?"

Overhearing, Zoë assures her, "The *Athena*'s super-tough exterior was designed to hold together, and our plasma and electromagnetic shields will protect us from high velocity impacts from space particles."

"But it's never been tried before."

"I know that. I need absolute quiet. I need to listen to the intercom by the engine for any signs of trouble," snaps Zoë.

Nervous and excited, we silently watch the clock for the final few minutes. All the normal sounds seem enhanced. We hear clicks and various motor sounds, and occasionally running water. At a new sound, I stare at Zoë questioning her with my eyes, but she remains steadfast, shaking her head.

Then, Zoë counts down out loud, "10-9-8-7-6-5-4-3-2-1."

The *Athena* engages immediately. We feel a jolt and then the acceleration.

"It's OK to talk now," announces Zoë. Lilian plays "Good to be Alive (Hallelujah)" by Andy Grammer.

Except for the initial jolt, the *Athena* runs smoothly, and all soon start to relax. Then some become restless and move around. After five and a half hours, Lilian announces, "We're almost at cruising speed. Hold on. No more g in five minutes."

In five minutes, Zoë says, "Phew, it worked! We're still attached. All gauges are where they should be."

NASA radios, "We're all breathing a sigh of relief down here. Over."

"Us too. Getting back to normal. Over," I radio. I pat Zoë on the back, "Amazing job."

Grinning ear-to-ear, she sighs. "Damn, it really works."

As the adrenalin leaves, my eyes get heavy and I yawn. Ava chides, "You made sure everyone was scheduled with a decent eight hours sleep, except yourself, eh?"

"Maybe." I yawn again and go to my quarters for a short nap. I get a late start on my next shift.

SIX

Mars and the Asteroids

In the next few days, we prepare for our first planned visit to another planet, Mars. One purpose of this visit is to allow us to abort if needed. Fortunately, the engineers repeated diagnostics indicate no signs of failure.

As we orbit Mars, I make a log entry, "December 25, 2046, 0300 hours Eastern Standard Time. We are in low orbit around Mars. All systems go. Time to test out the shuttle *Chidiya*. Pilot Emma Kelly and geologist Kiara Williams will deliver supplies to the SpaceX colony and return with rock specimens." Everyone else is on the bridge to watch or assist.

I radio Emma and Kiara who are strapped in the *Chidiya*, "Emma, are you ready? Over."

"Sure thing. Over," radios Emma. The bay door opens. The *Chidiya* is on its way down for her maiden voyage to the Martian south pole. Emma wears positioning goggles through which she can see her position in blue and computerized instructions in bright orange.

"How was the take-off?" I ask.

"The *Chidiya* exited the bay as expected. Instrument readings as expected. Over."

We watch as they enter the thin atmosphere. In a few minutes, Aurora announces, "Exit and descent are perfect on my sensors."

"I agree," says Lilian.

"We see you on our monitors. Looking good. Over."

"Everything fine in here. Out," radios Emma.

"NASA, are you watching all this? Over," I ask.

A few minutes later, "Yes, all systems read fine from Earth. Out."

In the *Chidiya*, Kiara exclaims, "Wow! Look at those Martian canyons, shaped like giant spiders, and the dark rocky mounds. Can't believe I'm really seeing Mars up close."

"Yep. Flying over Mars, it'll be hard to top that," says Emma, "Now let me find the settlement. It's supposed to be by a frozen white lake nineteen kilometers in diameter."

In a few minutes, Kiara shouts, "There it is!"

Emma radios, "Got a visual on the lake. Going in for a landing. Over."

As they approach, Kiara comments, "Their little village looks like an upside-down egg carton."

The *Chidiya* makes a perfect soft landing on the rust and tan compacted soil of the prepared airfield. Emma drives smoothly past the solar power field to dock at the main entrance.

As she exits, Emma says, "Hello! Martians."

"Greetings Earthlings," says a resident smiling. The new arrivals instantly attract the curiosity of the settlers.

"Merry Christmas!" says Kiara handing them the sweet butter cakes that she had baked.

"Happy Holidays," says their leader. Then, they shake hands while introducing themselves.

A smiling woman offers, "Please join us for my chewy homemade cookies and some punch."

"Thank you, ma'am." Kiara obliges and takes a bite. "These taste heavenly."

"Take some back with you," the woman says.

"So, you're off to the Ross system?" asks the leader.

"Yes, certainly are," says Emma. The settlers continue to ask questions about our mission, which Emma and Kiara are happy to indulge.

After about an hour, Emma says, "It's almost time for us to return. We haven't even unloaded your packages."

"Thanks so much," says the leader. "We really need these medications and other supplies. These are a life-saver. We've a small token for you too." Some settlers unload the supplies while the leader gives Kiara a wrapped gift. "Go ahead, open it," he urges.

"OK," says Kiara.

"I'm curious," says Emma.

Kiara unwraps the box and finds, among the sealed Martian rocks, chucks of olivine and opal. "These are too nice. You want to give us these?"

"Happy to. There's fourteen of each of the olivine and opal—one for each of you brave ladies."

"Thank you, but can we accept them?" asks Emma holding up an opal the size of a walnut.

"Believe me you've earned them," assures their leader.

"Oh, you're so nice," says Kiara. They hug good-bye. "Good luck."

"You too," he responds. Emma and Kiara return safely to the *Athena* where we chat about the visit, while enjoying the cookies and precious stones, which we opt to study for the benefit of the space agencies.

After another week, everyone, including me, has relaxed and adjusted to the new schedule. We start to develop social groups. Emma starts her rock band. Vivian starts a book club and most of us join. Ava leads a voluntary devotional time for spiritual studies once a week during the middle of the day shift.

Before going to our first devotional meeting, Ava and I listen to a radioed news broadcast. It focuses on poverty and race relations after a recent Black protest in Toronto that became violent. With the increase in world population, the living conditions of the impoverished residing in inner cities have been deteriorating. The inner cities are predominately inhabited by minorities. After the closure of a few major employers, there were recent protests extending to Pittsburgh and Detroit.

We walk to the chapel where I confess, "I was always afraid of the Blacks and told to avoid their neighborhoods. They seem scary in all the news stories. They must hate the Whites."

Ava argues, "I don't think they are any scarier than any other group of people. There are real issues, like the wall they're building around the poorest neighborhoods, but I think the press sensationalizes animosity to attract more viewers."

"I remember hearing news stories on robberies and shootings. What about the murder of your own husband on a mission?"

"That was due to poverty. We had many, many close friends in Cameroon, very nice and friendly people who welcomed us with open arms. Do you know any Blacks socially?"

"No, I grew up in a very small francophone town. There were no Blacks there. I only know Kiara, and I do not *really* know her."

"Is she scary?"

"No, that's silly. She is petite and friendly, not at all scary. I've never heard her even say a harsh word to anyone."

"Uh-huh," remarks Ava.

"Well, she does wear a lot of make-up and stuff. It looks unprofessional and it's a bit much for out here."

The discussion stops quickly as the other devotees—Lucy, Bella, and Kiara—enter the chapel. Ava focuses our attention on King James Bible readings that center on the unity of all peoples: Psalm 67:4, "O let the nations be glad and sing for joy: for thou shalt judge the people righteously and govern the nations upon earth;" and then Romans 2:11, "For there is no respect of persons with God." We have a lengthy discussion. It is obvious that Kiara has a thorough knowledge of the Bible and compassion for the less fortunate. I really like the idea of harmony of all peoples and races, but the strife seems endless; I'm just not sure if harmony is possible. At the end of the meeting, I return to my duties and activities, but think about Ava's comments.

There is much to do. In the first weeks, we unpack our personal items, which for some include materials for a favorite art or craft. Evelyn sculpts clay; Ava knits and crochets; and Arla draws. Kiara brought watercolor paints. She paints a serene Southern forest scene featuring a swamp chestnut oak on her quarters' paper wall.

"Your painting is beautiful, exciting yet calming," says Bella.

"Incredible. It looks so real," remarks Lucy.

"It brightens up the track," says Evelyn

Their talk awakens Harper, who looks at it sleepily and asks, "Can you paint one on my wall?"

"Mine too," says Lucy.

"Thanks, and sure, I can paint outdoor scenes to keep it consistent."

"I'd love a scene of life on the open prairie. I miss hunting and fishing, but mostly just being outdoors."

"I like cuddly mammals," says Lucy.

After Kiara finishes painting her wall, she starts to paint a midwestern horizon with wild mustangs near a creek for Harper. Kiara also starts to paint a scene with baby forest mammals —cubs, fawns, raccoons—playing together in a Garden of Eden for Lucy.

After a month in space, our hair needs trimming, and Kiara is happy to help with this too.

"I have to chat when cutting hair—like at a real hometown salon," she says.

I ask, "Why did you learn to cut hair?"

"When I was in middle school, I hated school and blew it off. My parents were getting divorced and my world came apart. Then I tried hairdressing and cosmetology in ninth grade and did fine. I liked it."

"But then you changed your mind?"

"Yeah, I was living with my aunt and uncle. 'Cause I did well that year, they took me and my brother to Bryce Canyon National Park and the Grand Canyon that summer. Thought it'd be all sand and boring, but I loved it! I could just stare for hours at the orange and white Claron Formation of limestone, siltstone, dolomite, mudstone—been hooked since."

"What's your favorite—rock, I mean?

"I don't really have a favorite. I like any crystal, especially gems, but what I really like is the whole scenery. I started painting landscapes—studied art with geology in college."

"Your paintings are amazing. Are you thinking of painting professionally?"

"Not really, I just like to paint when I'm in the mood. I do dream about retiring to a cozy little painter's cabin near Bryce Canyon. Just give me an easel and a rocking chair—and lots of friends stopping by."

"Sounds nice. I would visit." I really would. I've come to respect and like Kiara. I don't see skin color or her make-up anymore. I've become accustomed to her femininity. I see her as part of us, a *bona fide* member of the *Athena* crew. I can be very wrong about people and feel ashamed that I ever thought less of her.

At the end of the first full month of our exploratory journey, we have a scheduled close study of the asteroid belt. We slow down to analyze two large carbonaceous aqueous subtype asteroids on which NASA hopes to confirm the presence of a significant amount of usable water. The first of the grayish, cratered asteroids is shaped like a flattened skull, the second like a porous hiking boot. Before making the trip, Kiara, Lilian and Aurora make a detailed graphic model for the pilot goggles. Then, Emma and Kiara bravely depart in the *Chidiya* to obtain rocks for geochemical analysis and other studies. Because there is neither air nor heat on the asteroids and very little gravity, a walk outside the shuttle would be dangerous. Instead, Kiara operates the robotic arm of the *Chidiya* to drill and collect specimens. All systems perform as expected during the excursions. Kiara happily reports that the rocks on both asteroids consist of a mixture of usable water ice with carbonates and clay. Vivian tests the specimens for organic compounds but does not find any. They submit complex and thorough scientific reports on each asteroid, which I approve and transmit to Earth.

One of Lilian's tasks it to produce audio-visual educational broadcasts to send to the space agencies. She produces her first half-hour broadcast featuring Aurora providing background information on the asteroids and then Kiara and Vivian explaining their findings and impact of a water supply to future manned missions to the outer planets.

There are no more planned excursions in this solar system. For all of us, our first month in space has been an enormous learning experience in terms of day-to-day living, interpersonal relations, and scientific discovery. This is only the beginning of our voyage through the solar system. It will take us another eight months to get to the wormhole near the Kuiper Belt.

seven

$\sim\sim\sim\sim\sim\sim$

Life on the *Athena*

In the months that follow the asteroid excursion, we settle into a new way of life that becomes ordinary. During our shifts, the engineers work on maintenance and the scientists on approved projects. Most of our experiments are set up and we prepare daily logs and reports for NASA. For two hours of our shift, we break from this work and exercise. I enjoy quietly jogging around the ring on the track and watching the farm develop.

Botanist Bella Garcia has the most dramatic project. She uses a mini robot she named Roberto to plant seeds. As it rolls on the soil, it can measure the amount, depth and distance to plant each seed perfectly. All she needs to do is enter in the type of seed. Roberto can take soil samples and advise on ideal pH, nutrient requirements and water levels. Bella and soil specialist Evelyn Miller have done extraordinary work, though Bella asserts that horticulture is easier in space without weeds, pests and blights. They can also time the lighting, temperature and water perfectly for optimal results.

The arboretum's twigs sprout leaves and look more like dwarf trees. We have pine nut, filbert, hazelnut, almond, apple, pear, plum, cherry, apricot, peach, and banana trees, as well as fig and sugar cane. The arboretum is like a small park complete with a few cushioned loveseat benches. To enhance the effect, the ceiling is white, and the walls are a light blue on the top half and light green on the bottom. All create a perfect ambiance for relaxing, reading and eating.

Our fields are a functioning mini ecosystem. There, Vivian grows medicinal plants. Bella planted herbs, aloe, legumes, soy, millet, pincapple, berries, grapes, potatoes, stevia and various vegetables. In my jogs, I take in the earthy smell and extra oxygen. The docile honeybees are flying near their hive. Occasionally the rabbits and chickens are scurrying about, eating the parts of the plants that we do not need. They fertilize the soil, with the worms. I occasionally see fresh eggs in the nests. Lattice fencing and push-button gates contain the rabbits and chickens as directed by Bella and animal biologist Harper Anderson.

In addition to work and exercise, we enjoy meals, conversations and hobbies. We radio our families and entertain each other. Often after meals, we play games. I like playing chess, especially with Riya, my toughest challenger. Zoë brought a dart board and Riya brought poker cards and chips. At the end of her shift, she generally initiates a quick game of either five-card draw or seven-card stud. Aurora, Harper, Zoë, and I play with her regularly.

This time, we decide to play blackjack. We place our initial stake—one blueberry from our share of the harvest. Riya shuffles two card decks together.

Aurora comments, "This game favors the dealer."

"I'll hold at seventeen or over," offers Riya.

"I don't have much time today," says Zoë.

"We'll just play until we're out of cards. Do you want to cut?" Riya asks me. I'm closest on her left.

"OK," I say and cut the deck. Then Riya deals each of us two cards facing up and herself one card facing up and the other facing down. I get a seven and nine.

Riya asks me, "Do you want one more?"

"Sure, hit me." I get a ten. "I'm out." Everyone else loses to the dealer, except Zoë. Riya places the played cards in a discard pile.

"Another round?" asks Riya. We nod and contribute a blueberry, except Aurora who puts in two.

"Oh, a big-time gambler," remarks Riya. She deals us each a card facing down. I get a four and eight.

"Twenty-one," says Harper proudly.

"Me too," says Riya, "Tie." She collects all berries except Harper's.

"Damn. Not really a win. That sucks!" snaps Harper.

"Calm down, it's just a game," retorts Zoë.

We play a third, fourth and fifth round generally all losing to the dealer.

In the sixth and last round, Aurora bets ten berries. "Are you sure?" asks Riya.

"Yes, better odds, now," says Aurora.

Riya deals each of us two cards. I get a seven and eight. Then I'm dealt another seven. "Not for me. I bust. I always lose at blackjack."

Harper is next and after getting a losing card. "Yah, and you're bad luck."

Then, Zoë loses too.

Aurora has a two and a three and signals for a hit and gets a seven. She sees that Riya has a seven. Aurora pauses and signals a hit and gets a six. She pauses longer and then grins. "Hit." Riya deals her an Ace.

"How did you know?" questions Riya overturning her Ace.

"It was probable. Thanks for breakfast," she says smiling as she gathers all the berries.

"That was fun," I say.

"You cheated," complains Riya.

"What do you mean?" asks Aurora.

"You counted cards."

"There were one hundred four in two decks."

"We all know that. I mean you remember them and intentionally tally and calculate probabilities—a practice banned in casinos."

"We're not in a casino, and my mind just does, on automatic."

"Ha! You can't win against a total geek," says Harper.

Zoë notices Aurora frowning. "Aurora, stay just the way are. After we get back, you and I are going to Vegas, and we're going to win big! Probably won't allow us in a second time—Anyways, I've got to go now. Running a full diagnostic today."

"I'm headed that way too," I say.

"Are you going on?" asks Riya. "Can I join you?"

"Sure."

As Riya, Zoë and I open the portal to leave the dining hall, we hear screams in the gym. We rush over and see Emma and Lilian on the exercise floor wearing virtual reality headsets, augmented reality goggles, full-body suits and haptic gloves. Lilian is squatting on the ground with a handle aiming at an invisible enemy. Emma jumps behind her and wrestles down an invisible assailant.

"Gotta watch behind you!" yells Emma

"Thanks, I'd be dead—again."

"Yep!"

"Here they come!" Emma looks around them and starts shooting also.

"They're everywhere!"

"Stay away from the volcano!"

"I feel the heat."

"Ouch! That hurt. One snuck up and scratched me."

Suddenly they stop and stand up. "Game over," says Emma, "That was a fast half hour." She and Emma are the masters. They take off their goggles. "Oh, hi," says Lilian.

"Good morning," I respond. "Who were you fighting today? Pirates? Aliens? Demons?

"No, dinosaurs. Raptors," responds Lilian.

"Ready for the diagnostic?" asks Zoë.

"Yep," says Emma. She and Lilian remove the gear and wipe it down. Then Emma, Lillian and Zoë open the portal at the other end of the gym and head for the bridge.

"Are you doing the spacewalk or flight simulation today?" asks Riya.

"Neither, it's my SWAT day," I respond, "I set the simulation for two for one half hour." We put on the gear.

"Do we need anything else?" asks Riya.

"Yes, can you get the car please?" I ask.

"Sure," Riya pulls up two chairs and sits on one.

"Remember to stay on this floor area. It's a small play zone for this. Ready?"

"Of course."

I start my favorite simulation program fighting realistic villains. NASA welcomed these games for training, for exercise and for developing hand-eye coordination. The programs also encourage us to work together to accomplish a mission.

During the first few months in space, through our work and games, we have been developing strong teams, particularly, Bella and Evelyn, who have been working closely developing the farm. Also, for a few months, they share a secret. Tucked away in the back corner of the arboretum and covered with lattice, strictly against NASA policy, they have been growing a marijuana plant. Bella had hidden the seeds and wrapping papers. Now a healthy, leafy plant is growing superbly. They have a dried leaf and make their first cigarette. They take turns toking out of view of any camera and under a vent to hide the smell.

"Did someone install more lights?" asks Bella.

"No, I don't think so."

"But is seems brighter."

"Yeah, and that tree looks like a big flower, pretty," says Evelyn grinning.

"You're right."

"Or like your t-shirt. What is that?"

"It's tie-dyed." They talk about the beauty of nature and people.

"You think people will improve in the future?"

"I don't know, smarter, healthier probably, but could get worse. Overcrowding—no nature—makes people cranky, cold to each other. Maybe the past was better."

"If you could live in the past, which time period would you pick?" asks Evelyn.

"1960s, sexual freedoms, new ideas, fun clothes! Modern world but only one-third the population. Do you think we could go back in time?"

"Hard to say, if we went through a black hole or Einstein–Rosen bridge. But we'd get really, really long. Wouldn't that look groo-vy. We'd die of course, but if we came out the other end in a previous time, we'd live again. Just think about it." They pause deep in thought.

Bella agrees, "Yep, we'd have to travel back in time. Nice colors probably trapped in there too. Wonder if there would be music, space resonance?" Bella slowly gets up, takes out her classical guitar, plays some old folk tunes. "I want to write a new song."

"I'm feeling a sculpture." Evelyn gets some of her modeling clay and makes elongated human figures. She'll later bake them in her oven and paint them in 1960's psychedelic colors.

Bella writes a poem and then sets it to a folk melody for her classical guitar and for Vivian on flute. Later, they entertain us during a meal attended by almost the entire crew.

Bella announces, "Here's my new song entitled 'Friendship'."

Vivian begins with a relaxing flute solo, then Bella plays guitar and sings:

"Until the day before
Until the sun greets us
Reminding us there are other things to worry about
We were walking side by side
As we talk about heaven and get about anyway
Reminding us there are other things to worry about

Get about anyway
Until the sun comes back
Get about anyway
Until the day before

(Bella breaks for another flute solo by Vivian)

We get together to share a meal with games and laughs
We stay up all night to cry and

Laugh about the things we heard about and
What we will do in each moment,
Until the sun sets
Reminding us there are other things to worry about

Get about anyway
Until the sun comes back
Get about anyway
Until the day before
Get about anyway"

The song terminates with a flute and guitar melody.

After it ends, we all clap enthusiastically. "That was sweet," gushes Lucy hugging them.

"You're so creative," adds Kiara hugging them too.

"Thanks for letting me record. I was running out of ideas," says Lilian.

"Reminds me that I miss home, the sunshine and open prairie, family," whines Harper.

"Yeah, I missed my nephew's high school graduation," says Zoë.

Riya sighs. "My cousin was married yesterday. They sent a video, but it's not at all the same."

"I know it. It's my husband's birthday and I really miss him. Wish he were here," laments Arla.

"Could we share him?" jokes Evelyn.

"You're terrible," says Arla who can't resist laughing.

"Five months is a long time without a man," complains Bella.

"You're not kidding," adds Emma.

"One would be desirable on occasion," I confess.

"Which occasion?" asks Evelyn lifting her eyebrows up and down a couple time.

We barely have conversations with our family on Earth anymore. Most don't live near any U.S. space station. Even when they make the trip, it takes a couple hours for our radio waves to travel to or from Earth.

To help with the homesickness, I declare June 25 mid-year Christmas and bring out surprise care packages for everyone. They contain photos and other items that had been packed ahead by family and friends. Everyone enjoys their cards, chocolates, candies, photos, trinkets, fancy toiletries, or clothes. The new items freshen our stale quarters or lab stations. I especially love the family wedding photo from my aunt, the expensive Chanel jasmine soap and lavender shampoo with conditioner from another aunt, and two knee-length fleece-lined t-shirt pajamas from my dad. He also included a super-soft stuffed polar bear. It is comforting to think he is looking after me—that I'm still his little girl.

After seven months into our journey, Lilian decides to interview me in my captain's chair about our journey thus far. "Captain Camille, what is your overall evaluation of this project?"

I say, "Great! I feel we are very lucky that the journey thus far is going as well, if not better, than expected. The *Athena* and the shuttle are functioning perfectly. There are hardly any glitches. We feel safe. The experiments are progressing well, and all are motivated."

"What does a team leader do?"

"I make sure we move forward in our mission, and that all cooperate toward our goals. Communication, fairness, and trust are key."

"How's the crew?"

"Everyone's physical and mental health is optimal. We are working diligently on our projects and developing skills in new areas. Our minds are also challenged with some games, arts, clubs."

"Any regrets?"

"Yes, we miss our families. However, though there is the homesickness and some bland days, the crew members are bonding and optimistic. Life is calm, and often we have fun. We are excited to be moving to the Ross system and focused on our mission."

"Thank you, Captain," concludes Lilian, "It's a wrap."

eight

Distress

Eight months into our journey, a couple crew members experience significant emotional stress. After her personal radio time, I see Arla run crying from the bridge to her quarters. She flings a photo of her husband out. I learn that her husband had just sent a "Dear John" radio message indicating they "should see other people"—a very poor choice of words.

She is obviously distraught. I want to talk to her, though I'm not sure what to say. I sit beside her, holding her hand. "How are you?" I ask.

She mumbles, "How could he? We were so happy. I thought he'd understand." I resist the temptation to tell her all men are jerks and provide examples from my past. She needs someone to listen to her unique story.

"Talk to me. Understand what?" I ask.

"We honeymooned at the Great Barrier Reef; it was completely awesome—the colors, the fish, the coral. He was so sweet. I thought he'd support my dream to study oceans on another world. It'll boost my career—help *our* lives. We could go anywhere, do anything after."

"But—," I say.

"Says he found someone. Already! It's just been a few months!"

"I'm so sorry."

She starts sobbing. "I want to be alone, OK?"

"Of course, anytime you want to talk, I'm here."

Emotionally exhausted, she cries herself to sleep. I feel for her and am frustrated with men. I work off my anger by slaying a shipload of virtual pirates.

Our conversations often center on men. During our shift change, I meet with my friend, Ava, for coffee and conversation in our lab. Ava has a quiet and gentle way about her that makes it easy to confide your deepest thoughts. When I imagine a big sister, she would be just like Ava. With her body language, she lets you know that you have her undivided attention.

I ask, "Why are men so cruel?"

"What do you mean?"

"I try really hard, but like with Arla, why does every man I'm with turn out to be such a disappointment?"

"Do they?"

I nod. "If there is a room full of nice guys, I will always attract the one wolf. Not sure why."

"Maybe there's a reason. You told me your mother died of alcoholism when you were a child. Was she hard to live with?"

"Not sure of the connection but yes, you never knew what her mood would be. Sometimes when she was angry, she would spank me, unless I hid in the lilac bushes."

"And full of compliments, was she?"

"No, it's like everything I did was wrong, probably why I'm a perfectionist now."

"And then she died. How did that make you feel?"

"Really sad—like I was not worth her giving up the alcohol and staying alive for."

Ava explains, "Alcoholism is a debilitating disease. It may worsen over time, but that has nothing to do with the worth of the alcoholic's child. You cannot change a person, who does not want to change, by being perfect. Think of a physically abused child. You wouldn't say that that child is unworthy, that she deserves being punched."

"No, certainly not!"

"It seems that your low self-esteem has affected your choices. You may have been picking guys who treat you the way you feel you *deserve* to be treated. You need someone who cares to treat you the way you *want* to be treated."

I pause to think. "True, but I do not want a boring door mat either. I like self-confidence, adventure, passion—someone who cares about me, but who can also think for himself. Someone with spark."

"So, someone not too hot, not too cold."

"Exactly. Do you think that's possible?"

"Sure, I had a marriage like that."

"So, the love of your life and you could never think of anyone else."

"I wouldn't say *never*."

"Thanks for the insights Ava. You look tired. I let you get some sleep."

"Good night, or morning for you."

The space programs do all they can to promote physical, mental and emotional help, but for an occasional few, the strangeness, the confinement and the loneliness of space are overbearing. After eight months in space, I'm concerned about Harper who seems to be experiencing long-term emotional stress. Though Arla mostly recovers in a month, Harper has been getting increasingly worse. By being vulgar and insulting anyone who disagrees with her, she has become the black sheep among the crew members. She barely sleeps and when she does, I can hear her toss and turn. She constantly talks about how life was better before and "sucks" now. Evidently, she really wants to be home, but there is no turning back now. She always looks at me angrily, probably for pushing us forward.

More serious concerns are also emerging. For the past couple weeks, Harper has been complaining of hearing knocks on the airlock door near the farm. Our shields should protect us from any small space debris. Our sensors should be able to detect and divert us from anything large enough to be a threat. There is no physical cause for such noises.

Two weeks after Harper complains of the noises, Vivian reports a strange conversation after she and Vivian finish working in the farm. Vivian's medicinal herbs are planted close to the barn where Harper spends most of her time. Lately, she prefers her animals to people. Part of Harper's work is to socialize the farm animals. She and Vivian often pet the nocturnal rabbits and visit with the chickens to keep the animals calm and docile. The rabbits, being English angora, need daily grooming, and must have their coats blown out every three months. They are molting now. Harper is combing and plucking them carefully to harvest the wool. Then she places the wool in her mini processor to wash, spin, air and pack before she preserves it by freezing for later use as liners or yarn. Vivian asks, "Does plucking out the hair hurt them?"

"No, they like it."

"Can I help?"

"No, you have to be experienced to not to pick the short, new hairs. That would hurt."

"Ah." Still, Vivian enjoys petting the rabbits.

"Did you hear that rumble?"

"No, just the usual sounds of the *Athena*."

"It must be the dragon again."

"What's a dragon?"

"A large flying animal."

"I know *that*, but what do mean by a dragon in the *Athena*?"

"It's not in the *Athena*. It's outside. Look at the dents in the ceiling. It's climbing over us," Harper informs her.

"I don't see any dents."

"It's past," says Harper, and then to the rabbit, "I won't let it eat you."

"I've never seen any dragon outside."

"I'll show you." She finishes with the first rabbit and sets it down.

"OK?"

Harper brings Vivian to a portal. "See, there behind the white cloud."

"You mean the Milky Way."

"See, it hides. See the red eye in the middle?"

"I see a bright red star."

"That's what it wants you to think."

After they are finished, Vivian comes to see me to tell me about their conversation. I agree it's strange, but say I would talk to our astrophysicist, Aurora Yazzie, and chief engineer, Zoë Dimitropoulos, just to rule out a physical cause. I arrange to meet with them in the Bubble. I ask, "Harper saw something. This may sound strange, but is it possible that some space debris, somewhat resembling a dragon, could be out there pounding on the *Athena*?"

"Are you serious?" asks Zoë.

"Yes, apparently it has a red eye and hides in the middle of the Milky Way. Anything *remotely* like that possible?" I ask, realizing the question sounds outrageous.

"Maybe she sees the red supergiant Antares, a binary actually, in the constellation Scorpius, the Scorpion's Heart. It's about six hundred light years away though," suggests Aurora. "A living dragon? There aren't even meteoroids or comets anywhere close—a dragon." She shakes her head, then starts to grin, then giggle, which turns into an uncontrollable belly laugh.

Zoë adds, while smirking, "Maybe she dreams a knight in shining armor will visit her too."

"I take that as a no," I say, and then ask Zoë, "So nothing pounding on the ship, enough to cause bowing?"

"No, we'd all know about it. The sensors would have picked something up." Zoë can barely answer as she starts to laugh with Aurora, and then says dryly, "You can't be taking this *serious*. Want evidence? Maybe you and Harper should suit up to hunt the dragon, look for tracks, droppings."

"Sure," jokes Aurora, "I hear they're golden."

"Isn't it *eggs* that are golden?" asks Zoë.

"Maybe. Does it matter?" asks Aurora. She and Aurora guffaw, and I can't help but chuckle too.

Finally, I say, "This really is not funny. Vivian says Harper seemed convinced." After we return to the ring, I mention this and Harper's negative attitude to Ava, who agrees to monitor Harper closely for depression and hallucinations.

nine

The Wormhole

After nine months of space travel, we approach the wormhole. We are excited to receive a congratulatory transmission from the U.S. President and the Canadian Prime Minister, thanking us for our bravery and efforts and encouraging us to move on for humanity. I send back a polite message thanking them for their confidence in us.

Astrophysicist Aurora Yazzie, geologist Kiara Williams, and biochemist Vivian Li finish up observations and analysis of a few of the closest Kuiper bodies. They return through the tube to prepare their reports. Our videographer, Lilian Jones, is happy to have new material for her last monthly broadcast until we return from the other side of the wormhole.

We slow the engine and plan to coast in. Aurora, Kiara and I enter the Bubble and stare at what looks like a round train tunnel encased in a cloud of dancing Las Vegas lights. "Inside the tunnel, it's so dark," I say.

"Looks ominous," says Kiara.

Aurora assures us, "It won't stay dark, the wormhole bends at about the middle, and we'll see the stars and Ross system then. It should take only about two weeks to glide through."

"But it is only one thousand kilometers wide, possibly unstable, and may contain debris and harmful radiation. I understand that its gravity can be extremely strong," I say.

"I know, we'll be staying in the exact center to even out gravity, tricky because it's very narrow," explains Aurora.

"What would happen if we hit the side?" asks Kiara.

"There are no exact answers," replies Aurora.

"Would the gravity compress us?" I ask.

Aurora answers, "I don't know. How wormholes bend through space is still a mystery. Even if we were able to pass through the side unharmed, we aren't sure where in the universe we would be. We could find ourselves hundreds of light years off course."

I look in the opposite direction, "Good-bye Sun." At this distance, the sun resembles a bright star. We take one last look and return to the bridge.

We send our last radio messages home for the next six months. I send my dad a transmission in French. "Hi Dad, this is the big moment, a major reason we are here, almost to the edge of our solar system. Wish you were here to see it. All the brightly colored gases shimmering around the tunnel are very beautiful. I probably cannot get any messages in the wormhole and it's a long wait from the other side. You probably know that already. Wish us luck. I will be back here in six months to tell you all about it, same bat time, same bat channel. Miss the family. Love you. Kisses." The others transmit similar messages, hardly able to remain stoic.

We assemble on the bridge. Aurora, Lilian and Emma make speed and direction adjustments based on our latest observations. Due to numerous conjectures on wormholes, we send in a tiny probe to test elongation and radiation. Hours later, it comes back indicating dangerous levels of cosmic radiation. We would be at the high end of the safe radiation limits inside the *Athena*, with her thick walls and shielding. I make a log entry, "September 9, 2047, 1100 hours Eastern Standard Time. The probe tests were successful—no gravity distortions or ship-penetrating radiation in the center. We expect that our plasma shield and thick walls will protect us. Radar and lidar detect no harmful debris in our path. All systems are a go. Out." I give the signal to Emma, and we enter the mysterious darkness, apprehensively.

Our troubled crew member Harper was missing during my transmission. At the end, she runs past us at full speed, streaking along the track, screaming "Nooooooo! Run from the dragon's lair!"

She reaches life support and starts flipping switches and striking the equipment.

I run to her. "Harper, stop, you will hurt yourself and the life-support unit."

"No, go back!" She is about to break a unit. Emma surprises her, knocks her down and holds her in a body scissor.

"We need to get her to medical," I say.

After a struggle, Emma maneuvers Harper to standing in a full nelson. Then we each hold an arm and take her kicking and screaming to medical. There she has a fit of delirium, screaming about attacks on the ship until she exhausts herself into a deep sleep.

I say, "Someone needs to watch her 24/7."

Vivian, who had followed us, offers, "I'll watch her until Ava wakes up. Poor thing. She's really scared."

"I'm sure. Thanks Vivian, I need the engineers on the bridge. When Ava gets up, Emma, you should have her check you out too."

"Sure thing. Some of those kicks smarted."

"Thanks for your help stopping her."

I wake Riya, and she and Lilian carefully check and recalibrate the life-support units, shaking their heads. They fix a broken control panel and some tubing and later report that all is in order.

This incident does not help our mood in the mysterious wormhole. During the entire first week, we feel an emptiness, even creepiness as we are swallowed by the darkness. We had been accustomed to seeing whirling stars out of the portholes, but now there is nothing. It seems endless. Going to the Bubble to observe only makes me feel worse, as the hole to our universe gets smaller and smaller.

After a week, we reach the bend, and there is no light from the universe at all. I ask Aurora, "How can you tell where we are in the wormhole?"

"Gravity should be even in the middle."

"Should be?"

"We don't really know."

"I know I really don't like this," I say as a shiver crawls from my arms down my spine. "It's foreboding. How can you tell we are even moving?"

"We are. Hear the engine?"

"Yes, but . . ."

A few hours later, Aurora announces, "We're past the bend! Come see the sunrise or the Ra-rise." The entire night team cheer as they watch it on the live camera.

Harper opens the hatch and flies up the tube to get the full view from the Bubble. I chase after her, and Aurora follows. Harper stares at the bright light on the edge of the opening, much like our sun, but glowing red. Aurora says, "Once we exit the wormhole, we'll be less than three hundred million kilometers from the exoplanet Ross? It should take just over two weeks to get into orbit."

"It feels good going toward something," I say, "Ra is amazing!"

Aurora warns us, "Don't look at it directly without sunglasses. I'm setting a telescope toward the exoplanet. The Bubble is less protected from the cosmic radiation than the rest of the ship. This will take about a half hour, and then we have to leave." Harper and I watch as Aurora, in communication with Lilian, sets the scopes.

The day crew, excited to have Ra in view, decide to celebrate the "Rising of Ra" with a real meal from our farm. Kiara and Bella had dug up and washed potatoes and are now gathering fresh vegetables. Evelyn is in the kitchen area preparing the meal. While waiting for the deep fryer to cook the potatoes, she is having fun working with clay, forming Egyptian god images as center pieces for the table in the dining hall. She has made Ra, the falcon-headed god; Hather, the cow goddess; and Bastet, the feline goddess. She is now shaping Anubis, the jackal god. At the same time, she is listening to music about the Sun to form a varied playlist for dinner. She includes classics like "Here Comes the Sun" by the Beatles and "The Song of the Sun" by Mike Oldfield and some contemporary songs. She is contemplating adding "You Are My Sunshine" and trying to decide on which version.

As I'm jogging around the track, I notice a smell coming from the dining area—burning! I rush to the kitchen. I hear Evelyn shout, "The fries!" as she rushes from the far end of the dining hall. She is panicked and grabs the fire extinguisher. I quickly put the cover on the fryer, extinguishing the fire, as she sprays me all over with foam. I stare in shock.

Then I say dryly, "Well, you did manage to get some foam on the stove. You know you are not supposed to use foam on grease fires."

"Oh, right. I'll clean it up."

I feel ridiculous but can't get mad at Evelyn; she was surprised and trying. Then, I hear a strange bang. "What else did you do?"

"It's not me."

I receive an emergency signal on my communicator, wipe most of the foam off quickly, and rush to the bridge.

Arla and Lucy have been monitoring instruments in the bridge. They also heard the loud bang from the tube. Lucy immediately rushes to close all hatches. Arla triggers *Athena*'s emergency alarm system, waking everyone. She quickly sends out a mayday, though the radio waves travel in a straight line and cannot travel over the bend. Surprised by the farm portal closure, Bella and Kiara call Arla asking for information and Arla tries to explain. Everyone heads for the bridge. Zoë and Aurora check their stations in the adjacent engineering section and are frantic.

"The gauges are off! The ones that monitor Superman. This makes no sense!" mutters Zoë.

"*Athena* is drifting off center," says Aurora. Lilian and Emma try to restore the *Athena*'s course, but it does not change. Aurora warns, "At this rate, we'll hit the side in seven hours."

"As a precaution, we should put on our g-force suits," advises Dr. Ava Campbell. We rush to do so.

I ask Zoë, "What's wrong?"

Zoë answers, "I can't tell exactly without looking closer."

We go to a porthole and she shouts "Hell! There's a big hole in the cylinder, at the bottom near Superman. I need to see what happened!"

"Are you going through the Bubble tunnel?" I ask.

"Negative, the spoke rotator engine is just to the bottom of the connection; I can't access the engine from there. There's also a thick wall sealed to protect the upper tube and the Bubble against heat and radiation. I'll need to go in through the zipline on the lower spoke." She grabs some tools and a communicator, and we quickly walk to the spoke access airlock.

"Are you really thinking of ziplining over there?"

"Do you have a better way to get there?" I see no other options. "Don't worry, I practiced this before."

I state, "Protocol says no one outside alone to make repairs. I should go with you."

"For what? I won't be *outside* for long. I'll make repairs on the *inside*."

"I'll go with, I can help," offers engineer Riya Patel.

"Yes, better you should go too. I help you suit up," I say.

None of us have ever gone on a real spacewalk before. I work with Zoë and Riya to be certain they have everything connected properly, double-checking each step, annoying Zoë in the process. It takes four hours to suit up properly, for pressurization and nitrogen removal, to prevent the bends. I attach the SAFER (Simplified Aid for EVA Rescue) joystick and backpack to her. SAFER contains small jet thrusters to move around in space should the zipline fail.

I start to feel unusually weighty. "You nervous?" I ask.

"I'm excited actually," says Riya. "You seem more nervous than we are. We've got this."

"I'll feel better when you are back."

They enter the inner hatch to the airlock and secure it. Anxiously, I watch them, but they proceed fearlessly. They wait ten minutes for the air to get sucked back into the *Athena*. Then Riya opens the outside door, where the cosmic background temperature is a mere minus two hundred sixty degrees Celsius. Without a suit at this temperature, in one to two minutes, organs would freeze up, skin would be frost-bitten, the nervous system would go into shock. A person would be dead within three to four minutes. Knowing all this, Zoë steps out, with Riya following and securing the second hatch. It takes five minutes to zip across the spoke to the central tube. Then Zoë opens the portal to the tube, and they enter that airlock. After a few minutes, Zoë gives me a thumbs up from the blast hole.

I return to the dim and quiet bridge. Even in my g-force suit, I start to feel a strong force pulling me in different directions. I breathe deeply to look brave in front of the crew as I sit in my chair. Zoë and Riya stay in radio contact with Emma and Lucy on the bridge. I try to listen for progress reports, but because all the scientists are asking questions simultaneously, we can barely hear the radio.

I order, "Everyone, please no questions! We will answer them later. We cannot hear to work. Everyone, but the engineers and Aurora, go over to the far left, to the labs, and strap yourselves in."

Soon, it's quiet and I can hear Zoë say, "Damage is extensive. Over."

"We still get no readings here. Over," radios Emma.

"I'll work on that first. You should be able to soon. Out."

"There's no power to the life support systems. They're on emergency back-up—only good for five hours. I'm switching us to main battery-power," announces Lucy.

Emma radios, "Zoë, there's no power going to life support. Over."

"Roger," radios Zoë, "Lots of loose wires here. Riya's all over it. Out."

We hear occasional status call amongst the engineers. It seems to be taking an extremely long time. After twenty-five stressful minutes, we see the familiar blinking lights.

Emma radios, "All gauges are on. Over."

"Riya and I found and fixed a half dozen lines that were severed. Is power back on? Over."

We hear the familiar hums. Lucy radios, "Power is back on too. Switching from batteries."

"Copy that." I can feel the release of tension.

In five minutes, I radio Zoë, "Time is up. The warning lights indicate dangerous radiation levels."

Zoë responds, "It's a real mess. I need to connect the guidance system. It needs repair and rebooting. I'm rebuilding the inside. Parts are too cold and need to be warmed up. There's no time to go back and forth. We fixed the wiring so no need for two of us out here. I'm sending Riya back now. Over."

"Zoë, we can use the thrusters. Get back. Over."

"No, we'd use all our fuel, and they're not designed for this gravity. Over."

"We feel it, but you are in the danger zone. Over."

"I know, stop interrupting me," radios Zoë.

"Permission to stay not granted! Over," I order.

"Dammit I see the radiation alerts! No time to argue with you. Need to get this working."

"Zoë!"

"No time! Out." I sigh and shake my head.

In the tube, Riya asks Zoë, "Are you sure I should leave?"

"Yes, go now. I don't need help with the rest. It just takes time. I'm partially protected in here."

On the bridge, I ask our medical doctor, "Ava, can you help Riya with her suit and check her out."

"Yes, of course," responds Ava. She walks like someone trudging through snow.

Lucy informs me, her voice shaky, "I ran a full diagnostic of the electrical system. The main ventilator has not kicked back on. I don't hear it. I'll check it out—maybe blew a transformer switching over."

"Yes, do that," I say.

Zoë is in the tube for another half hour and is still in constant radio contact with Emma on the bridge. She asks them to try to maneuver the *Athena*, but nothing changes.

"Damn, the guidance system is working. What's stopping it? Over." radios Zoë.

"My gauges indicate guidance is fine too. Is it something else mechanical? Over," asks Emma.

"Maybe. I'll look around outside. Over."

I can see the worry return on everyone's faces and hear a few whispers. My stomach is tight, but I try to appear calm.

Lucy returns, "I can fix the ventilation. It's the transformer. Food storage unit is off too. To replace the transformer, I'll need to turn off the power to the bridge briefly."

"Can it wait until we are stabilized?"

"It's not optimal, but it can wait another hour."

The system flashes red and the computer indicates that we are approaching dangerously close to the side of the wormhole.

"We need to move away from the wall now. We're at three g. Its gravity will be strong enough to cause significant damage in seventy-five minutes," warns Aurora.

I radio Zoë impatiently, "Zoë, how much longer? We are dangerously close. Over."

"It's a complete mess here. I'm outside removing shrapnel from the main joint. Superman can't maneuver. It may take an hour. Over."

"Hurry," I say looking at my worried crew.

"Wasn't planning on napping. Out."

Everyone is quiet, still too nervous to speak. After a disturbing forty-five minutes, Zoë calls in, "I cleared out the shrapnel. Try it. Over."

Emma does, but reports, "No change. Over."

"Roger, I'll check the rods and arm," says Zoë.

"Copy that."

Zoë moves over a meter, opens a panel, and radios, "Lower control arm is bent. They stored spares parts here. Spare arm looks fine. I'm working on replacing it. Should only take a few minutes."

"Thank God," I say to Emma.

After fifteen minutes, Zoë radios, "This better work. Try it again. Over."

"Wilco," says Emma.

After a minute, she smiles and radios excitedly, "Gauges say we changed course, three degrees away from the wall. Over."

Aurora confirms, "We've slowed our approach to the wall." I can hear whispered hurrahs from the scientists and see they're smiling too.

"Can you give me the data to recalculate our course?" asks Lilian.

"Yes, I'll send them over to you," says Aurora.

"Let me know if you can't get her back to center," orders Zoë. "I'm looking around—unbelievable! Over."

"Wilco," says Emma. "Whew, it's stuffy in here."

"We steady now?" asks Lucy hurriedly.

"Yes, I think so," says Emma.

Lucy trudges to the far end of engineering. Abruptly the lights and all power turn off. Most gasp. Others shriek.

Lucy shouts, "It's only me! Give me a minute to replace the blown coil in the transformer! I switched life support to emergency back-up. It's just the lights. Their back-up must be expired." We see her in the light of her portable lantern.

"Give me a warning next time!" yells Emma.

"I did! It'll take just a sec."

"You freaked me out," says Emma.

"and a few others," I add.

"You frickin' gave me heart attack!" complains Harper.

In a minute, the lights and all instruments come back on. "OK, the ventilator works now. I'll recharge all emergency back-up batteries."

"Many thanks Lucy," I say.

A few more minutes and Aurora reports, "We're perfectly centered."

Emma radios, "We're where we are supposed to be. Over." Everyone cheers and rushes in for hugs.

Zoë radios, "Great, I'm heading back. Big problems here. Out."

I meet Zoë at the airlock and help her take her suit off. Because she looks ill, I take her to medical. Ava examines her, taking skin and blood samples.

I ask Zoë and Riya, "What does it look like in there. What is damaged?"

Zoë answers, "Everything. There's much more than I could fix. The device creating the magnetic field that stops the plasma from hitting the reactor wall is damaged. I cannot control the flow into the reactor because the mechanism controlling the amount of fuel that enters the reactor is also damaged. The spares blew out. In a couple days, the plasma will overheat and become unstable. It'll be like a giant explosion."

"We have to sever the reactor?"

"Yep, but it gets worse. The reactor was designed to detach from the *Athena* so it could be used elsewhere if the ring were in stationary orbit. The blast destroyed the controls for the mating adaptor. We'll have to sever it manually with hand tools."

"What do you think caused the blast?"

"It must be sabotage and look what I picked up in the debris." She shows me a pocket notebook with diagrams and Chinese writing.

I take it. "I will give it to Vivian and ask if she can make sense of it. Sorry Ava for disturbing you, I let you do your work."

As I leave, I hear Ava tell Zoë, "You have been exposed to much more cosmic rays than recommended. I want to keep monitoring you. Rest here. Let me know immediately if you experience any nausea, vomiting, or diarrhea."

"Will do," says Zoë too tired to argue.

I immediately return to the bridge to inform the rest of the crew of our situation.

"Thanks for being here everyone. I apologize for being short earlier. As you know, we had a critical situation. I would like to express my sincere gratitude to Emma, Riya, Lucy and Zoë for their competence and calm, and for Aurora and Lilian for keeping us on course." Everyone cheers.

I explain the engine overload and other damage and then open the floor for discussion.

"Without Superman, we could not reach Earth before our food supplies run out," advises Riya.

"We should try to go back. Maybe someone can meet us," suggests Harper.

"I'm not aware of any deep space craft even planned at this time," Riya counters.

"The sun's rays are too weak in the outer parts of our solar system for the *Athena*'s photovoltaic solar panels. We'd run out of power in two weeks, maybe three," adds Lucy.

"Once we leave the wormhole, Ra will be strong enough to energize the solar panels," says Aurora.

"They'll just be able to provide power when we leave the wormhole, but will become more efficient as we approach Ross," clarifies Lucy.

All signs indicate that Ross is probably survivable," says Vivian encouragingly.

"What if it's desolate?" asks Harper.

"We should be able to reach Ross in roughly five months without Superman," advises Lilian.

"Seems we won't have enough power for my plants. I'll prepare them for a long winter," whines Bella.

"The good news is we still have about fifteen months of food," says Riya.

"Going back is impossible. We must move forward to Ross," I conclude. "Are we all agreed?" Everyone, except Harper, nods or orally agrees.

"Zoë found this notebook. Vivian, would you help us decipher it?" I ask.

She skims through it, "Yes, of course. I may need Riya or Lucy's help interpreting the diagrams."

"Good, thanks. We need to remove the now dangerous reactor, using just hand tools. It cannot be done in the half hour time limit. We'll each need to take a shift. We all trained to do this type of work at NASA. We'll go out in pairs of two—we have two space suits," I explain.

"I'll go first," volunteers Emma.

"I'll go with her," says Lilian.

"Arla, please help me schedule the others with an assistant to help them. It needs to be completed in two days," I order.

"Will do," she responds.

I assist Emma and Lilian as they spend four hours suiting up. Then they leave by the zipline portal, taking safety tethers and smaller tethers to attach a power saw and other tools.

Emma, wearing the SAFER pack, quips, "If you have to die, die beautiful," and glides confidently across the zipline. "I've been dying to try that." They hold on to the tube's external handrails and footholds.

After thirty minutes, they prepare to return. "Are you sure we can't stay out longer? It'll take forever working like this. Over," complains Emma.

I radio, "Yes, Ava's orders. Zoë's pretty sick, nauseous. Over."

We continue to take turns in pairs, with one wearing the SAFER pack for reassurance. Lucy and Arla make the second trip. Both excelled at these procedures in NASA's underwater tank. However, having to actually step out of the portal into the dark, empty space, terrifies Lucy. I can hear her breathing heavily and Arla reassuring her. Lucy was more than ready to come back after a few minutes. She returns, perspiring profusely, her skin a pale white, complaining, "It's nothing like training. There's just nothing out there!"

A few hours later, Evelyn and I are ready to go. She yells, "Whee!" on the zip line. To get to our worksite, she crawls like Spiderman, singing the Spiderman show theme song. Progress seems slow, and I'm very tempted to stay out longer, but Evelyn reminds me that it's too risky.

After a long, stressful day with luckily no accidents, the last pair dislodges the lower quarter of the central tube. We are elated to be safe but still sadly bid Superman good-bye. Zoë's life work was floating away, and I note a tear streaming down her face.

Vivian meets with me in medical where Ava is still watching over Zoë. Vivian has deciphered the notebook. She tells us, "It indeed contains detailed sabotage plans of a timed bomb placed around our fusion reactor. They purposely set the bombs to go off when we were out of radio transmission range. Wouldn't you agree from these diagrams?" She shows some diagrams to Zoë.

"Yes," sighs Zoë.

"Very disturbing. I will radio NASA as soon as we can," I say.

"Don't you find it strange, Harper's hallucinations. The dragon and the color red are symbols of China," wonders Vivian.

"Do you think Harper may have subconsciously sensed something wrong—something our sane conscious minds ignored?" asks Ava.

"Don't know, maybe it's too close to be just a coincidence," says Vivian.

"You may be right," I agree.

Then I return to the bridge to check on navigation. Aurora complains, "Ross shifts its position erratically. Sometimes it seems to disappear. Debris within the wormhole is worse—shifting or just vanishing altogether. I thought I saw a large metallic meteoroid, more massive than us and distorted, but it vanished like a ghost—just a blip."

"Spooky. Could it be our instruments?" asks Lillian.

"I doubt it—could be dangerous for collisions."

"Where is it coming from?" I ask.

Aurora shrugs her shoulders and says, "Wormhole gravity attracts debris."

She works closely with Emma and Lilian to make slight course corrections, careful to stay where gravity is weakest. They work opposite the newly trained pilot, Arla, and observer, Kiara, from day crew. Carefully, they detect and maneuver around objects.

Within a day of our spacewalk, we all feel nauseous and start to vomit. Dr. Ava Campbell determines we are suffering from acute radiation syndrome. She expects we will recover within a couple weeks. However, Zoë now experiences severe cramps, frequent nausea with vomiting, and watery diarrhea.

I visit Zoë who is still in medical and ask Ava, "How is she?"

"I gave her an IV for dehydration. She seems extremely nervous and confused and loses consciousness. She says her skin feels like it's burning. It's serious—radiation poisoning."

"She'll recover. Zoë's tough as nails. You can heal her."

"I'm not so sure."

I know logically that Zoë's condition is critical, but I feel that she'll pull through. I inform the crew and then spend almost my entire shift monitoring her. Lucy and Riya, Zoë's colleagues from NASA, visit as often as they can. Others stop by to ask how she feels. Bella brings a bouquet trying to smile, "Here you are, I salvaged some before we had to close down the fields."

"You guys must have more important things to do than to fuss about me," says Zoë brusquely. "I'll *be* fine."

"We don't have more important things," says Lucy softly.

Later when Lilian visits, Zoë asks, "Can you help me make an audio-visual for my wife Sandra and send it to her? Ava won't let me out of bed."

"Of course. Be right back."

After Lilian returns and sets up, Zoë orders, "Now everyone out!"

The next day, while Harper, Lucy and I are with Zoë, her body goes into convulsions. I run to wake Ava. "Please do something!" I beg.

Ava wakes quickly and rushes to examine Zoë. After running several tests, Ava says, "I'm sorry. She doesn't have much longer. There's nothing I can do but make her comfortable."

"This really sucks!" snaps Harper. She walks out and slams her fist against a wall.

I hold Zoë's hand. "Zoë, you can fight this," I whisper in tears. Lucy, also in tears, puts her arm around me.

"Don't you dare leave us!" begs Riya. Riya exits medical for the bridge where she says angrily, "Why did she tell me to go? We could have gotten it done together in half the time!"

Arla hears her and puts an arm around her, "You didn't know."

"If I had stayed, she might have made it. I just can't watch her like this. It's so not fair!" says Riya. Then, she breaks down and cries.

In medical, Zoë continues to worsen until she goes into a coma. We keep close watch on her. I keep asking Zoë to wake up. I thank her for all she has done for us, for saving our lives. Others stop by to talk to her and to thank her. Lucy and Riya stay the longest telling her how much they have appreciated working with her. They reminisce. We joke about her gruff personality. I hope for a reaction in Zoë but find none. Ava continues providing life support and offers prayers. We keep looking for signs of Zoë awakening.

Despite all our efforts, in three days, she dies. We are all stunned in disbelief and mourn the loss of our intelligent, brave and trusted friend. We have a brief parting ceremony as we allow her body to float into space, playing her favorite songs, including "Dream On" by Aerosmith.

ten

Out of the Wormhole

As we exit the wormhole, I send a quick dire transmission to Earth, a message they won't receive for eleven years, "September 26, 2047, 2000 hours Eastern Standard Time. Traversed the wormhole. Suffered destruction of Superman. Found sabotage notes in Chinese near blast site. The engineers performed remarkably. Lost Dr. Zoë Dimitropoulos, who bravely sacrificed her life to save ours. Not enough solar power or provisions to return. Proceeding to Ross 128 b."

The mood is still very somber after we exit the wormhole. Most of us still feel sick. We realize that we cannot get back home, probably ever. We will spend our lives celibate, something we never intended. We won't see our families or be part of their lives. I ache for my corny, aging father, who has always treated me as his little princess. I miss Zoë. Even the plants have started to die in the frigid cold, making the gloom even more dismal. The melancholy is inescapable. Hyper-Space is practicing the doleful song "Numb" by XXXtentacion expressing a hopelessness permeating the *Athena*.

There are many uncertainties about what our new home will be like. Is it hospitable? Are there deadly, flesh-eating microbes or unavoidable toxins? Can we really grow or find food? We hardly have a conversation without someone mentioning a fear or loss.

Still, we keep moving forward. Despite our mood, we maintain our survival instincts. Aurora reminds us that we need to change course in order to reach Ross because our direction and declination are off. With Emma and Aurora's help, Lilian has been busy re-programming the computer to direct the orbital thrusters to bring us to our destination.

We need to crowd the tropical plants in our living space. I raise an eyebrow to Bella's marijuana plant in the middle of her quarters. Though I question her about it, this infraction seems so insignificant now.

Two weeks after discharging Superman, engineers Riya Patel and Lucy Karlsson explain that with back-up battery power diminishing, we need to drastically cut our energy use. We become accustomed to living on bare necessities—less water, low light, no virtual reality, minimal experiments. Within a week, we complain mostly of being crammed and bored. We can't spread out. I can't run the track because half of it is closed off to conserve heat. I don't even read for leisure because that takes power too. We can play cards or chess, but that can only keep us entertained for a couple hours at most. We cut use of electronic exercise equipment, though we can still practice our martial arts, yoga or other floor exercises. With hardly anything else to do, the days drag on. I find myself watching the clock on the bridge and seeing only minutes go by. The crew is becoming generally either apathetic or jittery. There are petty arguments when others waste resources.

For the past couple weeks since leaving the wormhole, I've been moping. Today I'm playing chess with Vivian in the dining hall. Vivian calls, "Checkmate."

"Oh, missed that," I say indifferently.

"You didn't play too hard."

"I know. I do not feel like doing much lately. I think a lot about Zoë. I wish there was something I could have done differently. Maybe she would have come back in time."

"Seems to me there were no other options. Let's be real. You *know* Zoë. She knew the danger, and no one could tell her what to do."

"You are right about that."

"I think people might blame *me* because I'm of Chinese descent."

"No, I do not, and no one else does."

"But everyone seems so cold."

"I think everyone is depressed, worried, and maybe some others blame themselves too."

"I don't know. Harper always scowls at me."

"She always scowls at me too."

"True, I've seen that," agrees Vivian.

"I'm more worried about this mission, about us. I feel we are so vulnerable. I hardly sleep. My muscles hurt. Ava says there is nothing physically wrong with me."

"I think there's a lot wrong. Stress is a killer." She walks over to the kitchen cabinet. "I'm mixing you some turmeric, cinnamon and curcuma rhizome. Sprinkle it on your food."

"Should liven it up," I say concerned how it will affect the taste.

"And you too. Also, you should try acupuncture. Come with me to medical. It can help and it doesn't require electricity."

"OK—nothing else to do—surprised you have needles." We walk down the track to medical.

"Of course, NASA approved. It's proven itself."

"So, if I believe in the mystical flow of energy *qi*, it works."

Though I doubted its effectiveness at first, during the third treatment this week, I start to relax. "I do feel better," I comment.

"That's your endorphins releasing."

"I'm surprised a biochemist believes in *qi*, and traditional herbs," I say.

"My parents practiced and wanted me to learn Chinese ways and language."

"Thank them for me."

"I would watch them and was fascinated by how it works. I wanted to learn more, so I studied biology and chemistry. It is what lead to my doctorate."

"Biochemistry is amazing, especially how life ever even managed to start."

"Especially DNA, the code of life. With just four simple nucleotides, life reproduces. Parents determine 99.5% of their offspring," says Vivian.

"And it's everywhere, ribose even found comets. If it can exist in space, maybe we can survive space too."

After the treatments, I feel motivated, animated, and encourage the crew to think positive too. Out of a need to survive, I insist that we start intensely observing Ross. I ask Emma and Lucy to re-purpose all available batteries; the ones on the *Chidiya*, on the weather satellite, even from our communicators, Roberto and a cleaner. We plan to re-charge them when we approach Ross. We work out a schedule whereby we can carefully ration our energy supply. This new purpose seems to reenergize the crew.

In addition, I receive another unexpected boost elevating the mood of the crew. Animal biologist Harper Anderson, carrying a large crate, makes a proud announcement at mealtime. "I have some news. Though the rabbits were initially reluctant to mate in space, we now have two new litters born the same day. One doe has six kits and another seven. Now, I introduce them to you, because today, they are strong enough to be held."

Everyone in the hall rushes to see them. "Oh, there're so cute," coos Vivian.

"So fluffy," adds Lucy picking one up.

"Look how perky they are." Evelyn giggles. "Love those ears."

"Precious." Kiara talks to one as if it's a baby.

"They don't seem to have a care in the world," I say holding one.

"So snuggly, can I keep him in my room?" asks Bella.

"I want one too," says Lucy.

"Please, they're calming," begs Vivian.

"I have no objection. I'd like one too. It's up to Harper," I say.

"They do need more space," says Harper.

A couple weeks after requesting the planetary studies, I review the initial astronomy, geology, biochemistry, and weather reports. The next day, I gather the entire crew for a meeting to share the results. "Let's start with the astrophysicist's report."

Aurora says, "Ross revolves around Ra in 9.9 sidereal days, 3:2 spin-orbit resonance, meaning a Ross sidereal day is 6.6 Earth days long. The sunlight is 28.7 percent brighter. There is hardly an axial tilt; the seasons will be hardly noticeable. Mass is 1.324 times Earth's with density about 1.453 times Earth's. Also, there's no natural satellite."

"No reason to go looney," quips Evelyn, "No tides either."

"Actually, Ra's gravity causes significant tides," answers Aurora.

"Interesting. Are we still on course for arrival in four months?" I ask.

"In a month, we will travel through a strange cloud of fine particles. There is an asteroid belt, but in the outer circumference of the Ra system. I would have liked to find a planetary body to slingshot around, but there is none near our trajectory."

"Yes, we are fine and on course for arrival within four months," answers Lilian.

"Thanks. Next, let's have a summary on its geology," I say.

Kiara reports, "I want to thank Evelyn for assisting. A long land mass stretches from the north to the south pole. I searched for signs of tidal-flexing and super-volcanoes, like on Io, but did not see any. We confirmed the preponderance of heavy elemental compositions of carbon, oxygen, calcium, silicon. There are also high proportions of light and heavy metals, including the very rare iridium, osmium, palladium, platinum, rhodium and ruthenium. Percentages are on this pie chart. Smatterings of these metals are found on the surface, but given the density of the exoplanet, I would hypothesize that these heavier metals would be plentiful beneath the surface."

"Thank you, Kiara, and Evelyn. Can we have the biochemical summary?"

Vivian reports, "I worked with Bella and Harper assisting. There is a thick oxygen-nitrogen atmosphere, with water vapor, lots of water vapor. We noted strong signs of organic compounds. Here is a list of the ones we noted thus far." She lists some on a screen. "Unfortunately, there are also large deadly amounts of methane gas on the continent in the southern hemisphere." She concludes, "There has to be some kind of life down there."

"I agree," says Bella.

"I'd bet on it," says Harper.

"Ross must be stinky," comments Lilian.

"Maybe, but natural methane is odorless," says Vivian.

"But could Ross sustain human life? In any case, looks like we should avoid the southern hemisphere," asserts Emma.

"Thanks. Let's get the marine and weather reports."

Arla summarizes, "The surface seems to be ninety-four percent water, ninety percent ocean. The high vapor content would stabilize temperatures. The atmosphere is thicker than on Earth, but no runaway greenhouse effect. However, the winds may be more severe than on Earth, but not intolerable. There is a greater difference in air pressure, causing frequent high winds and storms everywhere. There are signs of massive hurricanes."

"I'd still take beach front property," says Evelyn.

"Me too," says Arla.

"Any other comments?"

Lucy says, "Yes. Ross is so close to Ra, it will be brighter than the Sun on Earth. Our solar panels are even now a bit more efficient but will function optimally once we approach Ross."

"This is overall really positive," notes Riya.

"Sounds promising," says Emma.

"Yes, I agree. We need to take a break from studies but can continue our observations in a couple months when the solar panels will provide near optimal energy. Really good work ladies." I approve the full reports and transmit them to Earth. Even with the temporary break from work and subsequent boredom, the mood on the *Athena* improves.

A few weeks after our initial reports, Aurora needs to conduct critical studies to fine tune navigation. She is a modest, introverted person of average appearance. Looking at her, the only memorable thing is her long black braid reaching down to her hips. Otherwise, she seems to fade into the background. By contrast, her mind is extraordinarily brilliant; she is a mathematical genius. In middle school, she had joined the math team and memorized *pi* to the seventy-fifth decimal place just because another student had memorized it to the fiftieth. She perplexed her high school teachers and won the state science fair in mathematics each year, and twice at nationals. After receiving a perfect math SAT score, she received a full scholarship to Princeton University. She needed accommodation there because, although she is fixated and excelled in math and astronomy, she did poorly in written skills, was disorganized, and forgot practical routine chores. In college, she could read any formula, including, though it took her two years, the proof for Einstein's theory of relativity. Since then, her own research has been ingenious. Aurora didn't tell me any of us these things. I had learned them when talking with her quiet, but proud, Inupiaq parents when they were visiting Aurora in Florida.

Today, Aurora is studying the Ross system and other stars for mapping. Because I like looking through the Bubble as often as I can, I decide to assist Aurora, though much of her work is beyond me. We look out at the stars and admire the similarities between the view here and the view from our solar system. Compared to the one hundred thousand light year expanse of the Milky Way, our eleven light year journey seems but a small step. The Milky Way looks very much the same, as do the distant stars and galaxies. Aurora points out how much the Centauri, Sirius, Epsilon Eridani and Cygni stars have apparently changed locations. Then she focuses a telescope briefly to view the Eagle Nebula and the Andromeda galaxy. She talks about multiverses and quantum entanglement, where information can be transmitted faster than light. She lost me with multiple dimensions beyond three-dimensional space, folding and time. We look out of the Bubble and wonder at the beauty and sheer vastness of the universe, feeling very, very tiny, but honored to be able to contemplate this small part of the entire realm of universes.

We see a shooting star and wish upon it. As we are about to return to the ring, we see a bright meteoroid speed past the Bubble. With our binoculars, it looks like an elongated basketball. Aurora runs it through the light spectra. She states, "Judging by the trajectory and light curve measurement, I'd say that's an ordinary iron rock meteoroid in orbit around Ra."

I complain, "Ordinary or not, that was too close for comfort. Hope we do not get any more of those."

"So, you don't want to hear about the metallic meteoroid that seemed to stall and then whizzed by here heading straight for Ross?"

"Thanks, but probably not. I'd rather sleep, and we do not have enough energy to study all the meteoroids that are probably out here."

Aurora sulks. "Just as well then, couldn't get much info on it—too fast."

"Carry on and let us know if we need to reroute around them."

"Of course."

I smile and offer, "You should be able to study random meteoroids in more detail in a couple months."

A couple days later, Aurora tells us, "We are in what appears to be the dust trail of a comet, only I haven't been able to find the comet itself. It seems to be in orbit around Ra, and we are intercepting its path."

"Why can you not find the comet," I ask.

"We weren't using all my equipment, just what's essential. Now, the dust cloud has become so long and thick it's obstructing viewing. The dust is microscopic in size and even our limited shielding can easily deflect it."

"Still, let's study it more closely," I say, "I ask Vivian and Kiara to help with the analysis."

Aurora, with Vivian and Kiara, study the mysterious dust. In a few hours, they give me full reports and summarize.

Kiara reports, "I detect silicates, chondrites, nickel, iron, magnesium and other metals."

Vivian adds, "I analyzed a variety of organic compounds, mostly methanol and ethane, but also complex hydrocarbons and amino acids and trace amounts of DNA and RNA components.

Aurora concludes, "The composition is more complex than the meteoroids or comets in our solar system."

"Are you able to detect a meteoroid or comet?" I ask.

"No." Kiara suggests, "The nucleus must have been the head of a comet, which disintegrated when hit by a meteor."

"I'd have to agree. We should study probability and mechanism of how the collision occurred," says Aurora.

"Maybe Emma can take the *Chidiya* out for a closer look and I can collect specimens," suggests Kiara.

"It could help explain the origin of DNA," says Vivian.

"This is extraordinary," agrees Aurora.

"The *Chidiya*'s batteries are not recharged and we can't spare the power. Have you ladies considered how dangerous this situation is?" I say a bit sarcastically.

"Ah, no," says Kiara.

"What's on radar and lidar?" I ask.

"Nothing," says Aurora.

"Well, that's good," I say.

"No, I mean they're not working. They were fine an hour ago. Maybe dust particles are blocking the units," says Aurora.

"So were driving blind."

"The particles that we detected so far have been microscopic," says Aurora defensively.

"I know, but what we don't know is what happened to the rock."

"True," says Aurora.

"Would you and Lilian please plot a course around this cloud? Get Emma to help move us if necessary."

"We'll get right on it," say Aurora. She calls Lilian to help her.

We hear clinking on the Athena. Looking through Aurora's workstation viewer, Kiara says, "I think I see a few dime-size fragments."

"That's not good," says Aurora looking in the viewer.

Lilian reports, "New course plotted. I initiated the thruster to move us out of the cloud."

A few minutes later, we hear pounding. "They're getting bigger, baseball size!" warns Kiara.

I put the ship on alert. A siren wakes everyone.

Arla arrives and radios a distress call. In a low voice, I ask, "Who are you expecting to answer that? Aliens?"

"Yeah right, I'm half asleep, force of habit," she mumbles.

"What's up?" asks Emma. The rest of the crew assembles near the labs adjacent the bridge.

"Lilian, please close all portals. Everyone, we are in the comet's tail. We had thought the particles were all microscopic, but they seem to be baseball size. Lilian plotted us a course out. Can I have the engineers at their stations to monitor any damage?"

Emma, Riya and Lucy go to their stations and start running diagnostics. "Sensors indicate damage to a solar panel," reports Lucy.

After a few minutes, Kiara announces, "The particles are fewer, but basketball size now."

"Sensors indicate damage to the thruster at three o'clock, near the bay," announces Emma.

"Make that two panels," reports Lucy, "No three, maybe more."

Bella glances out a porthole and then shrieks, "No! A spoke is severed!" The scientists look alert, and try to get a peek of the damage, but are otherwise quiet.

"We are now out of the cloud," says Aurora.

"It looks clear," agrees Kiara.

"Any more damage?" I ask.

"Nothing else detected," says Lucy.

"None here, but some units have switched to emergency back-up. We only have a few hours on that," explains Riya.

"Nothing else with propulsion," announces Emma.

"With the hits, we are drifting off course," says Aurora.

"As power is the most critical, we need to replace the solar panels with our spare panels as quickly as possible. Agreed?" I suggest.

"Yes," says Lucy.

"Definitely," says Riya simultaneously.

"Riya work with Lilian for optimal power usage, turn off everything you can," I order. "Everyone, stay here so we can turn power off everywhere else."

"I'm tired of this shit. We shouldn't be here," snaps Harper.

Ignoring her, I say, "After we fix the panels, we will need to work on redirecting the *Athena* and then fix the radar and lidar units."

"Right. At our reduced rate of speed, we probably don't need to be concerned about the spoke," advises Emma.

"No one *ever* frickin' listens to me," mutters Harper.

"We need two volunteers to repair the panels," I say.

Simultaneously, Arla, Riya, Evelyn, Lilian and Emma say, "I'll go."

"I need Lilian and Riya here. Arla and Evelyn can go first. Emma, we will need your expertise later for the thruster repair—maybe go with Riya if life support is stabilized."

They nod and Emma says, "I'm cool with that."

"Go through the Bubble with Lucy to get a visual before we close it down." They do and ten minutes later return.

"Did you see any further damage?"

"No," says Arla.

"I know what's needed." Lucy hurries to get tools and three panels.

As Evelyn and Arla suit up, Lucy helps them and comments, "I hate spacewalking."

"Not me. It's exciting," says Arla.

"For sure, it's awesome," agrees Evelyn.

"We'll have a camera on you, and you can radio me," says Lucy.

I warn them, "The maximum time for a spacewalk for repairs is five to six hours depending on radiation and how fast you use your air. Pay attention to the warnings."

After four hours, they exit. Arla tethers the replacement panels and wears SAFER, while Evelyn tethers herself and attaches their tools and other spare parts. They slowly arrive at the first and closest damaged panel and replace it in just under an hour.

"It's in! We replaced it. Piece of cake. Over," radios Arla.

"Great. It's working. That should keep us above freezing," assures Lucy. We breathe a sigh of relief and cheer.

They reach the second panel. They are out there for three hours. We watch Arla and Evelyn on the cameras. Some scientists nervously whisper. Others look bored. They become silent when they hear the static of Arla's radio. "That one was far and trickier, but we got it in. Is it working? Over."

"Yes. It's functioning. Over," says Lucy.

Then, they arrive at the last damaged panel. Arla radios, "This one is really mangled. We can't. We don't know how to even start fixing it. This whole area was hit pretty heavy. Over."

"Focus the camera on it, so Lucy can guide you. Over," I tell them.

"Roger. Our air and radiation warnings are on yellow," reports Arla.

"Come on in. Over," I order.

"Roger. We'll tether the panel out here. Out," says Arla.

"We should have enough power now for minimal life support," says Lucy.

"Just enough for the bridge though. Not enough for other areas like medical, warm water, kitchen use," says Riya.

"If we're off course, we'll need power for the thrusters too," adds Emma.

Evelyn and Arla return safely. After refilling the air tanks and pressurizing the suits, Emma and Riya prepare for a spacewalk to assess the damage to and repair the thruster. After an analysis, Emma thinks she can repair it. They head back for tools and parts. While still out there, Riya accidentally kicks the external exhaust for the excess waste management system. It leaks and they are hit by waste globules. They radio to tell us to turn off the waste evacuation system and let us know what they need. We place the items in the airlock. They pick them up and return outside to complete the thruster repair in five hours. They get warnings and opt to leave the waste system for later.

"Glad to have you back." I say relieved.

As the globules melt, Emma says, "Oh, that's so gross."

We clean the suits, check for damage and refill the tanks. "Lucy, have you determined what needs to be done to repair the last array?" I ask.

"No, I can't tell from here. I'll need to actually see it. I've gathered every tool we could possibly need. I noticed three other panels in that array were damaged, so we'll need to carry those out there too."

"Are you OK to go?" I ask.

"Not really. I have butterflies, but I know I have to. It's my specialty."

"I will go with you," I say.

"You'll be fine. Look how long we've been out there, and I'd go again," encourages Riya.

"How could you like that? The suit's more confining than this ship," comments Harper.

Lucy suits up carefully. "Promise you won't let me die out there," says Lucy.

"I promise. That is why I'm here."

On the spacewalk, she grabs her holds very tightly and babbles about anything. Soon, she seems to have trouble regulating her aspirations. Her nervousness is contagious. I find I must remind myself to take deep, relaxing yoga breaths. This last array, with the four damaged panels, is midway between two airlocks. It takes us more than an hour just to reach it. I notice that some of the handholds near the panel are also loose.

When at the worksite, I note, "They cannot rotate. I'll install the three over there. They seem straightforward. Do you think you can fix the one here that Evelyn and Arla abandoned and get the whole array so it can rotate?"

"Maybe."

"Careful, looks like multiple hits around here."

Lucy grips a hold and complains, "It seems wiggly. Wish there were more holds out here."

Then she struggles to dismantle the twisted array. Its rotating hub seems mangled beyond repair. She notes, "This part is dented and I have no replacement. I'll try reshaping it." After three hours in space, I finish replacing my three panels and join Lucy. She has inserted a panel and rebuilt most of the array's structure and hub. "Hub's not perfect." She tries inserting it.

The hub does not glide in easily. She struggles with it for about an hour. Then she receives a one-hour time warning and gets frustrated. She bangs on the hub's connector with full force, causing herself to jerk backward. The jerk requires her to increase her grip on her handhold, which comes loose. As she loses her grip on the *Athena*, she grabs for anything, but her forearm hits sharp metal, tearing her suit. She bounces off the *Athena* tumbling off to space. Her tether, which had been fastened to a weakened hold, dislodges. The jerk and tumble happened in a couple seconds.

She is pulling away fast as I start up my SAFER pack thrusters and unfasten my tether from the *Athena*. I reach for her, but she slips away from me. I grab her loose tether, pull her toward me and then tether her to me.

As I circle back to the *Athena*, I notice the tear in her suit. I instantly pull out the repair kit in the belt of my suit. Luckily only the extra outer protective coating was ripped. I seal it before the rip gets worse.

She looks terrified and starts to hyperventilate. At this rate, she will use up her oxygen too quickly. I try to calm her by holding her tightly as I use the SAFER thrusters to return to the *Athena*.

She grabs me and stutters, "I thought I'd float away forever."

"I will not let that happen," I assure her. I keep re-assuring her to calm her down and slow down her breathing.

It works, but then she moans. "My lower arm really hurts. I can't move my fingers."

Arla radios from the inside, "Are you secure? Over."

"Yes, now we are. Over." I respond.

"Scared us to death!" says Arla.

I consider aborting. However, we have such a small energy supply and her suit will probably no longer be serviceable. I ask Lucy, "Are you too cold? Can you continue?"

"I'm OK. We have to finish this. It has to be able to rotate. We need it, our bunnies need it."

"You are right. I make sure you stay safe." I inform the *Athena*, "We are working on the rotator hub. It's in place but not working."

I motion Lucy to hold on to a more secure location and tether her securely, wrapping the tether around her. I try to cheer her, "I feel like Snidely Whiplash tying Nell Fenwick to a railroad tie."

"Who?"

"It's an old cartoon about an inept Mountie."

"Never heard of it."

"I guess not everyone has a dad who loves old shows and made you watch them. Just stay here and watch. Tell me what to do." I notice her yellow warning light for air is on. "Lucy, you have less than an hour left. You have to breath more slowly. Do not move. I can give you some of mine if you run too low and we can use SAFER back if we have to."

"OK. I'll try."

With her instructions, I finish repairs to the hub and test it within forty-five minutes. I confirm that we can direct the array to Ra to energize the rest of the ship. Then I help Lucy, but my yellow light is on also. With Lucy's injured arm, if we return walking with handholds, it would take longer than one hour.

"Is your arm feeling better?"

"No, it's so bad, I can barely take it," she whimpers.

"We're heading back."

Soon, her red warning light comes on, meaning she only has fifteen minutes of air left. She looks panicked and is crying. "Oh no, how can I get back? And my arm, my arm is getting so cold."

"I give you half of my air," I say attaching a line to her air supply. I see her air supply increase. "Look. It's working. You'll be fine."

"We only have about a half hour."

"I will fly over." I start to release her from her tethers.

Lucy grab the holds tighter, "No, I can't let go."

"You cannot hold on to walk and we don't have time. I can fly us there much faster."

"No, I... I don't want to float away."

"Me neither, I will stay very close to the *Athena*, within grabbing distance." She calms down. I continue, "We did it before."

"You're right."

"Grab my tether. I tie it around your good arm, and I grab your tether."

"OK, don't let me go!"

"Never." As I ignite the SAFER thruster, I receive a low fuel warning.

Lucy is breathing too fast and depleting her supply again. In fifteen minutes, I approach the airlock, but am floating too fast and over-shoot it. I must circle around, miss again but am closer. The SAFER fuel gauge reads empty.

"Sorry, it's just a couple steps," I tell Lucy. She seems light-headed. I watch her carefully as we secure our footing and walk to the airlock. I press the button and open it. Lucy's air runs out just as we enter. She's gasping for air in her suit. I give her mine again.

In a couple minutes the airlock is saturated, I remove our helmets and say, "You did great."

She's white and stutters, "Never again."

Dr. Ava Campbell scolds me as she helps us with our suit. Then she checks Lucy and diagnoses frostbite and a fracture to the radius in her forearm. Ava consoles her. "I'll put your arm in a splint and sling. That should help relieve the pain. It'll heal soon." Everyone stops by to check in on Lucy, complimenting her for finishing despite her injury.

Obviously, the ripped suit is no longer safe to use. This leaves us with only one usable suit. Riya explains that the waste system should be an easy fix and offers to go out alone. She promises to use both tethers and the refilled SAFER pack. For these reasons, I let her go out, with Aurora and Kiara watching her closely. Fortunately, Riya manages to complete the repair in under two hours. Then she checks the nearby radar and lidar devices. She only needs to dust them off with air cans. She reenters without incident with Ava assisting. I'm happy to have everyone back inside.

On the bridge, Aurora is pacing back and forth, muttering to herself. I ask, "What's wrong Aurora? Why are you upset?"

"Just thinking," she says, and then answers, "It was my fault."

"We're all fine now. Lilian and Lucy can develop a multiple warning system for when the devices are not functioning."

"I always miss things."

"Everyone does sometimes. Remember Evelyn almost burning down the kitchen?"

"Yes."

"It happens. Everyone misses things. Are you OK to work with Lilian to plot us a new course?"

"Yes, I can do that."

"Then, get some sleep. How long have you been observing that dust?"

They plot the course. Emma engages the thrusters and places us on course to Ross. Meanwhile, I prepare a log and detailed transmission, including a report on the spacewalks, with a strong recommendation to provide more than two suits on space missions.

Suddenly, Lilian screams, "Harper's in the airlock!" With all this activity, we have ignored our sick friend Harper.

I order, "Seal it so no one can open the outside door." I run to the airlock where I see Harper in the chamber with no suit.

She is yelling hysterically, "Please, I can't take these walls anymore! Let me out! I'm suffocating in here!"

I try talking to her calmly and sympathetically, "Harper, please come in. I want to get out of here too, and we will, safely."

She gestures to me with her middle finger. "No, let me out *now*. You can't keep me in here! I can't take being locked up anymore."

"We can, together. Come in."

"I can't." She starts sobbing.

The air is being sucked out, and she could suffocate in less than ten minutes. I hadn't anticipated such an event and had not memorized the override sequence. The warning lights come on. I run to get my laptop from my lab and remove the laptop from its charge port, hoping it still has some power. "Yes!" I exclaim. I see

Ava. "Come, I need you. Harper is in an airlock." She follows me as I try to locate the override instruction file. Nervous, I drop my laptop and need to restart it. "Drat." I reboot it. "There it is. Argh, it's password protected." Hurriedly, I search for where I may have stored the password. "Found the password." We arrive at the airlock.

Ava peers in, "She's suffocating."

I start to enter the complex set of instructions. Panicked, I mess up and need to restart.

"Hurry . . . Hurry. C'mon."

"That's not helpful."

"She fainted."

Finally, I enter everything right and the portal opens. Emma arrives and the three of us carry Harper to medical, where Ava attaches a respirator.

Emma whispers, "We should lock her in the chapel for the remainder of the journey."

Ava shakes her head. "Solitary confinement will only worsen her already fragile mental state." Harper soon regains consciousness.

I'm trembling. "Are you OK?" asks Ava, putting her arm around me.

I exhale deeply and put my hand over my mouth. "I almost lost two in that airlock today."

"A copycat. She may try again." I work with Ava to arrange to have a back-up always stay with Harper.

We continue onward to Ross. As we approach, our solar arrays become more efficient. We still need to keep the electricity to the farm at minimum. However, we can charge all our empty batteries. Most of us can return to our work and hobbies. Kiara continues her watercolors on the paper walls; Evelyn asks for mischievous monkeys to remind us to laugh. Then Kiara paints a shepherd with puppies for me and seahorses for Arla. The anticipation increases as we near Ross. Our mood changes from lethargic to optimistically energetic. We, like the solar panels, being closer to a star, are now working at full capacity.

Part II – Welcome to Ross

eleven

Orbiting Ross

Just over five months after leaving the wormhole, we place the *Athena* into orbit, encircling, tethered by gravity. I feel secure, even elated, to attach to firmament. From the Bubble, we can see the perfect ball comprised mostly of ever-changing pink chiffon clouds over a sparkling crimson ocean with beckoning land mass spanning the hemisphere. Evelyn and I stare at this stunningly beautiful world. Overjoyed, Evelyn kisses Ross through the glass.

On the bridge, I make a log entry and transmission, "February 28, 2048, 0800 hours Eastern Standard Time, the *Athena* is in low orbit around Ross 128 b. Plan to make intensive studies of the surface of the exoplanet, including topographical and climatic maps. All systems go. Happy to arrive at last. Stay tuned."

After about two weeks of observation while in orbit, I seek consensus on our fate, and call a critical meeting of the entire crew in the dining hall. I inform the crew, "We should have had five months of fuel in our thruster tanks for orbit, but we used up most of the fuel to get here. Because the orbit of the *Athena* will decay, we will burn up. We need to decide where to go as soon as possible. I had asked for feasibility studies. Let's start with astronomical observations."

Aurora reports, "Ross has a protective magnetosphere as shown in this diagram. It is strong enough to deflect Ra's stellar wind. Magnetic north is forty-six degrees south of the north pole." She displays images of Ross with circular patterns around it. Highlighting an orbital path, she says, "This band is the best altitude to reduce interference on the weather satellite."

I continue, "Good news. Arla can you provide us with a summary of its climate?"

Arla presents. "It rains, all the time, except for at the poles and equator. With a very long day, the temperatures can significantly change during a single rotation. In the polar regions, there are ice caps, and the nightly temperatures frequently plummet to negative eighty degrees Celsius with the windchill. Temperatures rise to fifty-five degrees Celsius at the equator. At certain altitudes and moderate latitudes, the temperature is consistent and comfortable, a perpetual spring. The best climate would be around latitude twenty, maybe up to forty." She presents a chart of major wind patterns. "The winds seem subject to a Coriolis effect. The northern winds circulate in the north, while the southern winds stay in the south."

"Thank you Arla. Kiara, can you summarize the physical features?"

Kiara shows us a detailed topographical map. "Ross is only about six percent land, consisting of two major land masses and many islands. There are two continents: One mountainous continent to the northeast; and one low-land continent to the southwest. The continents are connected by a long snake-like isthmus. The southern continent has low hills but is mostly swamp, probably all sedimentary rock with a thick layer of mud. The northern continent has icy cold tundra in the north with plains to the south. Travelling south and east, there are several mountain ranges—some mountains appear to be dormant volcanoes—with numerous rivers. I would expect igneous rock, and metamorphic rocks too. Given the age of the exoplanet and its composition, it is likely that it would be rich in gemstones like rubies and sapphires. At the equator, there are dry hilly deserts up to and including parts of the isthmus. There are few crater impacts still visible. I'm happy to say that I detected only very low seismic activity and wouldn't expect any earthquakes. Overall, Ross is geologically calm."

"Seems a lot like Earth," says Harper.

"Yeah, I'd say so," agrees Kiara.

"Thank you, Kiara. Vivian what are your findings?"

Vivian adds, "I worked with Bella, Harper, and Kiara. We detected organic molecules everywhere. I'll put a list on the screen. We focused our search of basic toxins but found none, except toxic levels of methane gas in the south. Also, on the northern continent, Kiara and I noted small fissures of methane in the central plains, but the methane was non-existent in the east. Given the very low level of methane in the plains, we concluded that such fissures are rare."

Bella adds, "Despite the methane, the southern continent seems particularly biodiverse. I suspect these reddish-green areas contain plant life, but it's too early to say for certain. It's hard to peer down due to a thick atmosphere and constant rainfall."

Harper adds, "I would assume that the animal life on land would have evolved to adapt to the methane. I'm pretty sure I spotted what could be large animal life forms in the oceans. Too fuzzy to tell really."

"I can just imagine the murmurs among the religious conservatives if and when we confirm life on another world," comments Ava.

"I imagine some'll be shaken," says Kiara.

"Even so, we need to disclose our findings. I will transmit the full reports back to Earth, come what may," I say. "This is all the reports. I thank you for your hard work and contributions."

I continue, "Next, I would like to discuss how to proceed. I suggest we take the *Chidiya* and scout locations. A few can go initially to run more tests for toxicities. Then, we could transport a few of us at a time with essential items."

"I want to go," says Evelyn.

"Me too," says Harper.

Emma suggests, "It would be hard to bring all our provisions and equipment in the *Chidiya*. We have enough fuel for only a few excursions. Maybe I can eventually purify the local methane, make some engine modifications, and use some of it for fuel. But, why don't we take the *Athena* down, using the thrusters to descend from orbit and then to help us land? Then, we'd have shelter and everything all together with us."

I ask, "Is that possible?"

"We'd still descend fast, but Emma and I worked it out. We think Zoë was wrong in that the thrusters, the *Athena*, can withstand heavy g-forces," says Lilian.

"The *Athena* was to eventually retire on the Canadian tundra near Iqaluit in Nunavut as a tourist attraction," I say.

"Though the parachutes aren't installed yet and we're heavy," says Emma. "It won't be easy, but it's possible."

"The biggest issue is keeping cool," says Riya.

"Kiara, is there a flat location to fit the ring, maybe in the polar caps?" I ask.

Bella protests, "We couldn't grow food. Too cold."

Evelyn agrees, "No soil."

"A home only a Canadian would love," quips Harper.

Arla suggests, "Yeah, who wants to freeze on the caps, the tundra would be better. It's flat too."

Evelyn disagrees, "We'd have trouble growing anything in the frozen soil and high winds. Maybe to the south, looks like plains."

"Plains sound awesome," agrees Harper.

Vivian agrees, "I think so. But we had detected methane fissures. Maybe it could work."

"I don't think we should risk it. There may be lots more subterranean methane," counters Kiara.

"The southern continent is a definite no," says Bella. We use Kiara's map to look for flat locations, hoping for a large enough plateau in the mountains.

Then Kiara asks, "What about the crater in this high island at twenty-five degrees latitude on the east side of the mountain range, which could block the methane to the west? The island has a rolling flat-top hill that rises a kilometer above sea level and a mountain to the west. The crater on top of the hill looks like it's a kilometer in diameter. We should be high enough to be safe from ocean surges. The mountain and crater walls would protect us from severe hurricane winds. The crater slopes down sharply on the inside edges but then has flat concentric circles, like terraces, toward the center. Let me zoom in. Y'all see, there's a little lake in the center, no green. If it floods, I think the *Athena* should float, though I wouldn't want to test that on the open ocean."

Arla says, "I like the altitude, a little less air pressure, more like what we're used to."

Bella adds, "Lack of green may be a good bet that life is sparse there. It may be hard to grow food."

"On the other hand, if the surface has life, it could have predators," argues Harper.

"Then an island might be easier to defend than the mainland," adds Arla.

"Also, we'd be isolated and have less detrimental impact on the world's environment. Why do you think this spot is barren?" asks Bella.

Kiara conjectures, "It may be that the crater was made recently, past hundred years or so, and life hasn't spread there yet."

"It seems warm enough," says Evelyn.

Emma complains, "It's a tight squeeze but I think we could land the *Athena* there."

"Seems too tight," says Arla.

We discuss a few other locations but keep coming back to the crater as the best choice.

"Are we all agreed in support of landing the *Athena* in the crater? Say 'Aye'."

Everyone raises their hand and says, "Aye."

"Because we can only land the *Athena* once, as a precaution, we should first take the *Chidiya* down to the crater to test the air and soil for toxicities."

"Aye, aye, Captain," jokes Evelyn saluting.

twelve

Ross Landing

The *Chidiya* is departing for its first trip to the surface, with Emma as pilot. Evelyn and Vivian go with her to test the air and soil. Wearing protective suits and loaded with kits and sterile bags, they look prepared. As the rabbits have continued to multiply and we now have an abundance, they take one to test the environment.

During the descent, Emma puts on the positioning glasses, saying, "Yep, I look cool. Now, it's time to try out these fancy wings." A few minutes later, she comments, "Outstanding! They work like a charm, just like a bird's! This is even better than rocketing to Mars and the asteroids."

"Yes, but it's weird out there. The sky's so cloudy and red," says Vivian.

"It's different," agrees Evelyn.

"Evelyn, what's on your ancient songs playlist?" asks Emma.

Evelyn blasts "Born to Be Wild" by Steppenwolf and then "Fly Like an Eagle" by Seal as they swirl through the clouds.

When the clouds clear, Evelyn declares, "I see the island! See there with the sloping hill and the rust-gray stone mountain."

They land in the crater on the brick-red ground. The wings fold up perfectly. "That was my best flight ever! *Chidiya*, you're amazing!" states Emma. She looks around and comments, "The crater is not as flat as it appears to be from space. There are quite a few boulders along the rim. The *Athena*'s landing will need to be perfect."

They see a few isolated rust-green stalks. "Could that be wheat grass?" asks Evelyn.

"Wow, sure looks like it," says Vivian. The two scientists put on their helmets and enter the airlock.

As they exit the *Chidiya*, Evelyn states grandly, "That's one small step for me, one giant leap for womankind!" She steps out and falls forward, unaccustomed to her added weight. "Doh, drat."

Emma radios, "Are you OK?"

Evelyn radios back, "Yeah, I'm OK."

"Man, you're heavy," complains Vivian. She helps Evelyn get back up and they carefully step forward. "Ground's crunchy," comments Vivian.

Evelyn tests the soil for composition and toxins, and then concludes, "Soil seems to have essential minerals and nutrients. No toxins."

Vivian does likewise for the air. "Air consists of nitrogen (75.3%), oxygen (21.1%), with helium (2.4%), argon (1.1%), carbon dioxide, hydrogen other trace, but safe, gases."

They give Emma a thumbs up. Then Evelyn picks up some rocks, examines them and seals them in her bag. Vivian pulls up a stalk of grass as a sample.

"Amazing! Even up close, it looks like real grass!" remarks Vivian.

"Sure does," says Evelyn.

"Before we conclude, I'll test it and we can put it under a microscope," says Vivian.

Evelyn announces, "So all tests look good. Now for the real test." They re-enter the chamber and rest a few moments in the *Chidiya*. "I think it's time to free the wascally wabbit," says Evelyn holding the innocent creature. She brings the exposed rabbit outside.

The rabbit seems fine, curiously sniffing the air. Evelyn sets him down and shouts, "Be free!"

"Poor thing," sighs Vivian.

The rabbit moves slowly, sniffing at the strange grass but not eating it. They attentively watch the rabbit about a half hour and detect no ill effects. Then Evelyn grabs the rabbit and says, "Thank you for being so brave." She puts the rabbit in an isolation box before returning into the *Chidiya*. "Well, how awesome is that!" exclaims Evelyn.

"Success!" shouts Emma. She radios, "You're going to love this." She informs us of their findings.

I respond, "Glad it went so well. I cannot wait to analyze your specimens. Over."

When the *Chidiya* returns, they are greeted with loud cheers and pats on the back. I tell Ava excitedly, "Please check them and then come to my lab. We have to look at these."

Harper insists, "I want to see too."

"Sure Harper, come to my lab with me now." We immediately prepare to examine the rock and grass samples. Kiara takes some of the rock samples to her workstation. When Vivian is done in medical, she and Bella run tests on the grass in the biochemistry lab.

Harper and I carefully set up slides. When we look under the microscope, I say, "*C'est merveilleux!*"

"Whoa! This is so much more than we expected," says Harper.

"Even after all the searching for life in space, it's still hard to grasp," says Ava.

The researchers meet in the chapel to discuss their results. Kiara starts, "The rocks are mostly dark gray basalt or light grayish tufa, with one bright dolomite rock found by the water." Due to our white light, the rocks appear less red in our laboratory. "There should be caves close-by. I love spelunking. Anyone else up for it?"

"Sure, that would be cool. I miss the outdoors," I say.

"I'm in," says a jittery Harper, and then boasts, "Well, we found microbes, long thin ones meshed in a spider web and colonies of round ones." She shows them an image on her laptop screen.

"They metabolize nitrates. I believe I saw spores. They appear to be actinomycetes or fungi," I say.

"The grass has cells, with walls." Harper shows more images.

I add, "It's hard to tell for certain if they are harmful. We tested to see how they react with human cells and did not observe any adverse reactions."

"Wow! *Real* microbes," says Kiara.

Bella reports proudly, "Yeah, and Vivian and I tested the plant and found it similar in make-up and composition to Earth grasses. The grass appears greener in color in the white light of the *Athena* and we found chlorophyll and DNA."

"We have just found definitive proof of life on another world," says Vivian.

"It's just . . . just awe-inspiring! God choose to give us this marvel, life on another world," says Ava.

"I know. It's wonderful, divine even," says Bella.

"A-men, that's the truth," agrees Kiara. "Can't wait to show the others."

"It means we should be able to survive too and get out of this tin can," remarks Harper.

"I will send a quick note to Earth, full reports later." We share the findings with the others at a celebratory dinner with peppy music and excited conversations.

Then, in a few days, we prepare the tremendous task of landing the *Athena*. We set the weather satellite to transmit information back to Earth and to the *Athena* and launch it. We need to be certain everything is secure and ready. When we land, the ring will lie flat turning us to one side; our floor will become a three-meter-high wall, and a wall will become a narrow floor. We cannot have any debris on any of the surfaces or floors. We secure all our scientific equipment and personal belongings. Tidy Lilian assists Aurora, whose quarters are always the messiest. Bella and Evelyn cover as much of the frozen soil and plants as they can in the farm. Harper collects any eggs and makes sure her animals are safe.

When done, we put on our heat insulating g-force suits to start our descent.

"Are you ready?" asks Emma. This is going to be rough. I've slowed the stabilization thrusters. Our descent should start within a half hour."

After a minute, Arla confirms, "I checked. Everyone is ready and secure in a seat."

"Are you sure about this?" asks Lucy.

"Yes, Emma and I ran simulations. It's all pre-programmed but at twenty-five kilometers out, we switch to manual and she's all Emma's," says Lilian.

"I've got this. I've worked at high g," assures Emma.

After twenty-five minutes, Aurora announces, "We reached the upper atmosphere. As we fall, the outside of the *Athena* will get extremely hot, about seventeen hundred degrees Celsius."

"But don't worry. The thruster side was designed to take such extreme heat. Lucy and I are directing all excess power to the cooling systems," says Riya.

"Just like a shuttle reentry," says Harper.

"More like flying with multiple jet packs. Here we go!" says Emma.

Lucy asks, "Are . . . are you sure we should do this?" and bites her lower lip.

"We've already started down. No turning back now," I say.

Even with our suits, we can feel the increasing downward acceleration. Soon it gets harder to talk. I feel a rush of adrenalin like on a roller coaster. Most scream. I keep telling myself to breathe, to stay calm. It's hard. I watch the temperature gauge rising above 60 degrees Celsius. In four minutes, the *Athena's* computer announces, "One hundred forty kilometers from surface. Thrusters switching on."

The g force lessens, but the *Athena* starts to shake violently. Bella and others scream again. As the shaking intensifies, all my muscles tighten. Silently, I wonder if this was foolhardy and pray incessantly for this to be over.

Soon we hear it announce, "Twenty-five kilometers. On manual." I watch Emma as she quietly stares at the monitors while struggling to adjust the many levers, one for each of the thrusters. I know it's almost over.

We see flashing red lights and hear the computer warn, "Thruster six overheating. Evacuate." Area six is in the farm. I hear an explosion—more screaming as the Athena sways. I feel my heart pounding and remind myself to breathe.

The computer announces, "Course change needed to reach target." Emma flinches and then quickly readjusts levels until the Athena is stable. The computer announces, "Course on target."

All at once, we are jolted and hear a loud thud, cracking, banging and painfully loud screeching sounds of scraping metal. I feel my stomach in my chest.

Everyone looks pale. "What the hell!" shouts Harper.

"*Almost* a perfect landing," Emma says with a grimace.

"Whew," I say. Then we shout for joy as we practically jump on Emma to thank her.

Evelyn requests, in a mock British accent, "Please sir, I want some more."

"That was a rush." says Emma smiling.

"You're both crazy," says Bella. "That was terrifying."

"Thank you also Lilian, Kiara and Aurora. Excellent work. We owe you our lives," I say greatly relieved.

I check everyone and ask if anyone is hurt. We notice that Lucy had not jumped up and find her passed out. Soon Ava revives her and then checks us all for injury or shock. She announces, "No injuries— no heart attacks, though I thought for sure I had one."

"What was all that noise?" I ask. We squat and crawl to examine the interior of the *Athena*. We find a large hole and thruster shrapnel in the farm, and several small cracks in other parts of the ring. Throughout, cables and pipes broke and equipment malfunctions.

"This'll take some work," remarks Riya.

Then, ignoring any precautions, we exit the *Athena* and see that it landed as planned in the center of the crater. The ground is not perfectly flat everywhere under the ring. The ring is on land, but the central tube and Bubble are in the middle of the tiny lake in the center. Most of the ring is elevated by the thrusters or boulders.

Then we look around and start to relax. The *Athena* is nestled in a depression surrounded by a high, rust-gray rock wall under an open sky. We bask in the comfortable warmness of the ancient star. It feels awesome to hear wind instead of the constant hum of the Athena's various motors. Surprised and grateful to be alive, I take a moment to soak it all in. Kiara remarks, "It's a good'un. The colors form a nice composite scene, don't you think?"

"Oh, definitely," says Vivian.

Feeling giddy, I take in a large breath of fresh air and spread my arms wide, marveling at how much room I have and enjoy moving freely. Evelyn and Bella make a show of kissing the ground. Harper, and then others, run around gleefully as Evelyn sings the "Sound of Music" theme song, completely out of tune.

We all very much want to explore, but we have a tremendous amount of work to do. The *Athena* is topsy-turvy, and it is very difficult to move around in our ship. Our track has become a crawl space. I have the engineers repair and re-organize the *Athena*, with priority on water and food. They patch the tears in our new roof to protect against water damage. Then, they have quite a challenge rearranging the furniture and equipment from the walls to the new floor and constructing new pathways. Because our quarters are hard to access, we move our bedding to the arboretum, where the engineers rig two new showers from the sprinkler pipes.

The rest of us work on developing a food supply on the few sunny days and on our labs on the all-to-frequent rainy days. I direct and help with the work outside. We first need to take the heavy trees out, as they are now laying on their side and too tall to be upright in our flipped ship. We hurry to prepare the soil, mixing it with ours and transplanting what we can. To obtain a more constant supply of fresh vegetables, we plan to stagger planting seeds. With Bella's suggestion, we decide to use the area outside the ship along the crater walls for multiple rotating gardens of legumes/soy, vegetables and grain. We plant close to the crater's wall to give the plants partial shade from the too-bright Ra and to distance them from possible flooding of the lake. Bella worries about how our Earth plants will handle their new home, or what kinds of insects or other pests, if any, might damage them. We discover the lake often expands in heavy rains—probably why the ground is flat. Because water is heavy, and the plants need a lot during the hottest part of the long day, we dig irrigation ditches to bring part of the lake water to the gardens. We set up the grow lights for use during the extra-long nights. In addition to the land plants, Arla transplants some protein-rich seaweed to the lifeless lake. We hope all this will eventually produce enough to sustain us.

Life on Ross is difficult. We are not used to the gravity, which is thirty percent higher here than on Earth, and twice what we're used to. The ground is stony, and everything seems heavy. Though we try stretching, our muscles remain sore. "This is hard work," complains a tired Kiara.

Evelyn quips, "A strong man would be great right now, and I wouldn't use him just for sex."

With our help, Harper builds a stone fence around the ring to keep the chickens and rabbits in the inner circle, where they can get water on their own. She seems calmer, less argumentative now. She smiles as she cares for the animals and sets up the beehive in the budding fruit trees. We have about thirty rabbits, and many seem pregnant.

The chickens are laying eggs in hidden locations. In three weeks, we have chicks. Evelyn tries to round them into a pen, but they get away from her. She follows them around, walking like a chicken and asks, "You think they'll follow me if I look like their mother?"

Harper snorts. "Meh, try coaxing them with food."

Now that Harper seems happier, we allow her some time alone though she talks to herself occasionally. She uses her new freedom to take long walks alone around the inner perimeter of the crater. One time, after her walk, she claims to see a man watching us at the western edge of the crater. We rush to find him with our telescope and infrared binoculars but find no sign of anyone. We assume she's hallucinating—can't blame her, we all yearn for a man and imagine one from time to time.

Even so, I feel lucky that we are alive, and we have each other. One clear night, I find Aurora transfixed by colorful shimmering lights in the dark sky.

"What is that?" I ask her.

"An aurora. It's always to our north."

"I've not seen one like this. It's mesmerizing."

"Uhn-hunh."

We stare at it for a while and then identify familiar constellations. "In astronomical distances, we are not so far from Earth." I marvel at the lovely sky and this place we are calling home.

thirteen

Exploring Crusoe Island

A month after our landing, I'm still maintaining a log and sending occasional transmissions. "April 19, 2048, 1300 hours Eastern Standard Time. The *Athena* crew succeeded in making the *Athena* functional and planting seeds, many of which are germinating. We feel it's time to explore the island. We named it Crusoe Island, after Robinson Crusoe, because we assume it will be many years before we receive a return transmission, let alone a rescue. Morale is high, but we sure wish we could hear your voices." Even though our new transmissions cannot reach Earth for years, NASA must know by now that we have not returned, as planned, from the wormhole.

Some days, Earth and that life seem far away. I look at the picture of my family and wonder how old I will be before I see them again. My young nephews and nieces would be all grown up. I imagine what it would have been like to have my own family—a sweet, intelligent and devoted husband, tender children, a warm home with a dozen pets. I imagine myself reading to my precocious toddlers, puppy in lap, while my handsome husband prepares a tasty dinner. We would talk to each other tenderly about our day. My eyes water at the knowledge that this will never be.

On the positive side, our homestead is somewhat settled, and we are acclimating to the extra gravity. We decide to have a "Spring Seed Germination" celebration at 1800 hours and then take the next shifts off to rest from work and explore Crusoe Island. We bake a special dinner from our food stock, and it smells enticing. We decide to eat outdoors, because the weather is lovely. We chat about plans for the crater, like constructing a fence around the garden to keep stray animals out. I make a short speech thanking Providence and every member of the crew for their contributions. Then, the band leader Emma and Hyper-Space perform their own celebratory song with a loud heavy metal rock beat as Emma and Lucy sing:

Into the cold, cold darkness we braved,
raging power under our feet
We felt it, we owned it, we flew
into the cold, cold dark

There're a thousand battles in the dark
and we've fought a thousand'n one
In the cold, cold darkness we braved
Into the cold, cold dark

Into the cold, cold darkness we stayed
How long 'fore we see the blue again,
your face, your face again
Into the cold, cold dark

Into the bright, red light we braved
Fear, burn, anguish gone
As hope sprouts forth life
Out of the cold, cold, dark

Into the bright, red light we brave
Life can be won. Space, we 'vercome.
Time to fly again. Fly again.
Out of the cold, cold, dark
Fly again
Fly again

We clap and smile. Emma jokes, "Mwah! My adoring fans. All that in a day's worth of creativity." Then she continues, "And these next songs, we dedicate to our devotees. We've been practicing these for a couple months." They play along with "Fighter" by Manafest. We start to dance. After they finish that song, Emma announces, "The last songs we've been working on are by Skillet, 'Legendary' and 'Feel Invincible'." Then Evelyn puts on contemporary rock music. We continue with dancing and a few laughs until half of us, including myself, are too tired to stay awake any longer.

I wake up early, at 0100 hours, because the day shift—seven of us, Bella, Arla, Evelyn, Kiara, Lucy, Riya and I—decided to explore the hill outside the crater and hike the six kilometers to the ocean shoreline. For protection, we all wear long pants, long sleeve shirts and gloves and, as always, our dark sunglasses. We prepare makeshift backpacks filled with testing equipment, food and drink. We find a spot where we can climb out of the confining crater wall and peer over the top for a panoramic ocean view.

"Breathtaking," says Riya.

"Wow, it's endless," says Lucy.

"Love the shiny ruby waves with flakes of gold," says Kiara.

We cannot take our eyes off the beautiful expanse. As we descend toward the shore, we can feel the fresh wind cool our bodies and can smell the salty, perfumed air. We are surrounded by plant life, sparse like on a beachfront on Earth, but more plentiful than inside the crater. There is much more tall red grass. We also see three species of short, small-leafed shrubbery and another with puffy rose flowers, swarming with coordinated butterflies.

"Enchanting!" I say and we sit on the ground, being careful not to damage any of the plants.

Bella remarks, "Now I know why the bees are always up here." We examine everything avidly, discussing each, and take samples of the plants, the soil, the rocks.

"Truly amazing. Let's go down to the water. It looks safe," suggests Arla. A broken sandbar, about one hundred meters off the coast, protects the shoreline.

"Look at all the huge waves way out there. A surfer's paradise," says Bella.

We find a soft, sandy area, on the otherwise rocky beach, on which to sit and eat our meal. We are calmed by the familiar sound of the ocean waves repeatedly hitting the shore. We take off our shoes, roll up our pants and cautiously step into the water. We find what appear to be seashells and discuss the probability of finding animal life. We spend hours examining everything, packing a few samples for the others to see and for further study. Kiara and Arla have a sketch pad and are drawing the flowers, butterflies, seashells. I ask Kiara to teach me to draw when Arla stops to piece together bits of shells, which she postulates form one enormous nautilus.

Arla excitedly points out brown dolphins jumping on the other side of the sandbar. We can barely see them as they dive into the tall waves and come out spinning through the air. As we approach the water, they stop and swim upright as if to observe us too. However, they stay far offshore.

After a few hours, our food and water are used up and our packs are full of specimens. We don't want to leave the beach but are excited to show the others what we've found. Arla says, "It's amazing, so beautiful. I'm going to come out here every chance I get."

When we return, the night crew is amazed at our samples and stories. They, of course, are excited for their chance to explore outside our crater, which now seems monotonous. As I'm still wide awake when Ava wakes up, I decide to go to with them. Emma has managed to open the bay of the *Chidiya*. She, Lilian, and Aurora want to fly over Crusoe Island, check out the mainland, and then search for potential sources of fuel to the south. Emma is almost done retesting each component of the *Chidiya* and running safety checks.

On the other hand, Harper wants to hike toward the mountain to check for fauna and where she is sure she saw a man, twice. Vivian, Ava, and I agree to oblige her. Excited to explore, we start the trek upward to the west. After we climb out of the crater, we walk through a gently sloping hill full of rocks the size of chairs.

"What I'd give for my riding horse right now," says Harper.

"This is great. The air feels so fresh and breezy," says Ava.

"Here's an excellent view, let's rest and look at the ocean," says Vivian.

"Sure. It's fabulous," I say. We are in a scenic meadow of red grass and tall greenish plants with small scented purplish flowers, favored by another species of smaller, delicate, lilac butterfly. "Beautiful, *this* reminds me of the opening scene of "Sound of Music."

"Look at all the butterflies," says Vivian.

"It smells nice, like roses," says Ava.

We rest a moment, enjoy the view, and then continue our hike. As we walk, the plants and rocks are getting to be almost as tall as we are. "So, we do not get lost, let's follow this rivulet that feeds our lake. It seems to originate upstream at the mountaintop," I suggest.

The mountain gradually gets steeper and we need to meander around numerous large boulders. "Kiara was right about the caves," says Harper. Then, she excitedly points downward. "Deer tracks!"

"For real! They are tiny," I say.

"You really think there're mammals here?" asks Vivian.

"We saw what might be some in the ocean," I say.

"What else would have made those tracks?" Harper insists.

"That would be nice to see, eh," says Ava.

"Let's be really quiet," suggests Harper.

After a while, our trail becomes rockier, without much more plant life, except for the omnipresent grass and short trees. We climb a tall boulder to look around for possible deer. From our vantage point, we can see the *Chidiya* take flight. Showing off, Emma swoops down to us, and we wave as they fly overhead. I watch nervously as she approaches precariously close to a tall protruding boulder. Suddenly, I spot what looks like a person falling.

I hear Emma radio, "What the hell was that!"

I radio her saying, "We check it out! Over."

Vivian, Ava, Harper and I hurry to go to the site where we think the person fell. I jump off our boulder, and because I'm the fastest, get there first.

I'm astounded to find what looks like a muscular human male moaning on the ground. He stares at me in fright, and I stare back at him in astonishment. I notice immediately that he has a big bump on his head and is bleeding profusely from his arm. Immediately, I rip my shirt to make bandages and apply pressure to his arm. Still, he faints before the others get to him.

"The bleeding is stopping," I say, as I continue applying pressure to his wound.

"We should still get him to medical to check out that bump," says Ava.

"He seems heavy," says Vivian.

Harper says sarcastically, "No man here. So, what's this short-to-average height, tan to chestnut skinned, black haired, unshaven thing?"

"You were right Harper," I say.

Vindicated Harper says, "I'll look around, see if there's anyone else." She scouts around and shouts. "Found his cave!" She returns soon and announces, "I don't see signs of anyone else—seems he's alone. But there are signs, food scraps, that he's been here a while, probably as long as we have. He's got spears, a pack, blankets."

"Can't leave him out here alone. But how can we get him down?" asks Vivian.

I say, "It's possible. Please bring two of the longest spears and the largest blanket to make a stretcher."

"Wonder why he's here?" says Ava.

"He's been spying on us," asserts Harper.

"Why?" asks Vivian.

"Don't know," says Harper.

"No matter, he needs our help," insists Ava.

"Agreed, we should help him," I say. After the bleeding stops, I lay out the spears and wrap the blanket around them. Then we remove his bow and quiver and lift his heavy, dense body onto the blanket. Each of us lifts an end of the two spears.

We trek the circuitous kilometer back to the *Athena* and place him in a bed in medical. Ava asks us to stand back while she manipulates the medical scanner, which forms an arch over his motionless head and shoulders. We watch as she moves the scanner slowly from head to foot and reads the results.

"Well?" I question, "He sure seems human."

"Per the scanner, I have to agree," affirms Ava.

"That's not possible, is it?" asks Vivian.

"Well, it has to be," replies Harper.

"We should take further tests," advises Vivian. While Ava disinfects the wound on his arm, Vivian and I take scrapings for examination.

Meanwhile, the others have landed and are eager to see him. Emma says, "I think I scared him. What a hunk too! How long before he wakes up?"

Ava answers, "I don't know. If he's human, and he seems to be, I'd say he has a concussion with loss of consciousness due to trauma and blood loss. I can give him additional oxygen in the chamber. He seems dehydrated, so I'll give him an IV with iron and acetaminophen. But first, he stinks, can someone help me with these clothes. We can put a gownie on him."

"I'll do it," offers Harper.

Harper helps Ava and even sponge-washes his very dirty and sweaty body, disinfecting various cuts and scrapes. Then we move him to the isolation bed and Ava sets up the IV. The bed was designed for women, and he barely fits. Then Harper takes his nasty clothes and blanket to launder. We stay and stare at him in amazement.

I decide to test him for possible dangerous microbes, take a few more swabs, and bring that and my finds from our hike to my lab. I start about twelve cultures for each sample in sterile, nonselective, blood-enriched media and in different environmental conditions—light–dark, room/body temperature, oxygen levels—and carefully label each petri dish. I quickly review the nineteen phyla of the thousand bacteria on human skin and opt to classify the alien bacteria similarly. Because I'm now getting tired, I decide to study the alien humanoid and my specimens further the next day after I get some sleep.

After a restless sleep, I wake up, and the first thing I think about is the stranger. I briskly freshen up with a washcloth, tie my hair back in a braid, brush my teeth, grab a coffee and scurry to see Ava while I'm still in my t-shirt pajamas and bare feet.

After sipping my coffee, I ask Ava, "How is he doing?"

She smiles. "Fine… sure gets plenty of curious visitors."

I can see that his arm has been stitched and his cuts bandaged, and ask, "How is the treatment going?"

She answers, "Very well. I think he should be regaining consciousness soon. He almost did earlier when Vivian was treating him with her skin salve and acupuncture. Vivian thought he seemed tense, found quite a few knots in his muscles."

I notice his well-developed muscles, "Seems we should have a security protocol once he wakes."

"Seems like a good idea, but I've been with him for hours now and need some rest. Can you watch him?"

I stare at him and say to Ava, "Sure!" surprised at my enthusiasm.

Then I sit beside him, staring but not quite believing he's real, thinking for a moment that we must all be hallucinating. How can there be such a human-like being here? I have so much to ask him: Where is he from? What are his people like? Why was he here? I notice I forgot my communicator but assume one of the crew members would be by shortly to peek at, or clean, or cure, or poke, or study, our guest. The curious ladies, who had been observing him with fascination, have, after several hours of gazing, moved on to chores or other projects.

fourteen

Abduction

I take a short break from watching the humanoid to check on my samples and cultures in my microbiology lab adjacent to medical. I set up spreadsheets for comparative growth charts and statistical analysis. I'm looking forward to discovering the fascinating differences in our epidermal microcosms.

As I return, I'm suddenly attacked from behind. I jab hard repeatedly with my elbow, but my jabs don't seem to faze the attacker. I try to flip the attacker across my back, but the attacker is too stable. I'm hit on the back of my knees, causing me to fall to the floor. Then I'm flipped on my back and the attacker sits on my stomach. I can now see that my attacker is our humanoid guest. I try punching his wound and poking his eyes, but he quickly grabs my two wrists in his powerful grip. I yell, and he covers my mouth. I bite him; he slaps me hard. He grunts something. Covering my mouth again, he ties my hands with the IV cord, holding one end in his mouth. He quickly tears his gownie and uses it to gag and blindfold me. Then he lifts me up and carries me as he frantically searches for an exit. He finds an opening in the broken ring, and drags me, struggling to get loose, out into the darkness and pouring rain.

When we are out of hearing range, he checks the cord binding my hands and again drags me by the excess. He's practically running. I can't see anything, and I bump painfully into rocks or whatever else might be out there. I try to resist several times by pulling back, but he yanks me forward. This goes on for a few kilometers until I hear the surf. He stops and releases the cord. I decide to make a run for it. I try to run along the shore to anywhere but here, but I smack hard into a rock. I can feel his powerful arm around my waist as he drags me back. He tosses me onto what feels like the wobbly hard floor of a boat. My face throbs from having bumped the rock. I think it's swelling. I feel blood dripping from my forehead. I'm angry from this treatment and regret not having taken safety precautions sooner. I should have had someone with me and a taser or tranquilizer. *I should know better.* Now, I'm trapped. I know my friends won't be able to find me in the rain and dark. We're moving; the swaying causes me to feel nauseous. Then, I start to shiver from the cold rain.

We reach shore. He continues to drag me like before but at a slower pace. He stops on a couple occasions, and I hear him drink and eat, but he doesn't offer me any. I wonder what he plans to do with me. Does he intend to rape me? If so, why continue dragging me? Am I to be sold as a slave? Is he from a tribe of cannibals taking me to feed his family? I obsess over not knowing what he wants. We travel like this for what seems like a miserable ten to twelve hours. The fear had initially increased my adrenaline, keeping me going, heightening my senses, but now, I feel exhausted. My feet and legs have grown numb. I can barely keep moving.

Suddenly the rain stops, and I assume we're in a cave. He stops, and we rest. I'm exhausted, thirsty, famished and shivering again. I have a severe headache, feel faint and lie on the ground. He removes the gag over my mouth and gives me water to drink. I ask him why he's doing this, but he articulates nothing. I wonder if he even has language skills.

He forces me on a soft covering and wraps himself around me. I sense he is shivering too. I stay awake a long time, afraid of what this monster might do to me but need the warmth from his body. After he falls asleep, I try to loosen the ties but can't. Finally, I resign myself to spooning, sinking into his bulging arms. As it gets colder, I move closer, backing into him. In a few minutes, he touches me with his penis. I whimper and struggle to move away. He seems startled and pushes away. He gets up and away from me. I hear him grunting. I try to ignore him, roll into a tight ball, and shiver, until I fall into a fretful sleep.

Later, he shakes me awake and drags me again. It's not raining. After almost another day, I no longer hear the wind and assume we are in a cave again. Occasionally, I hear a stream or a trickle of water. I'm so thirsty. My throat is so painfully dry, that the sound of water drives me crazy. I ask him where he's taking me—no response. Desperately, I ask the same question in French—still no response. Finally, we seem to arrive at his destination.

He is talking to someone with a deep voice, someone who seems to have just awaken. I start to figure out what they are saying. They seem to be talking in a strange French dialect. My captor utters, "We need to show that they can be defeated. I demand a pubic execution after what they did to Thérèse and our two . . ."

I gasp in fear. I can't imagine what this is about.

The other man seems stern and argues, "You know our customs demand a trial for that." He walks over to me, lifts my face, and says, "Only a barbarian would beat a women's face."

"I didn't beat her. She hit a rock—on her own."

"I'm taking off this ridiculous blindfold."

The other one looks like my captor, only cleaner and older, gentlemanly. The gentleman examines me with curiosity but doesn't make any threatening moves.

I look around. We're in a dolomite chamber lit by candles. There is a large tapestry on one wall, paintings on the other walls, a polished marble table and chairs, an inlay bookshelf with several old paper books, a rococo china cabinet and a fireplace. The fire feels warm and smells like pine. I move onto a soft rug in front of the fireplace and exhausted, I lie down.

After a few minutes, the gentleman declares, "She's way too scrawny and worn out to be dangerous." He moves to me and unties my hands, saying, "You both stink. Go get Francine and Marguerite." My captor leaves and shortly two attractive ladies arrive, and the

123

gentleman orders, "Get her cleaned up and fed so she can coherently stand trial in the morning."

"Yes, right away," says the older lady.

Turning to my captor, he asks, "Can she speak?"

"Yes, I heard her once, but couldn't figure out what she was saying."

The ladies, dressed in silky robes and almost as muscular as the men, take me through a long, dark passage to a secluded chamber. At this point, I'm too faint to resist. The chamber has a hot spring from which I drink voraciously. The younger lady indicates with hand gestures that I should get in. The water tastes and smells of minerals and feels soothing on my body, which I can now see is almost completely covered with cuts and bruises. They talk to each other in whispers. Then they bring me a towel and a stiff linen robe. I take off my own wet pajamas and notice they are torn beyond repair. Because these are the ones my dad had sent me and I desperately want him to protect me now, my eyes well up with tears.

While I'm still light-headed, they place me in a prison cell with a jar of cool fresh water and a food like stale, crusty bread. It's a small, dank cell of stone with one door and one narrow opening like a window near the ceiling. A bit of light filters in. There are stones in the shape of benches on each wall just wide and long enough to sleep on. I relax a little now that the brute is gone, and the other alien humanoids don't seem as intent on torturing me.

I wonder why these aliens speak French. Have they been listening to French radio waves from Earth? Could Stephen Hawking have been right that we shouldn't broadcast our presence all over the universe? Sorry Carl Sagan, no benevolent life out here. I don't see any electronic devices. It seems so improbable that they would have a radio. Everything else here seems so primitive. I drift off to sleep, unable to make any sense of all this.

I'm awakened by two burly, armored knights and brought to an impressive, brightly lit dolomite chamber. It looks like a royal reception hall, with an aisle leading to a throne at the far end. The air is heavily perfumed. About twenty adults, dressed in robes of fine linen or furs and sparkling jewels, are standing on both sides of the aisle, staring at me. They seem cold, even angry. I hear a murmur of whispered gossip. The two ladies from the previous evening, now even more finely dressed, walk proudly in front of me, and the two knights walk behind me, sword in hand. All the people are of short-to-average height and look like they spend their lives lifting weights in a gym, the women included. I feel extremely puny and insignificant in my drab robe. My head and legs still hurt as I am marched toward the throne. I remind myself to keep breathing deeply—yoga breaths—and manage to make it to the throne.

There I am placed beside my captor. He seems a bit older than me and is now clean, shaven, and dressed in a luxurious fur-lined purple robe. He stands by the throne where the gentleman, also in a long purple robe with jewels and a crown, is seated. I assume he is their king and my judge. Above his throne are ornately decorated words in French: Liberty, equality, fraternity. I feel equal to a French Revolution royal being brought up to the guillotine. I presume my chances in this trial are slim to none. As I face my captor, my stomach is in knots. My knees feel like they will give out from under me as I stand motionless.

A herald announces in French, "All bow for King François V, presiding."

The king announces, "Welcome esteemed citizens to the Court of Carcassonne. I open these proceedings. The marquis has requested this trial. The accused and accuser face each other." So, my captor is a marquis, and he looks furious.

The marquis says proudly, "Sir, I humbly plead for the court to order the execution of this woman for the murder of our people, for an attempt on my life, and for witchcraft."

The king asks, "Can you speak? What is your plea?"

They are all still speaking French, so I decide to respond also in French. Trying to sound confident and brave, I stammer, "Yes, I can speak. I plead that I'm not a witch. I . . . I have never killed or even tried to murder anyone."

125

The king states, "I confirm that the accused pleads not guilty. Let us hear the evidence."

The marquis speaks, "Sir, may I remind the delegates of Carcassonne of the death of the hunters and our ambassadors, and the slaughter of twenty-five innocent people in the outdoor market, including my wife and two children. Four weeks ago, I was sent by the king to investigate the new object from the sky that landed in the sacred circle of our ancestors. There I saw strange creatures and plants and a bevy of gaunt witches—no men. They speak a strange language. There was demonic music, satanic dancing. Her dragon surprised me and tried to kill me. They took away my dignity, placed me in a crystal coffin and injected embalming pins in me. I was fortunate to escape in the dark with their leader."

The king asks, "What is your defense?"

My mouth is almost too dry to speak. I swallow and barely manage to say, "I do come from a ship from the stars. I'm sorry for your immense loss, but we came in peace. We know nothing of the violent acts that happened here."

The king states, "The accused claims an alibi. Bring in the witness to the murders." We wait as a boy, who appears to be about twelve years old, enters. The king says, "Please describe the murderers at the market and what happened. Remember you must tell the truth, Étienne."

He speaks nervously, "Sir, there was a big ship from the sky. I saw men get out. They were skinny, tall, pale. They had short thick spears. The men tried to get the women to go into their ship. They wouldn't. Then, they were all dead—my aunt, my cousins too." He starts to snivel.

The king asks, "Were any of the killers women?"

"Sir, no, I don't think so."

Looking at me and the marquis, the king asks, "Do you have any questions for the witness?"

I'm too nervous to think of any and shake my head, and the marquis says, "No questions sir."

The king orders, "The witness can leave. Do you have a rebuttal?"

The marquis responds, "Sir, her coven is mostly scrawny and light-skinned. We can conclude they are related to or supporting the murderers, probably their mates."

The king asks me, "Have you assisted the killers?"

I can barely stutter, "No, sir. I don't know who they are."

The king proclaims, "There is no evidence that she was present at the murders or assisted them. We will move to the test for witchcraft." I remember the European and Salem witch trials, so I dread this test. He asks, "Why are you all women?"

I think, how can I explain this? "Sir, umm because it was practical for traveling."

"What did you do with your husbands?"

"Sir, I never married. We prefer sailing in the stars."

"Sounds too strange. Will the cardinal step forward and examine the accused?" An old man, dressed in a baroque red robe, moves forward, and stands next to me.

"I will look for the marks," he states and examines my skin. He looks down the inside of my robe. I can feel every muscle of my body tense up in humility and anger. I want to slap him, but don't dare move.

The cardinal announces, "I have found no demonic markings, only scrapes and bruises. Now, recite the Lord's Prayer."

I'm puzzled and so nervous that I draw a blank. I try to remember my childhood catechism class. The cardinal looks impatient. I almost say, "Hail Mary full of grace," but stop myself—wrong prayer. It slowly comes to me and I timidly recite:

> "Our Father, who art in heaven,
> Hallowed be thy Name.
> Thy Kingdom come.
> Give us this day our daily bread.
> And forgive us our trespasses,
> As we forgive those who trespass against us.
> And lead us not into temptation,
> But deliver us from evil.
> Amen."

As I recite, the cardinal sprinkles water on me, which makes me wince.

The cardinal examines me again, mumbles that I have no burn marks, and proclaims, "No marks. The prayer is close enough. The forgiving trespasses and deliverance from temptation verses are most significant."

I breathe a sigh of relief. A witch is apparently a spinster who wouldn't be able to recite the prayer and would be burned by holy water when trying. I'm relieved to have passed the test, without drowning or stabbings. As I realize that I messed up the prayer, I wonder whether the cardinal believes in witchcraft, or is just trying to pacify the royal family. I recall that any error in the prayer would have been a sign of a witch, but I'm certainly not going to correct him. I think this whole thing is beyond insane, like Alice in Wonderland, and begin to wonder if I'm dreaming, maybe crazy.

The king asks, "What are these strange animals?"

"Sir, they are common species from my home. The plants are from our home too. The plants and animals are a source of food and medicine."

The king turns to the marquis and asks, "I presume there are different plants and animals in different lands?"

He answers, "Sir, yes, of course."

The king asks, "What is this music and dancing?"

I assume he is talking about the Hyper-Space performance. I explain, "Sir, some people from my world like that sound. We have the freedom to express ourselves in any way we want. The music was in thanksgiving for the germination of our plants."

The king grins and declares, "We are farmers and have freedom of speech too." I start to think that maybe I can prevail in this ridiculous trial. Turning to the marquis, he asks, "Do you have a rebuttal?"

The marquis insists, "Sir, they are strange—scrawny, celibate, weird."

The king concludes, "That's not enough. The witchcraft matter is settled in favor of the accused."

I say softly, "Thank you, sir."

Sternly, the king asks, "Why did you attempt to take the life of our beloved marquis?"

"Sir, it was an accident. Our dragon is controlled by one of us, and she was playing with me. We had not seen the man on the rock above us. As soon as we saw him fall, I ran to help him. I stopped his injuries from bleeding. We didn't see any of his people and didn't want to leave him unattended. I thought he might die if left alone after his fall. We brought him to our ship to be sure he would recover. The covered bed was to protect from possible diseases—him from ours and ours from his. Also, it allows us to enrich his oxygen due to loss of blood. The needle provided him with water and iron, something he needed to restore his lost blood. It is how we provide our medicines." As I speak, I see the marquis' face gradually soften.

The king motions for the marquis to approach closer. He and the cardinal examine the marquis' wounds carefully and the cardinal states, "I see the wounds are deep but healing quickly."

I look directly at the marquis and plead, "We weren't trying to scare or hurt you, just curious, and trying to help. We're not killers. We can't even kill the rabbits, the animals that we brought with us for food." He lowers his head, averting my eyes. Turning to the king, I beg, "Sir, if we wanted to kill him, we could have. Why would we bring someone in who could attack us later, if we had malicious intent?"

The king asks, "Do you have a rebuttal?"

The marquis says softly, "I have nothing further to say." I'm relieved and assume this ordeal is done.

The king proclaims, "Because she saved the life of the marquis, he is obligated to stay with her, protect her for the rest of her life. Miss, do you have anything further to say?"

"Sir, I don't . . . I don't need a protector, at least not him. He dragged me here against my will . . . molested me. I just want to return to my friends. I don't want *him* near me."

The king asks, looking irritably at the marquis, "Is it true, that you molested her?"

Surprised, the marquis says defensively, "Sir, I had to sleep beside her in order to prevent her from running away. We were wet and cold so slept close. It was in the middle of the night. I fell asleep and forgot where I was. She has Thérèse's hair and skin color. I touched her and beg the court's forgiveness."

The king angrily declares, "The punishment for rape is banishment, or because neither of you are married, marriage. Marquis, which do you choose?"

The marquis asks, "Sir, may I request a rebuttal?"

The angry king says, "I disallow it. Choose!"

The marquis says reluctantly, "I am bound to protect her and choose marriage."

"What say you?" asks the king to the cardinal.

The cardinal states, "I consent."

The king proclaims, "May the court record that the marquis is married to the accused."

I decide this isn't a dream, it's a sick, twisted nightmare! I blurt out a firm protest, "No, I don't consent! That's not possible! I never accepted!"

The king states, "You are in my land. My orders are not refuted. The punishment for your outburst during this sacred hearing is imprisonment. I will throw your husband in prison with you until you forgive him."

"You cannot do that."

"I just did."

I beg quietly, "Sir, please, please don't order that."

He says firmly, "This hearing is over."

I'm taken back to the cell with the marquis where I pace in frustration, testing the door and window for possible escape. Failing to find one, I sit as far away from my captor as possible and stay on guard. We sit silently for a long time. I try to comprehend what just happened. Overwhelmed by the events of the past few days and lack of sleep and nourishment, and eventually, with nothing to do, I collapse into a deep slumber.

While I'm sleeping, the king comes quietly to the door. The marquis gets up and places a blanket on my exposed body while walking silently to him. The king whispers, "Marquis, what the hell? You're my heir. What are the people going to think about *this*? Kidnapping and rape are serious, even if she isn't one of us."

The marquis responds apologetically, "I don't know, Uncle. I was blind with rage when I took her. I couldn't think straight. During the hearing, I realized I really screwed up. I couldn't lie. I didn't actually *penetrate* her. I can't believe you'd think I would do *that*."

"Ah, you've been different—hostile, more aggressive lately. I misunderstood then?" asks the king.

"Yes, but if I completely denied her accusation, you would have had to punish her with ten lashes for making a false accusation in court. I've done enough to her already. I *was* horrible. I was willing to take the hit. I really didn't know she was trying to help me."

"You're impulsive, but I know you are always trying to protect our people. The attacks weigh heavy on you—on us all. But you need to use your head more and your passion less."

"We *have* to stop them. *No one is safe.*" After a pause, the marquis asks, "Do you really think she'll ever forgive me? Not that I mind being in here, that's not important. I've slept in a lot of worse places."

His uncle laughs, "Yes, I know. You've been everywhere. I'm glad you chose marriage. I'd hate to never see you again."

"Me too, thanks for a choice."

"I know it's too soon. Could have done worse. She's articulate—scraggly, but feisty—nice muscle in those legs."

"Guess she's OK… I'm not ready for a wife and then, I'd prefer a woman who *likes* me," complains the marquis.

"I'd assume she doesn't *like* any of us. Whether she'll say she forgives you depends on how much she wants to get out of here."

"Yeah, I think she's loving it here."

"I don't know if I totally trust them either. I want you to learn as much as you can. You said they are all women. I'll have a few single men return with you to seduce them to get information—probably won't be too hard to find volunteers. They probably have strong weapons that keep the others away. *They can control a dragon.* We need to learn their military secrets, make certain they're not collaborating with the others, and maybe even smooth things over, make an alliance ourselves. I want you to take her back as a goodwill gesture."

"Risky, but OK. I'll find out what else I can," says the marquis.

"Thanks. Her face looks bad. Francine told me she has scratches and bruises all over. We'd look better if she healed first. It'll be easier on her to return by canoe. I'll arrange one. Later."

"Later."

Long afterwards, I wake up. My captor brings me strange bread and a thin-skinned, melon-size fruit with water. I'm starved and I grab the food immediately. The bread is tasty, and the melon is sweet and juicy with a slight tanginess. It wouldn't matter if they tasted horrible, I would have still eaten all of it.

Then he dares to sit beside me and says softly, "I'm very sorry for the way I treated you. There's no excuse. I don't expect you to forgive me, but if you pretend to, we can get out of prison, and I'll take you home. It's my duty now, to protect you."

"Go away! You cannot keep me here."

"The king can," my captor states, walking away.

I can't even consider him protecting me and am insulted that he would think I would want him anywhere near me. He's the only one I ever needed protection from. I fume for a long time.

Later, overwhelmed by curiosity, I ask him coldly, "Why do you speak French?"

He looks puzzled, "We always spoke French. We are French."

"It's not possible. France is on another world."

"Our elders say we came from another world nine kingships ago. We flew here with white wings." This makes no sense. They think I'm a witch, so maybe they think they are angels.

Then he asks, "I assume they have names where you come from?"

"Yes, mine is Camille."

"I'm Marquis."

"I know," I say, and walk away. This is all the friendliness I can handle.

Later I start wondering how he knew that *we* "speak a strange language". His cave was too far away from the *Athena* to allow him to hear us and I barely spoke. I eye him suspiciously and wonder how close to us was he this past month. I have a creepy feeling that he must have been skulking around our crater. It gives me the shivers to think he may even have been inside the *Athena* itself.

After a couple days of silence and fuming, I realize they have no need to release me and my stubbornness is not helping anyone. If they want to attack the *Athena,* they can find it, and they don't need me to be there to do so.

I whisper to Marquis, "I give up. You can come back with me, but understand that I'm *not* your wife, never will be. I hate you and don't ever *ever* hit, or even touch me again. *Clear?*" I'm determined there'll be no Stockholm Syndrome, no bonding, for this perverse captor.

"Yes, that couldn't be any clearer."

Marquis calls the knights, and we are allowed out of the cell. The two ladies greet us and then, take me through a medieval castle of polished stone. The walls are decorated with colorful paintings and delicate tapestries. There are also numerous long bows, swords and spears; it seems they are planning for an attack.

As we walk, I overhear the older lady whisper, "Be careful around her. I don't trust her. I believe Marquis. She *is* connected to the others, who destroyed my husband. She must be. Why else are they here?"

The younger one whispers, "But the court found her innocent."

"She seems to have bewitched *them*. She couldn't even say the 'Our Father' right."

"A lot of people can't."

"Careful. Don't look directly at her. Don't listen to her. Men can't read women, but *I* can sense it. She lied to save herself. I know it."

They take me back to the hot spring, where I freshen up. The young lady offers me the choice of a soft, pretty, but delicate dress or the same type of robe they had given me earlier. I don't want anything from them and choose the latter.

Then, a bathed Marquis joins me, and we head out through the throne room, which leads to a large central boulevard lit by many lanterns. I can now see that they live in a huge cave resembling a cross between a gloomy medieval castle and a lively Renaissance town. The castle's courtyard reminds me of the Louvre in Paris. Once outside the castle, I note small, fort-like windows for firing weapons. At the entrance to the castle is a large circle resembling a pendulum clock. In the center of the courtyard is a decorative ensemble of adult-size crystals.

The next chamber of the cave is a complete small village. On either side are smaller stone chambers roughly resembling cottages or small shops for a tailor, shoemaker, tinplate worker, blacksmith, glassblower, jeweler, cabinet maker, baker, and other artisans. Everywhere, people are busy at their trade and talking. Boys are playing hoops, tag and leapfrog, and girls hopscotch. Old men are playing bocce ball in a sand pit. The people stop to look at us.

One old man yells to Marquis, "Would you like to play, sir?"

"No time today," he replies.

There are jeweled objects of gold, silver and large gemstones throughout the boulevard. Slabs of dolomite and limestone brighten the dull gray basalt. The bakery smells so good it makes my stomach rumble. Marquis hears it, brings me inside the bakery, and orders a loaf of bread with meat and cheese.

Handing some to me, he asks, "Do you hate bread too?"

Taking it, I respond, "No, I've never been kidnapped by bread."

In the boulevard, a crowd of two hundred people of various ages assembles. The king, who couldn't possibly believe the lie that I forgave Marquis, makes a show of saying, "All is forgiven. It was a big misunderstanding. I wish the happy couple the best on their travels. I am sending the marquis to visit again her gracious people. This time, I am sending three goodwill ambassadors with the marquis bearing gifts for the beautiful Amazon warriors to rectify any misunderstandings." I'm glad we stepped up from witches to Amazons.

I don't trust their intentions, but I can see the king's mind is made up. I don't want to go back to the cell with Marquis again. His people seem a lot stronger than us, but so primitive. Still, there is not much I can do if the king wants to send all of them to attack our defenseless island, so I play along with the charade. I'm also concerned about the group that attacked them and want to learn more. Could we be in grave danger too?

The king leads the unhappy newlyweds and three ambassadors through the boulevard, arriving at a quay near a long, Viking style canoe in a dark, narrow, gently flowing river. The two ladies who cared for me and a few others are waiting. They bid Marquis and the ambassadors good-bye. The group seems curious about me. Marquis obliges them by introducing me. I don't really want to meet them but am polite. I'm impatient to get home and away from this dreadful place. They are all very talkative, wishing the men a safe trip. Marquis introduces the two ladies who cared for me as his sister, Marguerite, and his teenage cousin, Francine. Marguerite averts my eyes, but her perky young cousin smiles at me.

She says, "It's been my pleasure to assist you. It is our duty to welcome strangers. Here, I would like to give you this mineral water with healing herbs for your scratches."

As she hands me a vial, I say, "Thank you. I'm Camille, and you are certainly very kind." I also say, "Thank you too, Marguerite, for the assistance."

Francine says, "Have a safe journey, and come back whenever you like." She asks me many questions, about our home, the animals, my friends, our clothes, and I indulge her.

After I finish my long conversation with Francine, I back away from the large crowd. I overhear the tail end of a private and unpleasant discussion between Marquis and Marguerite. Marquis whispers, "Or, I may have been wrong!"

She counters, "Doubt it. She's fooling everyone. You should be with Collette, not *her*. I was arranging everything. She ruined everything."

He responds, "I don't care about your arrangements. As I told you before, I'm *not* interested in Collette. She's too young—even for Jean."

"You should be willing to do whatever is necessary to secure the allegiance of the Plains. They're threatening separation," argues Marguerite. Then she adds, "*The newcomers are evil.* I'll help arrange a force to get rid of them."

"No, don't. I *will obey* the king's instructions on this mission. This isn't your business."

"Everything is my business!" she retorts. After this, Marquis walks away from her angrily. I move quickly to the canoe and decide to never come back to this place.

fifteen

Return to the *Athena*

It finally seems time for us to get in the canoe. Marquis sits in the back to steer. I try to get into the front tip of the canoe. One of the ambassadors stops me and motions for me to get in the back. Gesturing to a seat just in front of Marquis, the ambassador teases, "Marchioness," and to Marquis, "Your wife belongs here with you, brother." Marquis shrugs his shoulders as I sit near him. The brother looks like a taller, younger version of Marquis. Unlike Marquis, the brother doesn't seem to have the weight of the world on his shoulders.

The ambassadors chuckle as they attach torches to the front of the canoe and drop a large bag in the middle along with various medieval weapons and paddles. After all the travelers embark, they push off.

Smiling politely, the brother says, "Allow me to introduce myself, I'm Comte Jean-Louis. Please, just call me Jean. If you indulge me further, allow me to introduce my friends, distant cousins really, Guillaume and Claude."

The two fair and handsome cousins smile and say, "Hello Marchioness, we are enchanted to make your acquaintance."

I retort, "Enchanted. My name is Camille Tremblay. Just call me Camille."

Marquis orders, "Let's proceed, gentlemen."

The young ambassadors all paddle on the side opposite to where Marquis is steering, causing the canoe to bump into rocks. Then they feign frustration, blaming Marquis for poor steering. After a time, they settle down and reminisce about the past pranks they had committed together. Their mood is jovial, and I start to decompress.

It's a long ride. I have nothing to do or see, just the dark water reflected from the torches. I find myself staring toward the lighted torches and at the men in front and their incredible physiques. I notice their bold tattoos, and I wonder if there is meaning in them. As I try to figure them out, I find myself staring.

Watching me, Marquis whispers a warning, "The punishment for adultery is death. It won't matter if you don't think you're married."

I whisper back caustically, "You're so barbaric," and sigh.

I try to focus on the flickering lights in the black waters. Bored, I take out the vial and place some of the water on the cuts on my limbs, finding it soothing.

Later I ask Marquis, "How long before we can divorce?"

He responds, "Not that easy, the king and the cardinal would both need to approve, and they rarely do. I've never seen it." I'll have to settle for a legal separation.

Marquis later asks, "So you don't believe in marriage?"

"Not forced ones."

"But otherwise?"

"Yes, a woman has to agree," I answer.

"Here, parents—or the law—protect their daughters."

"So, I'm *protected* by being led in the dark by four complete strangers. Would you feel safe?"

"I'd be concerned, but you are safe."

After a few hours, we enter the blinding sunlight and wince, even though we are shaded by towering rocky cliffs. Claude takes out five large-brim hats and we put them on. I feel like I'm finally free from prison. As my eyes adjust, I find this scenery both peaceful and awesome. I exhale smoothly and smile at the thought of going home.

Travelling past the cliffs, we see embankments on both sides of the stream. We travel on the narrow, slow-flowing stream for hours.

Sometimes, when the otherwise tall and stony bank is lower, I can see the outstretched plateau, tall rocky mountains to the north, and older rounded mountains to the south. The ground here seems a lot more fertile than on Crusoe Island. There is much more vegetation, especially tall grasses and fruit trees. It seems strange not to see or hear any birds. On the other hand, we aren't bothered by biting insects. There are brightly colored insects that resemble dragonflies and beetles. Overall, the ride is slow but pleasant in the warm sun. The occasional breeze cools us. The air smells fresh and perfumed with blossoms. The men are talkative, but I remain quiet in my thoughts.

A few plain-dressed harvesters check out the canoe and wave at us as we float by. The men wave back. Three smiling girls throw large, multi-colored flowers at them; I had just seen these flowers on the fruit trees. It seems here the trees have flowers and fruit at the same time. The ambassadors pick up a small bunch of flowers, kiss them in turn, and return the flowers to the girls, who giggle. Later, we interrupt two plain-clothed boys with large hats, fishing in the river. They appear to be about eight and twelve years old. Marquis decides it's a good spot to stretch out.

I approach the boys and ask in French, "How's the fishing?"

The older boy shyly answers (in French), "Good today. Is that the marquis?"

I respond, "Yes, he is."

His eyes grow big as he exclaims "Wow!"

Then he shows me his bucket with two fish the length of his forearm, explaining, "We need one more for dinner for our mom, dad and three sisters, but the marquis can have them if he wants."

Marquis grins, and patting the boy on the head, says, "Thank you, but no need, I would be happier if you take them to your family." The ambassadors applaud the boys on their abilities. Soon, the boys return to fishing as we move on downstream.

Later, we see a group of delicate, spotted, deer-like mammals that have come for a drink. I can't help but smile and think how peaceful they look. There seem to be whole families by the water, spreading their spindly front legs to dip their delicate heads quietly in the river. Startled by the canoe, they run, but not before Marquis, who had drawn his bow, abruptly shoots one, dropping it instantly. The men stop the canoe, gut the animal, and then bring the dead carcass into the canoe, startling me. Looking at it, I'm disgusted by the dead creature, whose accusing eyes seem to be looking directly at me.

After what must have been eight hours since we left the quay, they deem it time to prepare to sleep. The ambassadors help Marquis prepare the deer and cook it on a campfire in a cave. The fire smells of cedar, and the venison smells enticing. They invite me to share. It feels like a gourmet meal, even without tableware.

The men exit the cave to go skinny dipping. I can hear them splashing and laughing. When they return, Marquis offers, "Go ahead, I'll keep watch for you." My arms are red, and cool water would be refreshing. I undress and get in the water, keeping a watchful eye myself.

When I return, they set up their fur blankets. I move the bedding they give me as far as possible from all of them. Snickering at my refusal to be near Marquis, Jean teases him, "Trouble in paradise?"

Marquis responds, "A little."

They make me uncomfortable. I wonder what they will do to me, whether they are really taking me home, and if so, what will happen to my crew. Though I want to keep watch, I'm too tired from the sun exposure and soon fall asleep.

When I wake, I see Marquis making a small cooking fire in our cave. I'm relieved no one has interrupted my sleep, but still worried about our future. I'm anxious about the invaders and want as much intel as possible. I cautiously approach Marquis and say, "You're up early."

He hands me a cup of water and says, "Good morning. Fishing is better when it's quiet." He starts cooking fish with pancakes.

"I'd like to ask you some questions."

"Sure. Have a seat."

I sit on a rock beside him and ask, "Who are the men who attacked your family?"

"I don't know. They appeared from the sky about fifteen weeks before you did. They caused methane gases to be released in the air, killing hunters on the plains. We sent ambassadors to negotiate. My brother-in-law was one. The others kidnapped our ambassadors, turning them brainless. Later they died. Four weeks after they first appeared, the others rounded up women and children and killed them in cold blood.

"That's horrible. Is there anything you can do to protect yourselves?"

"It seems we are safe from them deep in the caves, but we can't hide there forever. We have to come out to sow, to reap, to hunt."

"How many are they?"

"I'm not sure. Étienne saw about ten men."

"What kinds of weapons do they have?" I ask.

"Not like ours, much more powerful."

I want more information, "You said they came more than once, how many times?"

"At least four times that we know of."

"Where are they from? How did they get here?"

"I don't know where they come from." He looks around and picks up a black, multi-eyed beetle, saying, "Their ship looks like this beetle, but large like Carcassonne. I only saw it once from far off."

"Do you know why they are here?"

He shrugs his shoulders and replies, "They take metals from the ground—gold, silver and heavy metals and gemstones—they're all quite common."

"Why did they attack you? Did you try to stop them?"

"I don't know why they attacked. We have enough metals and gems so, no. We tried to communicate with them, but they, like I said, kidnapped our ambassadors. Then they returned to the sky. Have you ever seen them?"

"No. It's been a while. Hopefully they are done here and will leave us all alone," I answer.

"I doubt that." His information was too vague to be of much use.

We stare at the fire while Marquis finishes making breakfast. The others wake up and start bragging and competing about their conquests of women.

I ask them, "What are you going to do to us?"

Jean teases, "I don't know. It depends on a lot of things. We're on a peace mission to make amends, and mean you no harm, if that's what you're getting at. We're just trying to get to know you. Why not have some fun too." Then he whispers, "Which one of us were *you* staring at yesterday? You can tell me."

I blush without responding. I have the impression these ambassadors are friendly, but shallow, real Casanovas. They don't seem too intelligent. I certainly don't trust their intentions, but they don't seem prone to violence either.

Jean explains, "No one would mess with the marchioness—not worth it. Several generations ago, a selfish king stole the beautiful wife of a jealous and respected duke. The king and duke went to war over it. Thousands were killed, including the king. It was declared by the cardinal, the new king and the people that adultery would be outlawed. Guilty parties would be put to death. No exceptions allowed. This is a tripartite covenant that cannot be broken."

"That seems harsh."

"Guess so, but no rules for single strangers," says Jean smirking.

"Just easy pickings, something for nothing," I say sarcastically, then shake my head.

After a filling and tasty breakfast, we set out on our way with the canoe. There is a waterfall ahead. The men need to portage the heavy canoe down to the river below. I carry down some of our supplies in a makeshift backpack. It feels good to hike for a while instead of being crammed in the canoe. I look back and see the water cascading about fifty meters down the basaltic rock. It forms a lovely thin waterfall. I'm mesmerized by the mist and steady sound of the crashing water. There are large, pretty flowers near the falls that I haven't seen anywhere else. An animal species, which appears to be translucent rotating bracelets, float about the waterfall as the wind and mist carry them. They remind me of floating bubbles. They land gently, elongate, and climb up, only to float down again. "What are they?" I ask.

Marquis explains, "Ribbons. The ribbons capture the flower pollen as nourishment and excrete the excess, seeding the steep sides."

"A perfect symbiotic relationship," I say.

With this drop, we leave the flat fields of the plateau and enter hilly, forested terrain. Below I see a forest of tall, thick, tree-like plants and other reddish vegetation, with meadows bursting with multi-colored flowers, like a vibrant Monet landscape. Everywhere there are sweet, calming perfumes in the calm breeze. I can hear many strange, gentle sounds—occasional chirps, hums, bleats, squeaks—but cannot tell who or what is making them. I ask about the sounds. Marquis points out several gliding rodents moving from tree to tree and a large, slow-moving herbivore, without front limbs, eating flowers on the edge of the forest.

The character of our once small, slow river is changing. With the drops in elevation and additional waterfalls, the river's flow speeds up. Also, additional tributaries widen the river to about the length of a hockey rink. The riverbanks shorten. Soon, the men are using all their attention and energy to navigate the whitewater's boulders and meter-high drops. I'm using all my strength to hold on to the canoe. Water splashes into the canoe and our feet get soaked. After a drop, my hat flies off. Quite a few times I think the canoe will fall apart. Frightened, I lean back into Marquis. However, the men seem used to this and shout in delight. They are completely focused, maneuvering precisely. After a while, rather than being stressed, I start to trust that we won't crash and break apart. We feel exhilarated, and finally, exhausted.

The wildest part being over, we go ashore for a break. When the men are resting, I find hand-size, brightly colored climbing marsupials with large ears and big, friendly eyes. They match the color of the flowers on which they are feeding. "They're just too adorable, and they're purring." I reach out to touch one.

Quickly Marquis pulls my hand away. He admonishes, "Don't touch any! The purring's a warning. They spit, and the spit is toxic. It wouldn't kill you, but it would cause severe acid burns."

"Oh, thanks for the warning."

After a few hours, the river changes again. It's becoming serene. Twice as wide, it starts to flow very slowly. The riverbanks have disappeared into marshy clumps. As we approach sea level, I can feel the heavier, stiflingly muggy air. The smell of the lower, dense, dark forests becomes more and more pungent. The number of insects has dramatically increased. We sometimes find it difficult to see as we pass through large swarms. We veer away from several large, four-paddled, omnivorous water horses. I watch them and note that their elongated heads act like shovels. They have sharp teeth for moving mud and grasping prey.

As we continue, new strange sounds—shrills, shrieks, growls—become increasingly louder. The ambassadors quiet their chatter to listen intently. In the still water, I see a huge snake, like an anaconda, with eyes all around its bulbous head. Marquis warns me, "Don't touch these either. These are vicious biters and have killed small children."

"Don't worry. I've no intention of going anywhere near it."

After it passes, they decide to break to sleep and drag the canoe onto the clay edge of a small patch of dry land. The exhausted men collapse on the ground. The trees block out the warm sun. I'm soaked and cold. I mention that I would like a campfire. Marquis hands me his flint. It takes me several tries to get a fire started in this damp area, and then a long time to find dry, woody plants to keep the fire burning. After I have a decent campfire, Marquis spots and kills a long, wide snake with his knife. They prepare it for dinner with their other provisions. I've never tried snake, even on Earth, but this one seems nourishing, though a little too tangy.

As we prepare to sleep, Marquis warns me, "Camille, stay close, there may be hungry predators out here." Remembering the creepy anaconda, I stay close.

Looking up, Claude says, "It's going to rain."

Using axes, they quickly build a triangular shelter, just high enough to kneel in, with two walls of fallen logs and a third long side open to the campfire. The site is slightly raised, and they dig a trench around the entire shelter to direct the rainwater out.

Guillaume suggests, "Camille, would you please find and pile up dry leaves on the ground as a barrier to dampness."

"I can do that."

As I pick up some wide leaves, Guillaume warns, "No, don't touch that plant!"

"Oh," I say dropping my large pile of leaves, "Is it bad?"

"No, only kidding. You can use that," he says chuckling.

Then they place the overturned canoe on the long side as a roof. We cover the remaining opening with sticks and leaves to finish the roof. They move the campfire to raised stones in the middle of the overturned canoe, just as it starts to drizzle.

Because their clothes are drenched from the rapids, they take out spare clothes from a bladder sack. I have just my wet robe and am starting to shiver even by the fire. Marquis hands me a large, dry blanket. I take it and go behind covered bushes to remove the robe. I wrap the blanket around myself like a toga noticing that most of my bruises and scratches are healed. My face no longer feels puffy. I return and hang my robe by the fire to dry.

The sky releases a steady light rain. We stay together, with the ambassadors Claude and Guillaume on one side of the shelter, Jean in the middle, and Marquis and me on the other side. I lie nervously on my stomach between the wall and Marquis, with our heads toward the opening and under the canoe. Because our feet would touch due to the triangular shape, I bend my knees lifting my feet.

Suspicious that it seems to be taking more time to return, I ask Marquis, "How much longer before we reach the *Athena*, my starship?"

145

"It takes longer by river—not the most direct route—but it's easier, especially when travelling east. We're in the river's delta, very close to the strait—should be on the island with just a couple more hours of rowing."

"Marquis, I am capable of surviving out in the wilderness. I've hiked and camped a lot. I really don't need any help out here. You could have just pointed me in the right direction with a backpack, a few supplies."

"Oh."

"I wonder, exactly what are your motives? Yikes!" About twenty slithering intertwined yellow snakes stand up like cobras and hiss just a few centimeters in front of me.

Marquis smiles. "They're harmless, just mating, or trying to."

During a break in the rain, I can see some shapes in the distance lit by a myriad luminescent, flying insects. I notice a few species of trees folding up like upside-down umbrellas, making loud creaking noises as their limbs move. Other trees expand as if to allow their leaves to capture the first morning light before the other trees unfold. The movements sound like creaky doors. Other noises keep getting louder and eerier as the skies darken. I feel myself tensing up.

He teases, "Are you sure you want to be out here alone?"

I don't answer. I do feel that I would rather not be out here alone, but I won't admit it.

For a long time, I try to sleep, using my arm as a pillow. It doesn't work. I find it hard to sleep this close to Marquis, though he is now snoring softly. The air is heavy, and the humidity stifling. Too many things are running through my mind. All the strange loud noises and unfamiliar creatures make me nervous. I tell myself that there can't be anything too dangerous, since they are relaxed and sleepy. I'm stuck here with this lunatic but at least he seems to have mellowed. I study him. He's attractive. I scold myself, No, don't even . . . Then I consider sneaking away by myself, but I don't know my way around this swamp. If he's not lying, I should be home to the safety of the *Athena* and my friends soon. Sneaking away doesn't make much sense. The others all fall asleep, but it remains a restless night for me.

I manage to doze for a while, but then wake up when I hear a branch crack and scan the surroundings. I notice the rain has stopped. Looking up, I also see piercing red eyes glaring directly at me. At first, they seem demonic and terrify me. I grab Marquis, but the glare becomes hypnotic, and I let go. I am fixated on them and get up quietly, dropping the blanket. The eyes are irresistible. I walk toward them in a trance.

Suddenly, an arrow grazes its body, breaking the spell. It snarls. I gasp at seeing the ghoulish, human-like face with long, pointed teeth. It has nasty, dark, flying insects swarming all around it. I stare at its hideous panther-like body and elbowed front legs. As it runs away, I see a tail like a rat's.

Marquis is up and beside me, bow in hand. I'm trembling. Putting his arm around me, he guides me to the campfire and places my dried robe on me.

Then he quickly wakes Jean, Claude, and Guillaume, saying "The felis are back!" This alarms them, and they are quickly wide awake. Marquis tells them what happened and that he wounded it. Claude warns, "You know he's found his prey and won't stop until he succeeds." Each of the men light a torch and start carefully scanning, in a creeping line search pattern, a quadrant of the swampy peninsula.

I ask Marquis, "What . . . what does this mean? What was that?"

"Follow me close." He continues checking the ground for footprints and replies, "It means you're in danger. The felis are the most vicious land creatures. They are fast, deadly and intelligent, and can hunt all night long by smell and sound."

"It felt like someone stole my soul."

"They hypnotize their prey, causing them to leave the safety of their homes. You're lucky you woke me up; usually victims don't give a warning. Once alone, the felis would pounce, sucking all the victim's blood, and then bring the corpse to their own to feed."

"Ugh, that's so awful."

"I didn't expect any here. Though, they prefer very humid environments and tall trees, swampy areas aren't that plentiful here on the northern continent. They mostly stay on the southern continent, which is ideal for them. The methane doesn't bother them. They don't tolerate the dry desert between us and them. Strange as it seems for a swamp creature, they hate water, can't swim."

"So why are they here?" I start to regain myself.

"If it's too hot and there are fires down south, they might travel north."

"Do they attack often?"

"They're nocturnal but not cave dwellers, which is one of the reasons we live deep in the caves. Generally, we avoid each other. I don't know why they are here again, but they travel in small packs, so there are probably more than one."

"What are you guys doing?"

"We're looking for footprints to get a clue as to how many there might be."

"Of course." Though part of me is thinking if he hadn't dragged me out here, I wouldn't have been here to be targeted. I decide this is probably not the best time to start an argument. Swallowing my pride, I sigh and say softly, "They sound terrifying. Thank you for stopping it, by the way. I'm glad I didn't face him alone," which was also true.

He tells me, "It's my duty, you know that."

"Come see these sets of tracks by the water," interrupts Jean. Marquis and the other men follow Jean.

"Must be two more," says Marquis.

"It's too dangerous to stay at camp. They may be watching us now," warns Claude.

Marquis insists, "We have to immediately track and kill the beasts."

I frown.

"I can see you're disappointed."

"I am. We're so close."

"We need to get rid of them as soon as possible, or they may attack the harvesters. They may even get to your island and attack all of you, though it's unlikely they will cross the strait, but then again, they got here. They could try to follow you there. We at least need to warn the harvesters that the felis are back in the area. They attack the most vulnerable, so those kids by the water will be their next targets."

I'm horrified at the idea of the felis on our island and the children's bloodless corpses and offer, "I understand. What can I do to help?"

"Not much. Because the felis don't swim, you should get in the canoe in the river with Jean as a guard." Pointing to the water, Marquis continues, "Jean, stay there and absolutely do not follow us inland."

"You got it." We get in the canoe. Jean ties it to a stump in the river. He warns, "Keep your eyes covered and stay under the blanket."

Otherwise, he doesn't utter a word. I peek out and see Marquis, Claude and Guillaume, get in the water and wipe mud on themselves. Then, they search on land for tracks. The ground is soft, and they seem to easily find tracks and blood stains of the wounded felis.

The tracks lead farther and farther inland. I soon lose sight of their torches. I wonder what is happening to them. Jean and I wait. It's been several hours, and we haven't seen or heard them. The wait becomes agonizing. I ask Jean, "Should we follow them?"

"Positively not." We stay alert to listen for any possible sign of their return but hear none.

Hours later, Jean and I are getting sleepy. We try to stop ourselves from dozing by pinching or poking each other. We make repeated efforts, but eventually sleep overwhelms us.

I'm awakened by a jolt—our canoe hit a stump and then gets stuck on shore. We are in a strange new location. I can see that the rope had come loose. As quietly as possible, I use a sharp knife to cut off the bottom of my long robe above the knee. I get out of the canoe and step into nasty, oozing mud. I loosen the canoe and direct it out. I quickly get back in, waking Jean. "Where are we?" he asks.

"I was hoping you would tell me. Do you see anything familiar?" I whisper.

"No," he answers.

"We're lost then."

"I think so. I don't know how to get back."

"Wouldn't we just float to the ocean?"

He responds, "Maybe or maybe not, because the terrain has low hills. Sometimes, the swamp is below sea level and dead still. It's hard to tell where we would end up."

"Let's find an island, inaccessible to the felis, and climb a tall tree to determine our location using the stars. Maybe we can find a recognizable landmark or the others. We might see their torches."

"Sounds like a good plan."

Finding such an island proves difficult. After several hours, we settle on a site that has just a single access point. Watching closely, we bring the canoe to shore. Jean washes off his scent in the river and rubs himself with mud. He carries his bow and arrows along with a spear and offers me the same. I never learned archery but grab a spear.

Leaving the spear at the base of a tall tree, I carefully climb to the canopy. I am happy to see the shimmering lights of the aurora to the north and confirm directions by looking at the constellations. I know the ocean is to the east and is now at three o'clock. I can barely make out a break in the trees at twelve o'clock, which I assume is the main river to the north.

I carefully, but excitedly, climb down, only to catch a glimpse of two large felis crouching low under Jean's line of sight and sniffing the air. They are coming straight for me. My hairs stand on end. I grab the spear. Averting their eyes, I watch their body movements intensely to determine their next move. As they climb a large tree and inch closer on a branch, I assume a defensive martial arts posture.

They pounce simultaneously at me. I quickly step aside and immediately administer a round kick to the mid-section of one of the felis, releasing a loud kyai. The force of the kick, adding to its forward momentum, flings the felis sideways, knocking the other felis in mid-air. Both flop down momentarily stunned. I quickly stab the closer one with my spear while an arrow flies close to the farther one but misses it.

As I try to remove my implanted spear, I spot the farther one snarling. We lock eyes, those piercing red eyes paralyze me. I freeze. I cannot move. I see a second arrow, harmlessly flying over it, but distracting its gaze. I hear Jean running to me.

He yells, "Get back!" I step back, as he steps in. The felis scratches his hand as he drives his spear into its chest.

I stand still and breathe deeply. Shuddering, I say, "Thanks" and hug him tightly.

He assures me, "It's OK, it's over." I feel comforted in his arms; I don't want to let go. After a minute, as if to break the intimacy, Jean excitedly says, "Thank you, too! Hell of a kick! Teach me that!"

"Sure, I'll teach it to you someday, if you teach me archery."

"You . . . you should have Marquis teach you archery, he actually hits his targets."

"He's good. Maybe. We should try to find them."

Before we leave, Jean slits the throat of the two felis to make sure they're dead. Then, I drop some liquid from my vial onto Jean's hand and wrap his scratches. I notice his lower thumbs are blistered from rowing. As we get into the canoe to head for the main river, I insist on paddling too. Because there is a third felis out there, we remain alert.

Jean and I arrive back at the river by our initial campsite. He insists on waiting there as Marquis had told him. It would have been an unbearably long wait, but Jean and I chat about everything and anything. He is the royal cabinetmaker and teaches me to whittle to kill time.

Finally, as the sun rises, Marquis, Guillaume and Claude return. We are all relieved and greet each other excitedly. I notice Claude has wounds and clean them with some of the liquid from my vial. "What happened to you guys?" asks Jean.

Marquis tells us, "It's a long story. The tracks got harder and harder to find. Still, we kept tracking the beasts inland. After several hours, we could see the tracks clearly and knew we were close. Claude found very fresh tracks. As he was about to signal us, a felis pounced on him, aiming to bite his neck. Claude lifted his axe, thwarting the felis as it scratched his arm deeply. It snarled and prepared to pounce again. Guillaume and I heard the struggle, came running, and I speared it, killing it. I noticed the second wound in the felis and knew it had to be the first felis we encountered. It must have been too weak to stay up in the trees. As I cut off its head, we heard an eerie loud howling."

"Glad you guys are alright and the other felis is dead," says Jean.

Marquis continues, "We decided to head for the howling but didn't see any tracks on the ground. After searching for hours, we noticed a few tracks, which indicated they were headed back to our original campsite. We hadn't seen any remains and knew they still needed to feed. We suspected they may have been luring us out, aiming for the easier target and decided to head back. Because we were getting dangerously tired, we built a raft so that one person could guard, while the other two slept."

"We fell asleep too," confesses Jean.

Marquis continues, "When we arrived back at our initial campsite, we found tracks, confirming our suspicions. You were gone. We assumed you had drifted and followed the current to find you. We didn't and came back here again."

Then Jean tells Marquis what happened to us and our defeat of the two felis. "That's really impressive. How and why did you learn to kick like that?" asks Marquis suspiciously.

"I just did when I was growing up, for self-defense."

Everyone, but Marquis, relaxes with our victory and is happy to finally leave this dank and creepy place.

sixteen

Encounters

At dawn, in the salt marsh, I see the *Chidiya* overhead. I'm so excited I try to stand up to wave, but Marquis holds me down. He complains, "You'll tip us over."

Just as he finishes his sentence, Guillaume stands up, waves and excitedly shouts, "Come get me you foul beast!" The canoe tips over.

Jean complains "We and everything—our blankets, our packs, our food—are soaked! Idiot!"

Guillaume exclaims, "That was so cool! I gotta ride that dragon!" Jean jumps on Guillaume and holds him underwater. Guillaume gets up laughing.

Emma swoops down again and we wave at each other. I see her on the radio. Because the grassy marsh contains tall plants, she doesn't have a place to land. I'm so happy to see Emma, I don't even argue when Marquis offers a hand to help me back in. "Thanks," I say and shout, "Yes!" with my arms high in the air, grinning ear to ear.

In very little time, the canoe reaches and crosses the choppy strait. I feel queasy, and Claude gets sick. We land, secure the canoe, and then walk to the cave Marquis sheltered in. The men stop to drink and freshen up in a nearby rivulet. They find their driest, least smelly outfits and change, smearing some of the sweet-smelling purplish flowers on their clothes.

Claude brags, "I'll sweep them off their feet with my poetry and Cyrano de Bergerac lines." The three ambassadors start arguing incessantly over who has the smoothest pick-up lines.

"Are they always like this?" I ask Marquis.

"Afraid so," he responds.

Then, I laugh softly and grin. Marquis notices, "You have a lovely smile. So, what's so funny?"

I reveal in a whisper, "I'm the only one who speaks French."

"Right, I remember." He grins ear-to-ear and does not give away this secret.

Later, on the mountainside outside the crater, Kiara, Evelyn and Ava rush out to greet me with outstretched arms. We hug tightly.

Ava cries, "We were so worried about you, so happy you're alive. You've been gone more than a week. We've been out looking for you, just called Aurora and Vivian in." Kiara and Evelyn repeat the sentiments and we all hug.

I say smiling, "I'm so happy to see you again."

Ava says, "Tell us about your companions."

I state, "This is Marquis. They think he's my husband." My friends give me a questioning look. I clarify, "We're definitely not romantic. It's a long, crazy story. These clowns are Jean-Louis, Claude and Guillaume. They're ambassadors of goodwill." In French, I introduce my friends to the men, who give an extremely polite greeting in French.

I translate it and say to my friends in English, "They don't speak English. I see you have on your tasers, good idea, hopefully not necessary but you never know."

Ava tells me, "We all have one on. Arla had us prepare for hostilities. She and Harper have tranquilizers pointed at them, for safety reasons, just in case there's trouble. Emma will join them. Lilian and Riya will be watching everything from the bridge."

I say, "Hopefully all that won't be necessary."

Then Ava smiles. "We want to celebrate your return. The rest of us have been preparing dinner–even used fresh foods. Bella and Lucy are still in the dining hall." I translate the dinner plans for the men.

Ava adds, "Please ask them to leave their weapons outside." I translate.

The ambassadors readily comply over Marquis' objections. Then Marquis questions, "Many are missing, Why?"

I say, "Preparing dinner. Some may be sleeping."

He gives me a sarcastic look. "You expect me to believe that?"

"Do you really expect them to trust you?"

Guillaume says, "The ladies are gracious enough to prepare a meal, and we should be polite and thankful. Please, let's go return the sentiment with utmost graciousness and gratitude."

"I don't like this," says Marquis, but he drops his weapons too.

Not everyone is on guard. Kiara and Evelyn whisper to each other about the men and giggle. Claude is grinning with his eyes on Kiara.

We arrive at the crater, and the ambassadors are amazed at the huge spaceship in the center. Jean asks, "Did you build it?"

I answer, "No, just fix it."

Guillaume asks, "Where's the dragon?"

"Probably in its lair."

Walking past our gardens, Marquis says, "I like what you've done with this dull crater. It looks alive."

"Thanks. We all worked really hard," I say. They want to know what everything is. I don't want to divulge too much and indicate there will be time later.

Ava directs us to the dining hall, "Looks like it's going to rain, again."

I cry out when I see Lucy and Bella. We also hug for a long time.

Then I excuse myself to shower and change. The warm, clean shower awakens my skin. I feel like I'm peeling off layers of stinky sweat, mud, even blood. Disgusted by my own body odor, I lather thoroughly with my skin-softening, jasmine soap and use my lavender shampoo and conditioner in my hair. After blow-drying, it seems so soft and silky I decide to leave it down. I have nothing to wear befitting a welcoming party, hardly anything clean either. Therefore, I put on my cheerful, brightly colored spandex yoga pants and fitted t-shirt. I find no clean bra either. This outfit will have to do.

When I return to the dining hall, Ava, who had noticed Jean's and Claude's scratches, is applying proper sterile bandages. They have been trying to communicate with gestures, but this is not effective. I busily translate. The ladies excuse the lack of gourmet cuisine and prepare to serve homemade pasta with tomato sauce, nuts, and our garden radishes. I can also smell the aroma of the berry pies baking for dessert. Marquis insists we eat first. I suspect he's afraid we might poison them.

They are all eager to talk. I cannot keep up with the translations. Kiara suggests, "We should use our communicators' translation function."

"I'm not sure that's a good idea. As it is now, we can talk privately," I say.

"C'mon, we can't talk."

"Yeah, this isn't any fun," complains Evelyn.

"Please," begs Kiara.

"OK, OK."

I excuse myself to get my and the extra communicator, which had been Zoë's. I find Lilian and ask her to set them all to translate. When I return, I show our guests how to use them. They need to hold down a button and talk into it in French. Because of their unrecognized dialect, the words come out in garbled English on my communicator. I speak in English on mine. The words come out in perfect French on theirs, which is a dialect strange to them. It takes some trials before the AI adjusts. It seems slow to me, but our guests are wide-eyed.

"You can keep this one as a gift," I say.

"We have something to give you too," says Claude. He takes out a bag of precious and semi-precious gems and gives some to us.

As a geologist, Kiara is visibly impressed. She checks a clear crystal on a hard surface. It leaves a scratch. "Wow! A diamond. And these look like garnet and sapphires," she exclaims.

"They have a lot of them; they are not all that rare here," I say.

She asks questions about the gems, rocks and caves here. Claude is happy to answer all her questions. He tells her about his travels in their caves, and she says she can't wait to see all of them. The two converse, locked eye to eye in their own little world.

Aurora and Vivian return from their search and come in to greet me with hugs. They, too, check out our guests. Guillaume and Jean, in competition for the number of women they can interest, prefer to play the field. They flirt with all the ladies, who flirt back. The ladies enjoy just looking at men after being without them for so long. We ask a lot of questions about their life here.

"How do you live?" asks Bella.

"We are mostly farmers; we fish and hunt," answers Jean.

"What to you grow?"

Jean gives her details.

Evelyn asks, "How many are you?"

"About nine thousand people," answers Guillaume.

"Are you a farmer?"

"No, I live at Carcassonne. We're artisans. I'm a tinsmith."

When asked how they got there and why they are so like us, their answers are vague. They ask just as many questions about us. They seem fascinated by our world and our journey.

At dinner, Marquis stays beside me. He smiles at me and says, "Everyone here seems to really like you."

"I like them too."

Then he sniffs my hair and body. "Your hair smells nice and it's pretty like that," he whispers to me.

"Thanks."

He touches my hair. "It's soft."

Immediately, I scowl at him and he backs away.

Later, he accidentally touches my sleeve and I flinch. "Nice outfit. I've not ever seen anything like it."

Then he stares until I feel like his prey and ask snappily, "What do you want?"

"Nothing." He turns away and complains to Jean, "It's hot in here."

I whisper to Evelyn, "He's staring at me. Do I have some weird growth on me?"

"Only him," she responds and giggles.

He seems to be daydreaming. After dinner, he whispers, "You were brave, at Carcassonne and on the trip back. You're smart. I can see why you're the leader. I'd like us to work together."

"Marquis, I don't think—"

"Would you please grant us a tour of your impressive home?" interrupts Guillaume.

"Of course," answers Evelyn.

As we open the door to the hallway, the light hits Arla. Marquis notices her with a tranquilizer gun pointed at his brother Jean. Marquis instantly grabs Lucy as a shield and has her in a choke hold. We all gasp in shock.

Furiously, he says, "I'll kill her if you move." Looking at me, he demands, "Get me the weapon now!"

I beg, "Please let her go."

He glares at me, "You betrayed me, having us leave our weapons outside while pointing one at us."

I reach over to get him the gun, while explaining, "It was just a precaution." I try to calm him, explaining, "It cannot kill anyone, just put someone to sleep."

He shouts, "I don't believe you!"

Lucy struggles. He chokes her harder. She is turning blue. I grab the dart from the gun and inject it in myself, saying, "I'll prove it."

Ava shouts, "No, don't Camille!" as I stagger to the floor, with Ava breaking my fall.

seventeen

Trip to Safety

The fall shocks Marquis, who loosens his grip on Lucy, and she tasers him. Vivian tasers Guillaume and Evelyn tasers Jean. Kiara hesitates. Aurora reaches over and tasers Claude. Emma and Harper rush in quickly and shoot darts in each of Marquis and the ambassadors.

Ava and the other ladies go to medical. Shaking her head, Ava says to her unconscious patient, "Oh, Camille, the dosage was too strong for you, they were set for someone twice your size." She administers intravenous fluids to prevent dehydration and to stabilize heart and body functions. She sets up dialysis and prepares the respirator. Then she examines a shaking, crying Lucy and concludes that she is fine, just bruised and scared. Leaving the doctor and her patients in medical, the rest of the ladies meet in the bridge.

The stunned men are left in the dining hall as Lilian, who has been watching on the monitors, seals the doors. They are imprisoned there.

"Well, what should we do with them?" asks Arla.

"That one seems really unstable, dangerous," says Emma.

"No argument there," says Arla.

"But there are many more of them out there. What if they come looking for their friends?" asks Vivian.

"I can watch for them," offers Aurora.

"Still, how could we defend ourselves? We're probably going to be here a long time. We need to encourage positive relations with these people," says Arla.

"Right," says Evelyn.

"The others haven't hurt anyone. Kiara suggests, "I think we should talk to them."

"It seems they just want to be friends," says Bella.

"or maybe more," adds Evelyn.

"They're generous—," says Kiara.

"They're waking up," interrupts Lilian. The ladies listen to the men as they wake up slowly.

Claude says, "My head hurts."

"Ow," says Marquis, touching his head.

"Well," Jean states, "Mission accomplished, we learned about their weapons."

Guillaume complains, "No, we were supposed to *seduce* them to get the information. What the hell Marquis? What's wrong with you! We're supposed to build an alliance."

Marquis responds, "I reacted. I saw the weapon aimed at my little brother. I couldn't let them hurt him."

Claude looks around the dining hall and asks, "How do we get out of here?" They soon discover there's no way out.

On the bridge, Kiara says, hands on hip, "Well, that's just peachy."

"What scoundrels," says Evelyn.

"Let's leave them in there. Teach them a lesson," says Emma.

"OK," says Arla.

After a few hours, they discuss the situation again.

"I'd like my kitchen back," says Bella.

"Me too," says Kiara.

"I say we need to leave them there," asserts Emma.

"It would be unconscionable to leave the new visitors imprisoned without a substantial cause," counters Arla.

"I agree," says Kiara.

"Me too. The other three did nothing to hurt us. I think they were just as shocked as we were," says Vivian.

"And they're kinda cute, refreshing," says Evelyn.

"Like a tall drink of iced tea," adds Kiara.

"And interesting. We can learn from them," says Bella.

"We can let them out, on condition that the crazy one leaves this crater," offers Arla.

"I can live with that," says Emma.

"Emma, Harper and I will go talk to them. We should prepare for a confrontation, stay in radio contact," says Arla.

Emma, Arla and Harper, with a radio and armed with guns and tasers, cautiously open the dining hall door. The men step out. Using their communicator, the brash Guillaume exclaims, "So glad you decided to let us out."

"Want to be escorted back in?" asks Emma.

Claude asks, "What do you plan to do with us?"

Arla sternly proclaims, "You three gentlemen can stay as our guests, but the one that was here before must go! He's attacked us twice."

Jean argues, "You mean Marquis? But, it's his land, he's the heir apparent. He has the right to go anywhere, for whatever reason."

"Marquis must go!" repeats Emma.

"It's fine, she's right. I'll go, if I can just say good-bye to my wife," says a sullen Marquis.

"What, what wife?" Emma asks.

"I think he means Camille. I guess we could guard him," radios Kiara.

"I noticed he hardly took his eyes off her," radios Lilian.

"OK, just for a few minutes," agrees Arla. Emma, Arla and Harper, carrying their guns, escort Marquis to medical. Jean comes too.

Marquis sees the body very still in the isolation bed and asks quietly, "Will she die?"

"She's still in a really deep sleep. She's had too much barbiturate, but she'll recover," says Ava.

Marquis stares a long time and sighs, "She'll always hate me."

"You never know brother, you two did have a moment before getting here. She actually smiled at something you said."

Marquis turns to Ava and communicates, "Please tell her I'm sorry, and that I want to protect her. I failed miserably. I didn't intent for her to get hurt. She's pretty special. I know I'm going mad."

Emma retorts, "Going? You're definitely already insane!"

Ava asks, "Why is it that even when everyone was having a good time, you're so uptight?"

Marquis reveals, "We're all in serious danger."

Jean explains, "Others from the sky are attacking our people, releasing toxic methane, destroying our minds, attacking defenseless villages, killing us. Marquis' wife Thérèse and children were killed. He thinks you ladies were part of them."

"That explains all the hostility. Why didn't you tell us?" asks Ava.

Jean replies, "We didn't know you really, which side you're on."

"Good-bye, Camille. Don't hate me forever," whispers Marquis. He tells Jean, "I'm heading out to my cave. I don't want to spoil our mission."

After he leaves, Jean tells Ava, "He wasn't always angry and on edge. Before the massacre, he was serious, but we had fun. Now he's just quiet. He's the king's favorite to succeed him. We all respect him, but we're all worried about him."

"He has us worried too," says Ava. Then she asks, "Jean, have you ever seen these white dots on Camille's feet before?"

"Sure, kids get them all the time," answers Jean.

"What do you do for them?"

"Nothing, they go away on their own."

Ava and Jean gather and inform the others of the danger. Jean offers, "You could all come to Carcassonne. It's a castle in a cave, plenty of room. The others haven't attacked us there."

"If they're coming from the sky, the *Athena* can be easily seen," says Emma.

"It would be best to leave here," says Kiara.

"I'll scan the skies for signs of invaders," says Aurora.

Arla suggests, "Why don't we booby trap this place? If they do come here, we can get rid of them for good."

Vivian agrees, "I like the idea. Lucy, Riya and I can put together bombs." They explain the process to the others.

They agree that Guillaume and Claude should take Evelyn, Kiara and Bella to Carcassonne first. The three hurry and pack a few necessities. Bella whines about leaving her plants, but Kiara is thrilled.

The five leave immediately. Kiara and Claude sit close as he teaches her to paddle. They are practically glued together, except for the few times she stops to analyze rocks. Claude is enthralled with everything she says. To avoid waterfalls and swamps, Guillaume and Claude take a different, picturesque route through the southern mountains. The route contains more of the meadows and forests. The ladies enjoy seeing the sweet-smelling flowery meadows full of deer and other mammals. It's only a slight bit longer route, and Claude wants to bring Kiara alone to show her his hidden grotto. The men row until their muscles are numb and they cannot row anymore.

"We've reached the caves. This land belongs to my family," says Claude.

"Let's rest here. I'm exhausted," says Guillaume.

Claude squeezes Kiara's hand and says softly, "I would like to be alone with you."

She blows in his ear and whispers, "OK, I'd like that. I'm ready."

"I want to show you my favorite place, not only for the limestone formations but also the beautiful gemstones. I know you'll love it. It's really awesome," says Claude, "I'll pack us a picnic."

Kiara tells Evelyn and Bella, "We're going spelunking. Don't wait up."

Claude and Kiara each carry a lantern, and descend a long, winding tunnel through the mountain. They are giddy in anticipation, and Claude wants their first time to be special.

At the entrance to a second cave system, they examine and collect tiger eye. "These are nice!" says Kiara. After a few meters, she notes, "Look at this white and orange dolomitic limestone."

"I told you, you would like it. There's more."

After one hundred meters, she exclaims, "Turquoise. And for real, are these malachite and azurite gemstones? Can I take some?"

"Yes, of course. Gather what you want."

They stop and take samples. Then, he takes her to a large grotto.

"This is breathtaking! It's more magnificent than a fairy tale castle! I love the stalactites, stalagmites and flowstone formations. I've never seen them glistening with opal." She explores further. "Wow! It's speckled with rose quartz and calcite crystals. I'm completely amazed. I've never seen a grotto quite like this!"

Claude smiles and says softly, "Nothing is too beautiful for you." He grabs her in a tender embrace, which she eagerly returns. Then he puts down a thick fur blanket and prepares their picnic.

"This is quick, but I feel like I've known you forever."

"Like we're soul mates."

"Two peas in a pod."

"What?"

She explains and they giggle.

They ignore the food and lie down, caressing each other. He presses against her saying, "I want to be with you."

She takes both their clothes off slowly in a gentle tease. "I want you too."

They embrace each other, enjoy the passion, and then fall asleep.

After he awakens, he kisses her and wakes her gently saying, "You were wonderful, are amazing, and I would love to stay here forever."

"You are too," she says and then yawns.

"I hate to leave but we do need to get to Carcassonne."

After Kiara and Claude had indicated their intention to explore the caves alone, their travel companions found a clear, quiet pool near the opening to refresh themselves. Evelyn and Bella, who had been flirting with Guillaume throughout the trip, whispered and giggled. They took out a joint and explained the effects to Guillaume. Each took a toke, making them relaxed and hungry.

Guillaume asked, "What would you ladies like for dinner?"

Evelyn took her clothes off and responded seductively, "Dessert. What would *you* like for dinner?" and beckoned him to her as she dove into the refreshing pool.

Bella undressed too, asked, "Want a two-course meal?" and followed Evelyn.

Guillaume promptly took his clothes off and dove after them. Evelyn and Bella rubbed their naked bodies on each side of him. They wanted to make up for a year and a half of lost pleasures, exhausting Guillaume. After they delighted in their sensuality, the three contentedly devoured all the food in their packs before falling asleep.

After Claude and Kiara return, Guillaume goads Claude by bragging about his double score, but Claude doesn't seem to care. The five continue their journey, contently rowing to Carcassonne.

eighteen

Revelations

Several hours after the five left Crusoe Island, I wake up groggy in the *Athena*. I feel dizzy and light-headed.

I ask Ava, "What happened?"

Ava reminds me, "You hit yourself with a heavy dose of barbiturate."

"Oh, I remember."

"You're recovering nicely. I still recommend rest. Also, I noticed strange white dots on your feet, mostly near your toenails. Jean says they are common here and go away on their own. I examined a swab—looks like a yeast. I spread some clotrimazole lotion on the skin infection, but they don't seem to be going anywhere. So, I put sterile slippers on your feet. Here, take this pill, a dose of fluconazole. Keep your feet dry and change the lining of the slippers twice a day. It should help, though I'm not really sure what to do for alien yeast."

"Thanks, I'm curious. I check it out." I try to get up but feel dizzy. "—after I rest."

"Don't ever do that again!" scolds Ava.

"Did it work?"

"Yes, he let Lucy go immediately and we sedated them and locked them in the dining hall for a while."

"Good."

Ava describes their fear of attack and plans for an exodus. Although I'm feeling a bit overwhelmed, I agree with the plan.

"That Marquis seems taken in by you. He seemed very upset." She tells me what he had said earlier.

"Really?" I question.

"Well I'm not making it up."

"Sorry, I mean I'm surprised. Even though he may regret it, Arla was right to banish him. He's too unstable to stay with us."

In a few hours, I'm feeling better. I decide to stay close to medical and go to my lab. I swab my own feet and set up the yeast in dextrose agar plates. I store them at body temperature for further study. I look at the slides prepared by Ava and identify the floating piles of fuzzy white balls as single-cell pseudo hyphae, thirty micrometers in diameter. I agree they are yeast and then wince. I can see vertical hypha lodged in skin cells. This means they can hold on tight and maybe penetrate my skin.

I also examine the cultures I had prepared the week before. With Ava, I start to classify the hundreds of newly discovered microscopic life forms, starting with a few of the more prominent ones.

While I'm recuperating, the others are setting up booby traps throughout our homesite. I step out for a break and Arla tells me, "Vivian and I rigged some that can be detonated from Marquis' cave." She shows me where they are hidden.

Outside, I see Jean and Riya digging holes for land mines.

Jean complains, "Ah, I hit a rock."

Riya disagrees, "That doesn't sound like a rock. It sounds like metal."

They dig out a small dense silver box with panels and examine it. Riya figures out the latch and opens it. After a few minutes, a holograph appears, and they stare at it.

Then Riya shouts, "You guys *have* to see this!" She radios Marquis, "I found something for all to see! This means you too, Marquis. Come."

We assemble outside the *Athena,* with Emma, Arla and Harper armed and prepared for the unstable Marquis. Lucy looks at the silver box. "These panels look solar."

Marquis rushed down but approaches me slowly. He fidgets, looks down and speaks softly, "Umm, I was worried. I'm glad to see you up. Are you OK?"

"I'm fine."

Riya opens the box and a holograph appears with a sound recording. It takes us several hours to review it because the recording is in French and we need to use our communicators to translate. Attentively, we listen:

> The 25th day of November 2069. This a Captain Philip Landry of the French Space Program airbus, the *Champlain*. Our mission is to start the first human settlement on Ross 128 b and maybe determine what happened to the famed *Athena*. France has chosen one hundred one representatives, one from each of the French departments, fifty men, fifty women, and one priest. We plan to follow the same route through the Kuiper Belt wormhole . . .

> The 29th day of May 2070. This a Captain Philip Landry. All are ready for the trip through the wormhole. No sign of the *Athena*. The crew is excited for this most exciting part of the journey. Miss everyone at home. Pray for us. Here is a personal message from everyone on board, starting with the France Overseas representative from Guadeloupe . . .

> The 10th day of June 2070. This is Captain Philip Landry. We traversed the wormhole. We thought we saw the *Athena* but just a mirage. We crashed into what appears to be the debris from an exploding nuclear fusion engine. The *Champlain* is irreparably damaged. We are able to steer to Ross 128 b, but the wormhole is closing, and the *Champlain* is

falling apart, structurally weakened, life systems malfunctioning . . .

The 30th day of July 2070. This is Captain Philip Landry. Not enough fuel to stay in orbit. Life support is on bare minimum. We will fly as low as possible and parachute down with whatever essentials we can carry. We are aiming for the temperate region north of the equator for the best chance of survival. This is my final recording. God save us.

It takes us a while for our minds to absorb this. Aurora is the first to speak, "I knew it. There *were* temporal distortions in that wormhole."

Lilian says, "That would mean that the *Champlain* entered twenty some years after we did, but we exited years after the *Champlain*. We must have been in there for at least a couple hundred years judging by the current population."

Arla adds, "A meteor didn't make this crater. The *Champlain* did."

"Probably why the site is sacred," says Marquis.

We realize that the inhabitants here really are humans and are from France. Lucy looks at Jean and smiles, "We've been allies for a long, long time."

Young Jean flirts, "Do you want to seal the deal?"

All the ladies hug Jean and give him *bisous*, a standard French greeting of pecks on both cheeks, as Jean relishes the attention. The ladies have gotten used to his flirting, and he to them constantly brushing him off. He still enjoys flirting with everyone, except me.

I say, "I feel bad. It seems our damaged engine is what stranded your people here, with barely anything."

Marquis says, "Don't feel bad. Staying here seems to have been the plan, and it's not a bad place to be."

"It's interesting. All the survivors' advanced technology was destroyed. Over the generations, they modified their laws and culture," I say.

"It seems they now rely on pre-industrial age skills," comments Ava.

"Our first king was dubbed, the Professor of Antiquities. We are taught that he was one of the founders who flew down with the legendary Philip Landry. The professor brought down the sacred texts and taught us our ways, what it means to be French. He showed us how to survive. Since then, every king had to learn the sacred texts," explains Marquis.

"Part of, a lot of your history is missing." Turning to my friends, I say, "It seems their society is based on the books they preserved, probably a knowledge of French culture to the Renaissance and Middle Age crafts. I'm surprised someone still had paper books." I close the box, hand it to Marquis, and say, "This should be yours. It is your people's heritage."

He takes the box. "Thank you. Carcassonne will appreciate this."

"You're welcome, Marquis. That seems like a title. Do you have a birth name too?"

"Yes, it's François VI, but I much prefer Marquis."

"I like "Marquis" better too. I see you came down with bow and arrows."

"Sorry, I forgot. I always wear this, like clothing."

"I'm not mad. I was going to ask if you can teach me to shoot?"

"Now? Sure, we'll need to move somewhere out of the way. Do you have something soft we can use as a target?" I grab a meter-square piece of foam from our remodeling. We walk away to the edge of the crater and set the foam on a rock at fifteen meters.

He stands perpendicular to the foam, with his feet apart. "Stand like this." I copy him.

"Now hold the bow out with your left hand, place the arrow on the guide with the colored reed out, pull the string back to your eye until your right arm is high. Can I show you?" I nod. He stands right beside me, moving my arm. I must be used to him near me because it feels comfortable. "Close your left eye. Aim. Release." As I release, the string whips my elbow and I miss the target completely.

He laughs. "You shoot like Jean. Try again but turn your elbow downward." My aim is better this time.

Marquis asks, "May I help you with your finger position?" He is so close I can hear him breathe.

"Yes." As he holds my hand and moves my finger centimeters lower, I feel flush. Pretending not to feel anything, I tell myself to focus on my aim.

Then I try again, hit the side of the target, and exhale a "Yes!"

"Much better. Try again." I get the arrow closer to the center. "You learn quickly."

"Cool."

On my next try, the bow string hits my breast. Marquis teases, "If you were a real Amazon, you would cut off a breast for better aim."

"Not happening. I'll have to settle for being an army captain."

"You're a soldier?"

"Yes, I *was,* before our journey here."

Smiling, he says, "You walk proud like one—guess that's why my uncle thought you were an Amazon warrior. He likes you."

"Really?"

"He's usually a good judge of character. Why are soldiers here?"

I clarify, "I'm retired medical. We're scientists, engineers."

"And explorers?"

"Yes, definitely explorers."

"I like that."

I talk about our mission and practice until my left elbow is bruised, forefingers sore, and purlicue is raw. I have to stop and say, "Thank you. That was fun."

"My pleasure."

"I should go."

"If you must."

I'm afraid of where this might lead if I stay and find an excuse saying, "I need to check on my epidermal microbe classification experiments, my petri cultures."

"Don't know what that is but sounds important. Thank you for talking to me."

I reluctantly bid him good night and he returns obediently to his cave, alone, but smiling.

I return happily to the *Athena*, where Ava and Arla eye me accusingly. I feel like a teenager past her curfew.

Defensively, I say, "Do not look at me like that. Archery is a good skill to have, here."

"Of course," says Arla sarcastically. "Seriously, be careful."

Later, I contemplate what the revelation from the box means for our families. We will never be able to return to the home and people we knew, even if it were possible to somehow travel back to Earth. It hurts me to think I can never see my dad again, and that he spent the rest of his life never seeing his only child again. I will never see my relatives, never see their children grow up. Everyone I once knew back on Earth is gone, long dead, and buried. My stomach aches and my eyes swell as I realize a big part of me is gone. I mention this to Ava, who thinks it would be good to have a community funeral so we can all mourn our losses together.

The crew still at the *Athena*—Ava, Emma, Lilian, Aurora, Harper, Vivian, Lucy, Riya, Arla and I—build a large campfire to ceremoniously say goodbye, one by one, to our dearest loved ones from Earth. In turn, we write a name on a small piece of paper and tearfully recall why we love this person. We burn each paper, symbolically sending each to a better world. It is a very long, reverent ceremony, but a release we all need.

nineteen

Carcassonne

Far away on the plateau, the five canoers arrive trouble-free at Carcassonne. When they arrive at the dock, Guillaume announces, "We're here—none too soon, my arms are killing me."

"Doubt I could paddle another meter," says Claude.

"That seemed very much longer," complains Guillaume.

Still using our communicators, Claude suggests, "We should report to the king first. You ladies ready?"

"Sounds exciting," says Evelyn.

"The king is fair, but rather strict," warns Guillaume. "He expects exceptional manners."

"Good to know," says Kiara.

As they enter the castle, Claude requests an audience with the king.

Soon, he enters smiling, exchanging hugs and *bisous* with Guillaume and Claude, and says, "Welcome all of you. Please, come let me show you to my dining room." They walk to an adjacent chamber and the king closes the door. He asks, "Who are your companions?"

"Sir, may I present the lovely geologist Kiara Williams, soil specialist Evelyn Miller and botanist Isabella Garcia? Here, you need to speak in this and press this, so that they can understand you," Claude explains and hands the king the communicator.

"Certainly," says the King. He hears the translation from the communicator. His eyes open wide, but he remains poise.

Claude says, "Ladies, I present King François V."

The king says, "I am enchanted to meet you." He says leaning over to kiss each of the ladies' hand in turn.

"He's so eloquent," whispers Bella to her friends.

"A smooth operator," whispers Evelyn.

"We are happy to meet you too, sir," says Kiara. "Your castle is impressive, and these tapestries are amazing."

"Thank you for the compliments. They keep the cold stones warm," says the king. He motions to the large table and chairs and says, "Please, have a seat. Tell me about your journey."

Claude and Guillaume describe our journey and then explain our innocence and vulnerability against the others. Claude concludes, "These Amazons are not warriors, just scientists, and they need our protection."

The king states, "I promise they will be safe here, under my protection."

Kiara says, "Thank you, sir. You are too kind. Could I please ask your indulgence further to arrange for canoes back to Crusoe Island to get the others?"

The king replies, "I would love to indulge you, young lady, but have you noticed that the weather is turning? There are now severe thunderstorms in the southeastern sky. That is a sign that a major hurricane will arrive soon. We can only send the canoes after the weather clears."

Guillaume says, "Your majesty, there is something else. We, I mean Marquis, the marchioness and Jean, each killed a felis in the swamp."

"She did! Are there more?" asks the King.

"We only tracked three, but if they came, maybe others will come too."

"You're right. I'll order all the children to stay deep in the caves and recommend the same to adults, until hunters can ensure there are no more felis in the area."

After their meeting with the king, Guillaume and Claude take the ladies on a tour of Carcassonne. In the courtyard, they notice a strange circle in the center and stare at it. It is round and divided into six equal pieces, like a pie. The right half is bright, but the left half is dark. In each piece is a bold Roman numeral, 1 to VI, starting clockwise from the top right. Each of the six pieces is further divided, two thirds plain and one third striped. On the outside of the large circle, over each of the six main pieces, are the Arabic numeral one, starting at the top, and equidistant, the numerals up to five. The numerals one to five are repeated at each pie piece.

"What is that?" asks Bella, pointing to the strange circle.

"A week clock. See the pendulum?" says Guillaume.

"Yes, but I've never seen a clock like that."

Guillaume explains, "We start on day one on the bright side and represented by Roman numeral I. We have breakfast at sunrise, represented by the top Arabic numeral one, going to the right, lunch is at two, shops close at three. Quiet time starts at numeral four, when children are put to bed. That's about at the striped or sleep section. Five is mid-sleep. The next bright one-sixth piece is day two—see the Roman numeral II—again waking with Arabic numeral one. The bottom starts with sunset and the dark time. Our day of rest is at the dark Roman numeral VI, which represents the last of the dark days. The whole clock is a week."

"I understand," says Kiara, and to Bella and Evelyn, she clarifies, "Their week is a full planetary rotation, an astronomical day. A 'day' is just over twenty-six of our hours. Their hour is just over five of our hours. Not as precise as our atomic clock, but it seems more practical here."

As the ladies walk through the courtyard, they admire the large triple crystals. "Oh, look," exclaims Kiara, "One crystal seems to be blue anhydrite, one of strawberry quartz, and one of white selenite. Are the crystals over a geyser?"

"Right," says Claude, "It erupts regularly every year, every fifty-five weeks. Hot water spurts out. The crystals mark the site, so no one gets too close—they look good, I think."

"They're incredible and beautiful. This place has hot springs?" asks Kiara.

"Yes, healing baths," answers Claude. "I'll ask my sister Claudine to show you soon. Men aren't allowed in the women's baths and vice versa."

"Looking forward to it," says Kiara.

"Me too. I'm overdue," agrees Bella.

"I'm sure you'll like my sister. She's open-hearted, generous. She's the most important woman in the Carcassonne social circles. But don't get on her bad side; she's got quite a temper," adds Claude.

Then, Claude and Guillaume find a place for the women to stay. Guillaume opens a door to an upper room over a shop.

"Nice! Spacious beds and warm fireplace," says Evelyn.

"This big one is for Evelyn and Bella. I'll show you yours," says Claude to Kiara. "It's smaller, and close." They walk several meters. "Here it is. I'm just next door."

The ladies settle in and are comfortable. Claude visits Kiara often. Upon learning that she likes to paint, he sets up an art studio for her in his gem shop, where he makes jeweled objects.

Claudine enjoys being the first Carcassonne lady to meet the newcomers and introduces them as honored guests showing them the hot springs in which to bathe. The Carcassonne ladies provide delicate foods and proper fancy dresses. Kiara has fun returning the favors by styling their hair with ribbons and fancy accessories. The three newcomers are flattered by their invitations to the ladies' sewing circles and social teas, where Carcassonne's ladies inquire about the health of the marquis and marchioness and hope to learn interesting tidbits for gossip. The newcomers usually use their communicators but are starting to learn greetings in French. They talk about Crusoe Island and Earth, though sometimes this makes them homesick. They worry about how their friends are handling the storm and constantly inquire about getting help to the *Athena*.

Meanwhile, Guillaume brags loudly to a couple of his close companions about his double conquest and the strange herbs.

Marguerite has been staying aloof of the newcomers but listens for any negative gossip. She overhears Guillaume and starts to spread rumors, to anyone who will listen. She alleges that the newcomers are actually promiscuous witches with magical herbs, sent to ensnare the leaders of Carcassonne. Her proof is their black magic communicators. Moreover, she refers to the newcomers as usurpers defiling their sacred circle. One of her strongest supporters is the pious Nanette, who is married to the head of the royal guard, the nervous and always suspicious Comte Antoine. The two women have long discussions on the potential moral degradation from these strange witches and exaggerate their menace to Carcassonne society.

Marguerite hosts a big dinner of the noble families, including her uncle, King François V, and her cousin, Guillaume. She purposely does not invite Claude and the newcomers. At her dinner party, Marguerite frequently expresses her grave concerns about the so-called Amazons in order to garner support against them.

When the king hears her gossiping against the newcomers, he warns Marguerite sternly, "I understand you are suspicious of my guests. I have publicly given them my support. Do *not* keep this up. It is slanderous."

"But it's the truth. Don't you find it strange that the winds and even the felis are attacking us now? They must be conjuring them."

"These happened before. You don't know *that*. Your gossip makes me appear incompetent. If I hear another word, I'll send you away, immediately, to marry the widower Henri. He's here and tells me you proposed a marriage between our families to establish closer relations. He has asked my permission to marry you; he wants a wife for *himself* and a *tutor* for his children. As you know, there aren't many women out there. I'll consent if I must to keep you from causing trouble here."

"No, you can't! I don't want to live way out there. It's desolate. You can't expect *me* to live in a hideous underground hole, travel in smelly animal skin tents. It's so unclean. Henri himself is scarred, dirty and he has *seven* children! Young ones!"

"*You* should be willing to do whatever is necessary to secure the allegiance of the Plains. They're threatening separation," mocks the king.

Flustered, Marguerite argues, "Henri's uncouth—like Marquis. Marquis should marry his oldest daughter, Collette, and live out there, not me."

"Stop, Marquis is married."

"You can't be serious. She's a witch. I'm only trying to save Marquis, and Jean, and *you*."

"I am serious, and you aren't saving anyone. We can handle this."

"We need to launch an attack on them, to execute them, to stop them! You never trust me to handle *anything*. Why do you trust Marquis more than me?" whines Marguerite.

"He listens. He works hard. You don't. I'm warning you. Stop undermining my authority."

"Of course, I'll do as you order. But it's not fair. I'm the oldest. I have the right to be the next ruler of Carcassonne."

"You have no such right," corrects the king.

She only plans to be more secretive. She cannot send her brother off to the plains if he's still married to the witch. Marguerite and Nanette convince her husband Antoine that the *Athena* and the women aboard are a real threat. They hint that the king is possessed. Antoine secretly assembles a few soldiers to be ready for an engagement against the intruders. He is sure the king will soon see the need when he regains himself.

With the spreading rumors, Kiara, Evelyn and Bella receive less invitations and more suspicious glances. However, Claudine and her closest friends appreciate Kiara's help with their coif and continue to visit her and Claude. Her exceptional hospitality puts them at ease. In his shop, they admire how sweetly Claude and Kiara interact and her serene and skillful paintings. They spread their own view that someone so sweet and talented could not be malevolent. Soon Carcassonne becomes polarized.

twenty

Microbes

The hurricane winds that pound the plateau, ravage the coastland.
Crusoe Island experiences the brunt of the storm. As we expected,
we are protected from the storm surge by our altitude and from the
harshest winds by the crater walls. Arla concludes that we are in the
midst of a category five hurricane. We finish our projects indoors.
Soon, we use up all the materials and cannot make any more bombs.
The ladies pack to leave, though no one can go outside.

I ask Jean, "Why didn't we just swim across the strait to the
mainland and then hike?"

Jean responds, "The ocean waters contain dangerous creatures,
especially the kraken. We need to stay above the waters. Even then,
it can be dangerous because the kraken have long, tentacled arms."
He waves his arms imitating one.

As the wind howls and the rain pours, I look out into the dark
night toward the volatile Marquis and wonder how he's managing.
"He's alone up there. No human should have to be alone through
this."

"Marquis will be fine. He's been out in this type of weather
before. He has food and knows what he's doing. His cave is deep and
has interior rooms where he can get away from the winds."

"You're right. Nothing we can do now."

I have been wearing the medical slippers since Ava suggested them and have difficulty walking. "Funny shoes," Jean teases.

"The white dots keep getting bigger. They're now specks and keep growing. My feet are very itchy and red, driving me crazy. We've tried medicine, anti-fungal creams and powders, but nothing helps."

"Can I see?"

I show him my feet. "Ugly, no? It's probably from something from the swamp. It's eating my skin—hope it doesn't eat me alive," I say and bite my lip.

"I've never seen anything like *that*."

"I wonder why?"

"Don't know. We smeared that swamp mud all over ourselves."

"I didn't. You guys were more exposed than me. Can I take a skin sample from you?"

"Ah, why? Will it hurt?"

"I want to see if you have a microbe that repels this yeast. Humans are full of benevolent bacteria. Maybe that is why the yeast doesn't flourish on you. And, no it won't hurt, I just need to wipe your skin with a soft swab."

"That's fine then."

I bring Jean to medical and take a swab from his feet for study. It may take a week to grow enough to be useful. I meet with Dr. Ava Campbell and she suggests, "We should test the old samples from Marquis to see if anything interacts with the yeast. We need to find a solution soon, before you have permanent skin and maybe other tissue damage. Not sure what this would do in your circulatory system."

"I know, I'm worried. There are probably hundreds of different microbes here. I do not know if that even is a solution. I will ask Vivian if she has any ideas."

"She just told me that she has found a few white spots on her feet too."

"Oh, no."

"She took a shower in the stall after you did."

"So, it has been quarantined?"

"Yes, just now. Everyone else usually uses the bigger, more private, shower."

"There seems to be about a two-day, Earth days, incubation period before they are visible."

Ava and I develop a few experiments in the lab to test my hypothesis. It will take hours, even days, to watch how the microbes react. Due to the vast number of different microbes, I ask Harper and Arla to help catalogue the hundreds that we found on the Marquis cultures. Biochemist Vivian Li suggests another theory, that there may be something in their diet, something different that they secrete that may be suppressing the yeast. She searches for Jean and asks him for additional skin samples; this time it pinched.

After, Ava, Harper and I discuss plans with Vivian, we start talking about recent events and even some juicy gossip.

"We think some of Jean's flirting has been paying off," states Vivian.

"Not sure who he's with, but I heard loud, heavy breathing once in the sleeping quarters when I went to retrieve some toiletries," says Ava.

"Worse, I walked in on him in the dimly lit farm behind a lattice fence, kneeling, naked, thrusting into an ecstatically moaning woman bent on all fours." She mimics the sounds. "I couldn't see who because I was shocked and backed away," says Vivian.

"Did you hear anyone admit to it?" asks Ava.

"No," answers Vivian.

"Maybe, we should leave the consenting adults their privacy," I say.

"No way, we're not done. We want to talk about you," teases Harper.

"Why?"

"We want to hear all the details about you and Marquis," she asserts.

"You talked about what you saw, and the felis, but not much about him," says Ava.

"Not much there."

"Is he a marquis?" asks Harper.

"Yes, I think so," I answer, "He's the king's nephew."

"What's his real name?" asks Ava.

"It's François VI, after the king, but he prefers Marquis, his title."

"He's calling you his wife, seems there's *something* there, eh," says Ava.

"Oh God, I assure you there's nothing."

"Not buying that, the way he looks at you," insists Ava.

"Give it up, we want to hear *everything*," says Vivian.

"It is not like that. When he first kidnapped me, he *dragged* me—pretty rough too—not exactly a romantic stroll. We were shivering cold and he slept near me. We were touching but nothing happened, just too cold. Then he brought me to be tried as a witch and murderess of all things. I think his uncle, the king and judge, took pity on me. I was found innocent, but we mentioned sleeping together, and like you three perverts, the king thought there was more, and pronounced us married. Then he locked us up together, until I forgave Marquis."

"Weird," says Vivian.

"That sounds really scary," says Ava.

"It was."

"Do you think Kiara, Evelyn and Bella are safe there?" asks Vivian.

"The others there seem primitive, suspicious maybe, but otherwise OK."

"So, what did you *do* when you were locked up?" asks Harper.

"What does *forgive* mean?" asks Ava.

"*Forgive* apparently means I pretend to be able to stand him. I stayed angry for a couple days, but he said he would take me home. I agreed to go with him as long as he stayed away from me."

"I haven't seen such a temper in you," says Ava.

"*He was trying to have me killed.* At first, I said no because I was afraid of what they would do to you, but then I thought they could attack any time—and I missed you."

"And we missed you too," says Ava.

"And then?" says Vivian.

"We travelled in a canoe to a swamp. He was hunting felis and Jean and I got lost."

"Is that all?" asks Ava.

"Yes, they are barbaric."

"So, that could be a turn on," teases Harper.

"Not exactly, but he did save me from one felis. They are horrible. Marquis is amazingly fast with a bow and arrow, and accurate."

"Your hero," taunts Vivian.

"He is cute," says Harper.

"I guess he is," I confess, "The other guys kept trying to shove us together. I think they found it funny that Marquis was stuck with me."

"Doesn't seem like Marquis minds," says Ava, "A whole week close together and—"

"Nothing," I say.

"Must be that yoga outfit," says Vivian. My cheeks feel flush.

"Him Tarzan, You Jane. You *blush-ing*," teases Harper.

"He was smelling me! It was weird."

"He seems volatile. So why do you like him?" asks Ava.

"I do not."

"Sounds like a *denial*," says Ava smiling.

"No, but I guess coming back, I started feeling safer with him. He knows a lot about everything in this place. We can learn from him. He fits here. Hunts and even cooks, expertly. That swamp was really, really creepy."

"Or he's just the lesser of two evils," says Vivian.

"I'm stuck with him. They have strict rules against adultery and divorce here too. No one else can come near me. Breaking their antiquated rules can be a capital offense."

"So, it's him or no one. He doesn't seem like a completely horrible person. He probably has a severe case of post-traumatic stress," suggests Ava.

"Ah, I did not think of that. Makes sense. He is fine sometimes, even laughing in the rapids."

"You mean like whitewater canoeing. Sounds like a blast," says Harper.

"It was," I admit.

"So, what are you going to do with him now?" asks Vivian.

"No idea, he was ordered to protect me."

"You should give him a shot," advises Harper.

"No, how can I trust him not to snap? He has no self-control."

"You have a point," says Ava "and I'm calling it a day."

"And we have a lot of work to do," I say.

After the hurricane passes, those not in the labs clean up the mess left by the strong winds. After helping us clean up, Jean complains that he has had enough frozen food and nuts. He wants to catch fresh fish, after which he plans to visit his brother.

After a workday in the lab, Harper wakes Arla, and they tag along with Jean to the beach with their own makeshift fishing pole.

Jean laughs and teases, "You're not strong enough to bring in a real fish."

"Wanna bet," responds Harper.

Arla spots her favorite sea mammals swimming and jumping in the distance. "I love coming out here to watch them whenever I can. They look like dolphins, except with arms, humanlike head and torso," says Arla looking through binoculars.

Harper spots them too. "They seem to be playing tag."

Arla shakes her head. "No, there's a ball and each has a stick. They're playing toss, like seals." Arla and Harper wave at the dolphins, who seem to wave back.

Arla notices Harper's long fishing knife and asks, "How do you have a real fishing knife? That's too impressive to be NASA-issued."

"That is nice!" says Jean.

"It's mine, was given to me when I was twelve by my grandfather as a good luck charm, so I brought it with me out here."

After a little while, Jean has a bite on his pole, struggles and brings in a meter-long silvery orange fish. "These are the best." He does a preliminary cleaning. "I'll take this up and leave you some. Then, I'm heading out to see Marquis. I think he might like some company and gourmet dinner. I beg your leave. Good luck, ladies."

"Bye," they say simultaneously.

"Remember, stay out of the water."

"Of course," says Harper. The two are enjoying the warm beach and want to stay longer. They are determined to bring in a fish to prove Jean wrong.

Harper asks Arla, "Have you tried him?"

"No, seems too young. Actually, I prefer coming down here to the beach alone, with the sound of the waves, the cool breeze, the hot sun. It just feels romantic. I imagine this merman . . ."

"Uff-da, kinky, I'm tired of being alone. I need a real man, the real hard salami. He's much more gratifying—so hot!"

"You and Jean, well OK." Arla teases, "You'd make beautiful babies."

"Ah, no."

After a couple hours, they have a bite. It's smaller than Jean's fish but still respectable. It's a fighter. They pull hard, knee deep in the water. The fish seems to be weakening. Abruptly, it darts out toward the open ocean. Arla and Harper hold on tightly to the pole to not lose their catch, moving farther into the deep waters. Suddenly, a long arm with suction cups pulls Arla under water, and she disappears. Frightened Harper releases the pole and takes out her long fishing knife. A suctioned arm tries to drag her under water too. Quickly, she slices it. It lets go. She calls out desperately for Arla but cannot see her. The creature with the suctioned arms pops out of the water, revealing its monstrous hard shell and all ten of its six-meter-long arms extending around a huge orifice. Its beady eyes seem to be staring angrily at Harper. Trembling with fear, Harper walks anxiously back to shore and frantically calls out in vain for Arla.

Harper can see the dorsal fins of the dolphins rush to the spot where Arla was dragged under. She sees thrashing in the water and picks up the binoculars.

Peering through them, Harper sees a dolphin, holding a spear, what they had thought was a stick, with one arm and dragging Arla with its other arm to a flat rock protruding from the water. Though the dolphin is far, Harper thinks it is administering CPR. She adjusts the focus. The dolphin appears to be a man. Arla coughs and seems frightened. He rubs her gently on the arms until she is recovered and calm. He has a pleasant and friendly face with a concerned expression.

Harper yells repeatedly, "Bring her here."

He ignores her, takes Arla's hand, over her and Harper's protests, and drags Arla farther out to sea with his group.

Harper runs to tell us what happened. Desperate, I radio Marquis for help.

"Can you help us? What do you know about them?" I ask.

Marquis says calmly, "We've been coexisting with the sea people from the beginning. They stay in the ocean and seem benevolent. We don't interact much. I've heard of the sea people helping drown victims. The rescued claim that the sea people are hypnotic, calming. They generally just let us go. Maybe there are more kraken near shore, and they can't get to shore just yet. They're also known to be playful, but we've never heard of them harming anyone."

"What can we do?"

"There's not much we *can* do. She may need help returning from where they take her. Jean and I can search the coastline."

"Did you ever meet one?"

"Yes, when I was young. By myself, I had canoed too far out in the ocean. A small group redirected the canoe back to shore. They seem shy. I wanted to communicate with them, but one waved and they all left. They're very fast too. I wanted to follow but couldn't."

"That's reassuring. Thanks so much Marquis. We're heading out to look for her in the *Chidiya*, our dragon."

Emma and I search along the main coast. It soon gets dark, and it's almost impossible to see anything. We give up and reluctantly decide to return after daybreak.

We notice that the land is flooded from the hurricane. Emma says, "They won't be able to come out of there to get us with the canoes. The rivers are overrun and running too fast. Maybe we should evacuate using the *Chidiya* instead. We'll need to find a cave to hide it."

"The *Chidiya* may draw attention to where we are hiding. In any case, I'm not leaving until we find Arla."

"Me neither."

Our yeast infection is another reason for staying. Ava, Vivian and I are determined to continue running experiments on the stubborn alien yeast and we need our labs. Ava has been using cryosurgery on the larger specks to lessen the damage. It slows the growth, but Ava warns that there can be long-term damage to the skin tissue. Even with this, the yeast is continuously spreading to my ankles and getting larger on Vivian, moving from her toenails to the rest of her feet.

Vivian is testing for unknown biochemicals in her lab. She uses chromatography and mass spectrometry to separate molecules in her skin and yeast samples. She runs comparative tests for density, pH and color on the biochemicals. Then, she uses sensitive gel electrophoresis and emission spectroscopy instruments for further analysis. She compares these with the biochemicals in our vast electronic library. She isolates trace amounts of a new protein from Jean's skin sample and new organic compounds from the yeast. She now plans to try micro-experiments to study the effect of the new protein on the yeast compounds using the electron microscope and x-ray diffraction. If successful, she'll work with Lilian on a computerized model to elucidate biochemical pathways and develop nanoparticles that can identify and destroy the yeast compounds. Despite a few promising leads, at the end of three shifts, she concludes that her newly discovered skin protein did not interact with the yeast compounds.

Undaunted by failure and driven by the incessant itching, Vivian radios Jean. She asks, "How are you guys doing?"

"Good, good, and you?"

"Not so good. Tests have all been failures. Can you please come by and give me more protein samples for studies?"

Standing next to Marquis, he teases, "What's that, you want to study my meat?"

"Not exactly," responds Vivian, blushing, "I need your body—no, your skin—for samples, you know what I mean. Can you come after sunrise? I'm too tired now."

"OK, for tomorrow," he radios back. Then he says to Marquis, "See, she wants me—making an appointment."

During the long Ross night, while Vivian is running her experiments, Ava and I continue to study the effect of skin microbes on this awful aggressive yeast. However, my thoughts are on Arla. Harper is with us, but barely able to focus.

She complains, "Classifying bacteria is boring as hell."

"You can name one after you," I suggest.

"Oh, can I? Now there's a thrill."

"I would rather be looking for Arla too, but it's dark and we need light and should save the fuel for when we can see. Besides this yeast could be dangerous."

"I know. I didn't mean I wouldn't help."

"Thanks, I know not everyone shares my fascination for the microscopic world."

I check on the petri dishes and carefully measure growth rates. Then, I separate out the various strands as much as possible. I insert skin nutrients and close the dishes, setting them for ideal skin temperature and in normal air.

"I will help classify and every six hours, Ava and I will record and analyze growth rates," I tell Harper.

Harper asks, "OK, how do I classify this brown microbe? It's running, it's weird. Ha, I think I'll name it after you. Camillus Tremblay *curre*."

I say dryly, "Thanks. How is it weird?"

"It's ciliated—should be a paramecium but is not in a liquid—crawls on the surface of other bodies. Always seems hungry."

"You can still classify it in the phylum Ciliophora. I have not noticed it before. You say it seems hungry."

"Yah, see."

I look under the microscope and see the large, brown microbe swallowing a smaller round red microbe. "This must be it. It's oval, about two hundred fifty micrometers in length. Based on the ventral groove and distinct cilia, I'd say the common class Oligohymenophorea, maybe the freshwater order Peniculid, or maybe needs a new order. You are right about it being hungry. I will isolate and grow them with yeast."

After twelve hours, we have grown enough Tremblay microbe to take counts. I say, "This could be our answer. Let's check the dishes in six hours."

In six hours, I check the petri dish and the amount of yeast is reduced by three-quarters. I'm excited and quickly check a second control dish and see the same result. "Yes!" I shout.

Harper prepares a slide, "I see Tremblay *curre*. It seems attracted to the yeast. Now its encircling and swallowing it."

"The yeast and red microbe are the same size as skin cells. Wonder what would happen to skin."

"Be good to know," agrees Harper.

"I'll test it." I scratch my ankles.

"You shouldn't do that."

"Argh! Can't help it." I grab the anti-itch cream.

After twelve hours, we note that the flake of skin is slightly diminished in size too. I say, "These counts are very disturbing!"

I prepare a slide. "Huh, Tremblays seem to ignore the skin." I keep looking. "Oh no! Takes a while but it swallowed the skin cells too."

"Damn," says Harper.

"Agree," I say.

"Let me prepare the slide with the red microbe."

"Why, we already know Tremblay eats that one too."

"I haven't classified it yet." She prepares a slide of the red microbe.

We view it and determine it is a single-celled ovoid coccus bacterium. Harper says, "That's interesting. The coccus seems to be attracted to the Tremblay, which swallows it. I also see some cocci being ejected whole from the Tremblay."

"That is interesting. Let's keep an eye on them. I'll do counts."

After a few hours, Harper views the slide and says excitedly, "Tremblays are dying!"

I look at it, "Yes, you are absolutely right. It seems the cocci are a parasite eating its host from the inside. This may be the piece we need."

"I like these hunters. I think I'll name the cocci after me, Apud Anderson *venatrix*."

I prepare new slides for the scanning electron microscope and confirm my theory that we need both the Tremblay microbe to get rid of the yeast and the Anderson cocci to get rid of the Tremblay microbe.

I recheck the petri dish with the cocci and confirm that although the cocci had initially reduced in size, later their numbers increase.

I also prepare petri dishes of the cocci and skin for counts. "Can you prepare a slide with these two?" Harper does and comments, "The cocci and skin do not interact with each other."

I prepare several petri dishes to grow more Tremblay microbes and Anderson cocci.

Ava joins us in the lab, and I summarize our results. "I'm getting tired, didn't really sleep the past two days. Ava, can you check counts on the Anderson cocci and skin and run a study on which of your antibiotics would kill this new Tremblay microbe?"

"Yes, of course."

When I wake up, I join her and ask, "Any luck?"

"Yes, much. The Anderson cocci and skin counts remain constant. Also, both penicillin and cephalosporin kill the Tremblays, and the cocci."

"It's up above my ankles and really red. I've not much to lose. Let's apply some of the Tremblay."

"OK," says Ava. Wearing gloves, she mixes the microbe with a lotion and spreads it on me.

In two hours, I calculate a ten percent reduction in the white yeast. "Let's apply the Anderson cocci."

"Yes, here goes."

By the end of my shift, I note that the yeast is gone, along with the redness. I announce, "It worked!" Though it may be unnecessary, we apply the antibiotics to be sure the Tremblays die before they cause skin damage.

When Ava wakes up, we ask Vivian to visit to apply the treatment to her. The treatment works on her also. Harper, curious about our treatment results, joins us.

"Thanks so much for all your help," I say to Ava and Harper.

"Yeah thanks, it was so incredibly itchy," says Vivian

Even though during our journey Harper seemed hostile toward me, I reach out and give her a big hug. She smiles and says, "I'm glad I could help, seems like I caused only stress before."

"We still love you," I respond. Then Harper squeezes us, smiling. By sunrise, we inform the others that the yeast infections are cured. We can again focus on Arla.

twenty-one

The Rescuer

After the kraken attack, the sea people drag Arla through a break in the sand bar and then far out to sea. Up close, Arla can see that her dolphins really look more like humans, though with tails instead of legs. Though she is a strong swimmer, she cannot keep up with the group.

Her rescuer slows down to escort her. He brings her south to another island with a calm inlet. He's staring at her as he circles around, occasionally touching her skin and hair. She can check him out too. He seems mammalian and is naked, has male parts. He has a small dorsal fin on his back, pectoral fins on his lower torso, and a dolphin tail with flukes. His upper body seems human, except for the gills behind his elaborate helix. His skin is tan on the underside and darker on the back, oily, and covered with hairs like hers. He would be handsome, if he were human. He's not harming her and seems like a kid with a new pet.

Hours later, Arla tires and her stomach is growling. He notices and lets her go ashore on this island. It is full of flora and colorful turtles. She does not know what, if anything, is edible or toxic. The short fruit trees, grasses and flowers give the island a jungle appearance. Ra is setting, and she is getting cold. She is excited to find flint and uses it to start a campfire. She hopes her friends can find it, but the wind disperses the smoke. Then she builds a quick one-person shelter using one long, fallen branch, which she leans against a meter-high rock, forming a triangle with the ground. The ground beneath the branch is a little longer than her body. She adds branches to the sides, leaving a small opening. Then she uses leaves to cover the ground and top of the shelter, weaves a door from long leaves, and mumbles, "This will have to do." It's already dark and she's still hungry.

She hears her rescuer making oral sounds and goes to see him. He is carrying a small fish and seaweed, which he seems to be offering her. She goes into the water to get it and he pats her on her head. That seems to be a sign of affection, and Arla does the same to communicate a thank you. Using sticks, she cooks the oily fish with the seaweed and eats them. The fish is succulent and sweet.

It calms her stomach, but she is thirstier now. She goes inland a little way in search of fresh water and finds a rocky cliff with a short waterfall. She knows she should boil the water but doesn't have a container. She settles on digging a little well beside the running water and hoping for the best, drinks the sandy water.

She is chilled from her wet clothes. She returns to her camp and takes them off, hanging them to dry on a rock near her campfire. She's thankful there are no biting insects. She hasn't noticed any on Ross.

Arla doesn't see any sign of the *Chidiya* and knows they can't search effectively in the dark. She decides to wear her clothes on land but to take them off to visit her new friend in the water. It would be very lonely, except he continues to provide her with seafood and company. They notice small fruit, which are plentiful on the island, land in the water. He takes one, peels it, eats it, and gives another to Arla. She peels it, and though it tastes tart, it's also flavorful. She likes it. Sometimes, he touches and tickles her, and she returns the petting. She tries to communicate, naming things around her, but he doesn't seem interested in learning language.

After she is rested, he guides her on a swim to the east, reaching a rocky island. In the starlight, she could barely make out that the island is full of mammals that look like seals, only thinner, reddish-brown and extremely friendly. They have adorable black eyes and large whiskers. They wiggle harmlessly all over Arla and her rescuer. He finds a round rubbery nodule and tosses it to them. A large group of young seals dive for it, toss it back to him, making clicking noises. He gives the ball to Arla and she tosses it. To her delight, the seals chase after it and return it to her. They play at this game repeatedly. The seals never seem to tire of it, but after a couple hours, Arla's arm gets sore and they stop.

As her rescuer takes Arla back to her island, two young, orphaned seals hitch a ride on the back of Arla's rescuer. They join Arla on her island, snuggling with her as she relaxes. She finds them amusing and a comfort. Her rescuer brings Arla food, and she finds the seals are very greedy for her fish. She fusses at them to keep them away from her fire for their own protection. She can barely get a bite. Her rescuer notices and brings her extra. Then he leaves for a long time.

Tired from their swim, Arla goes to sleep until one seal nudges her awake. She hears a faint cry of distress. The other seal is gone. Arla follows the sound to a cave near the top of the waterfall. She says to the seal, "Oh! Poor little thing. You can't get out of that small hole." Arla climbs down to get it and it nuzzles her. "I like this cave much better than my puny shelter. Thanks for finding it. You can stay." She smiles and pets it gently.

She goes out to make a torch and returns noticing two openings in the back of the cave with openings to two larger rooms. One of the rooms has a long descending passage, which she follows until it opens to the ocean. "Nice! Thanks, little guy. I'm moving."

"I guess I should name you guys. Are you a boy or a girl? It's hard to tell. You act like dogs, so I'll name you Brittany for pointing out danger. That's a pointer dog for hunting by the way. I'll name you Setter, as in Irish Setter, for playfulness, no protection ability. I'd like to introduce you to my friends." Arla sighs, and then continues talking to Brittany and Setter, until she settles down again to sleep.

It seems like a day before her rescuer returns, but he seems eager to show her something. He excitedly reveals a handful of clear, soft gelatin, which confuses Arla. He blows into the gelatin, forming it into a clear balloon, and slides it over Arla's head. She panics though he tries to pet her arm reassuringly. Then he takes her under water. Arla starts to hyperventilate, but soon notices that she can breathe under water through the balloon. It acts like gills. She can also see, hear and smell under water. He's so excited that he does flips and swims all around her.

He takes her by the hand and directs her southward. They see a family of very large auburn whales, each with a pelican beak and fins like airplane wings. He stops to pet one, encouraging Arla to do the same. The whale feels smooth and calm and seems very gentle for its large size. Her rescuer grabs the extended side fin and places her hand on it too. Holding on tightly, they ride travelling about sixty kilometers per hour. When Arla looks at him, he holds on with just one arm. Then he lets go completely, catches up from behind the whale, jumps over its extended fin, grabs hold of the it again, and smiles at Arla. Then he repeats his stunt. After travelling about ten kilometers, he gently removes Arla's fingers from their grip on the whale.

He guides Arla down, where it is pitch black. Then she sees iridescent lights on a dome structure, which looks like an upside-down colander and is the size of a city block. As they approach, she sees it has square openings that lead to long hallways. She notices the structure is a living benevolent organism, which other sea people are ridding of irritants.

Her rescuer takes her through one of the long hallways, longer than any kraken's arm, to a large central room. In the center is a volcanic fissure providing warmth and yellow light. This inner sanctum is full of sea people of various ages. Most are sleeping, but the few who are awake seem to be communicating with hand gestures and movements. They all seem serene. A few parents appear to be caring for young infants and children, who are playing chase and other games. A couple of the sea people are beautifying the cells, another is making low, calming, melodious sounds. She sees hardly any personal material possessions other than their musical instruments. The place seems magical. The sea people stop what they are doing to look at the new visitor. Some reach out to touch her. He brings Arla to visit with each of the awake sea people. She learns some of their hand gestures.

When done, he returns Arla to her island, removes the bubble from her head, and pats it. Arla returns the gesture and kisses his cheek to say thank you. She marvels how these alien beings appear so humanlike.

When she returns to her new cave home, Brittany and Setter greet her with excited clicks and grunts. They seem elated for her return and bring her a nodule. She plays ball and enjoys their company but wonders if her friends can find her in here.

Later, on her island, a few hours before dawn, a secluded Arla awakens and gets fresh water. Her rescuer is there, waiting for her in the shallow inlet. He shows her snails, and they eat them raw. They feel weird sliding down her throat but taste good.

As he places a bubble on her head, he motions for her to go with him in the warm southern waters again. They explore a multi-colored reef lit by the same yellow light. They try to catch the beautiful fish and then dive through large schools just to watch them disperse. Arla rubs her leg against what looks like a hairy ball. It tingles and her rescuer strokes her leg gently. Arla wonders what his purpose in all this is and what he might want from her.

She wishes she could communicate with him. Swimming close to her, he wraps one arm around her waist, turning her to look at him. He pats her on her head, and she returns the gesture. Then she looks in his eyes and sees his passion. She feels an irresistible desire for him. He places an arm on a butt cheek and holds her tightly. He is rubbing his entire body on her and she hears a gentle voice in her head, "I'm in love with you and tried to communicate that to you with pats on the head, our signal for mating. But only now, your thoughts said you were ready. Or am I wrong? Shall I stop?"

Arla rubs her hands on his head, smiles and thinks, "No, I want you," and feels a calming, erotic sensation.

He communicates, "During intercourse, we are completely telepathically connected. I am called Tal." He reads her and can tell she couldn't see him as clearly, laughing at her mistakenly thinking they were dolphins.

She wonders, "What…what will you do to me?"

He explains, "I cannot harm you. My people are always empathic and slightly telepathic with mammals. Because of this, we cannot hurt a mammal. We had not meant to scare you by taking you away from your home. There were too many kraken near shore. After they devour everything, they will leave, and then I can take you back."

Reassured, she thinks, "I can finally thank you for saving me. Why did you risk your life?"

He communicates, "I have been watching you for a long time and became fixated. I was enraptured the day you were at the beach alone and masturbated. I had an overwhelming desire to get to the shore to enhance your pleasure." She blushes. He communicates, "I'm blushing too because our emotions are connected. We are one person."

Then he confesses, "I was testing our compatibility and your temperament with the young nocturnal seals. I think you're sweet. I was so happy to be able to have you meet my family. The telepathic bond is so strong, we mate for life. We don't understand the human concept of shame for nudity and copulation." Other couples are intertwined as they swim around them, and it seems perfectly natural, even beautiful, like a dance.

Arla thinks, "I love you."

She senses him saying, "I'm so happy." Arla and Tal swim with the others, mindlessly intertwined, experiencing repeated orgasmic pleasure.

She learns that his people are an ancient and peaceful people. "Because our star and world, which we call Serafia, are billions of years older than Earth, we have had a much longer time to evolve from our primordial soup. My people can travel across the universe in multi dimensions. I promise to teach you how someday. In this process, we use thought with ambient electromagnetism, thermal energy and low-level radiation and emit light and sound. We like to explore but prefer physically staying on the world of our evolution and letting our minds travel."

"Did you go to Earth?"

He continues, "Yes, often, we even influenced life on Earth. We've shared our DNA by placing it on comets. One hundred fifty thousand years ago, we decided to develop a creative Earth being like us, knowledgeable in the arts, music, poetry, sensual pleasure, and full of wonder. We provided our modified DNA to the primitive Homo sapiens species."

"So, we are very similar."

He informs her, "Yes, this new Earth species did develop, but sadly also used creativity to achieve new levels of violence. Some selfishly abused the gift of erotica. Most abuse their own planet and its environment. Now, humans have traveled through the stars and settled on our world. Though we view humans as our children and quietly help when we can, some are not as intended and hurt others."

Tal and Arla glide close to Crusoe Island. While still in her trance, Arla looks out admiring the emerald eastern sky at the first light of day. Then she looks up in dismay. She sees a menacing flying craft and worries about her friends. Tal communicates that emotional distress breaks the bond. The two separate, and he helps her back to her island, kissing her gently goodbye.

Part III — Attack of the Polyus

twenty-two

Capture

At first light, Emma and I hurry out to look for Arla again. We fly around Crusoe Island and then south along the coastline. We still see signs of flooding and are discouraged because there is no sign of her. We decide to search the nearby islands in the ocean.

Suddenly, an ominous black-winged object five stories high, appears above us.

"What is that?" asks Emma.

"Evade. It looks like it could be the ship that Marquis told me about." Emma immediately tries to circle away from it, but it quickly follows.

Aurora radios, "I detect an unidentified flying object near you."

"I confirm and am sending you an image. Over." Then our instruments all fail as something pulls us toward it.

I radio, "Mayday! Mayday!" There's no response. I say to Emma, "Not sure they got that."

"Probably not."

A door opens on its underside. We are sucked into a huge, brightly lit bay. A long metallic arm parks us beside small craft and large equipment.

An imposing man appears with two large Siberian huskies heeling on each side. He is about two meters tall and dressed in what could be formal military attire. He has what looks like a short, thick rifle holstered across his chest, another one on his hip, and a long knife on the other side. He is slender, has striking blond hair and light skin, and appears to be in his mid-twenties. Following the leader are six guards, similarly armed. All look alike except one massive, dark-haired guard standing just beside the leader and in front of the other men.

"Stay in the *Chidiya*," says Emma.

The leader motions for us to get out. We do not and he crosses his arms on his chest. We stall, pretending the doors are stuck. He and his guards aim their weapons at us. "I think it would be better to get out," I say nervously as we open the doors.

Smiling, he calls to us with a Russian accent, "Welcome to the starship *Polyus*. Captain Cami, I presume, and this lovely lady must be U.S. Air Force pilot Emma Kelly. I've heard so much about you. I'm Vladimir Budanov, and your biggest fan." Emma and I look at each other, perplexed. We proceed as he directs us through the bay to an elevator. At the elevator, he continues, "I understand you are martial artists. I suggest no tricks. You may not be familiar with these powerful weapons. They shoot concentrated UV light, nasty burns. I like these–very clean, cauterize wounds, no mess, no noise."

"Fascinating," comments Emma. She turns to the handsome but scarred, dark-haired guard next to her and asks, "Will you teach me to use *your* powerful gun?"

He responds seriously, "No ma'am."

Budanov snickers to Emma, "You don't want to mess with Mason here. He's tops in *real*-life hand-to-hand combat, very disciplined. All my men are fully trained to hit a moving target at one hundred meters. They won't be providing lessons."

She responds, "You're no fun. I assume I can't pet your dogs either."

"They are not pets," Budanov sneers.

"'Course not."

After the elevator door re-opens, we walk through what appears to be a spacious control room, with many stations and a floor-to-ceiling circular, dark-tinted window. In front of the window are two armchairs facing outward, with a small table in between. The room is almost all white and so polished, I feel we are stepping onto a cloud.

"This is my bridge," says Budanov. "Follow me to my conference room."

We walk into a lavish conference room with a large, perfectly polished black marble table. On the sides are black marble credenzas on which are statues and exquisite works of art encased in glass. I recognize the Fabergé eggs and tiny jewelry boxes. Famous paintings hang on two walls, "Moonlit Night on the Dnieper" by Arkhip Kuindzhi opposite "Black Square," by Kazimir Malevich. A painting of the *Polyus* hangs on the wall in between. There is another round, dark-tinted window on the exterior wall.

He says, "Have a seat ladies. Let's go get your crew." Then he calls, "Ida, show the actual *Athena*," and we see the outside of the *Athena* in 3D over the table. We can also see our crater from the window and that the *Polyus* is hovering by the *Athena*.

He continues, "Ida, connect to the Athena intercom system." Then he says in false politeness, "I welcome the lady astronauts as guests of the *Polyus*. I see seven of you on infrared and would be very offended if you did not join Captain Cami, Ms. Kelly, and me."

To me, he says, "Lovely old vessel, the *Athena*—quite a valuable antique. We will have to get a closer look later."

The crew of the *Athena* do not come out. He calls again, "I'm feeling generous today. You have ten more minutes to comply." He waits impatiently for ten minutes, and still no one comes out. He goes onto his bridge. I can see him point to a moving form on an infrared image of the *Athena*. He says, "I choose that one. Scare her. That will convince them." They shoot a laser and it hits near the form, which stops moving.

In the window, we see Aurora, Harper, Lilian, Vivian, Lucy and Riya rushing out.

Emma and I saw the laser hit in the 3D image, and I gasp, "Ava! What happened to her?" As Budanov returns, I beg, "Please stop. You may have hit our doctor."

"Body temperature's still normal. Probably, she fell."

Emma and I watch as his men exit, then force our friends to drop the gun and remove their tasers. Soon they enter the conference room.

Budanov says, "Welcome to my starship, the *Polyus.*"

My friends look worried. Harper starts perspiring and mutters, "No, no stars, no space. Dragon's back, breathing fire, crashing ceiling. Ava, Ava. Got to save Ava. No!" All stare at Harper, now wide-eyed and shouting, "How could you do that to her! Take that you kraken!"

She lunges across the room with an imaginary knife. His head guard immediately stands directly in front of Budanov as his guards take aim at her. As she circles around the head guard and almost "stabs" Budanov, an inconspicuous ceiling unit, which was yellow, turns red as it shoots her with ultraviolet light, causing a fourth-degree burn through her flesh to her heart. Shocked, she only has time to grasp her chest before her heart stops, killing her. "No!" I shout and run to kneel beside her. I take her pulse, though it is obvious there is nothing to be done.

Budanov coldly asks, "Anyone else?"

A guard waves a hand-head scanner over Harper and confirms, "She's brain dead, sir."

Budanov explains, "That's a shame. Our artificial intelligence is programmed to destroy any threat to me. I only need Captain Cami here, but you're all here because she may need a little encouragement. Guards, confine them below. Cami and I have to talk."

Budanov guides us to the bridge and then three male guards take my friends down the elevator. From the bridge, the male guards are watching them comparing the curves of each of the women. I see them take my friends down a narrow, drab hallway. Two guards grab the behinds of Lucy and Riya.

"Stop!" says Riya.

A guard complains "It's been months since . . ."

"Not our problem," asserts Emma stepping toward her friends.

Another touches Emma, and she promptly grabs his wrist, pulling it back to the point of pain. She kicks loose his weapon and gets him in a head lock. The second guard points a weapon at her, and the third at Riya.

He says firmly, "Back down, tigress." Emma sees the weapon on Riya and obeys, as he sneers, "She's a feisty one. Guess it will take a few of us to hold you down."

They arrive at a small bland prison cell with three rows of skimpy triple bunk beds. One guard smirks, saying, "Come on in. Home sweet home. We have work to do. We will be back to welcome you later."

In the cell, Lucy whimpers, and Aurora calmly hugs her.

"I can't believe Harper's gone," says Vivian sitting down with her hands covering her face.

"Hard to believe. Wonder what happened to Ava. I heard a loud noise and Harper and I ran toward it, but I didn't get to her," laments Riya. "I feel awful. I should have stayed."

"You probably would have been targeted too. It seems they have laser weapons," says Lilian.

"They do. This sucks," complains Emma, "We didn't find Arla either." She fumes and paces. The others stand or sit solemnly quiet.

They hear a voice from a neighboring cell, "Bad man." They peer into a high window and see three gorillas sitting in a similar tiny cell. Each is wearing dark bracelets on each wrist. They stink of sweat and dirt.

Emma says, "You're not kidding." The gorillas sign a hello. My friends, half-believing their ears, return the gesture.

"We brothers. Me Cain."

The other utters, "Me Abel."

The third utters, "Me Seth. Strong."

Tenderly, Lucy says, "I bet you are. Me Lucy." She pauses and asks, "Why are you here?"

Seth responds, "Bad man."

"How sad. You should be free in the jungles," says Lucy.

Emma supposes, "I bet they're using the poor beasts for experiments or manual labor."

"That's horrible," says Lucy.

Emma is restless and whispers, "There must be a way out."

A calm Lilian observes, "They are probably watching and listening in on us."

Emma looks at Lilian and whispers, "I can't believe we did all that, and no takers."

"At least we're together. Not sure what he wants with Camille, but it can't be good," says Lilian.

On the bridge, Budanov shrinks the monitor muting the sound and complains to Mason, "You were slow."

"You weren't in danger, sir. No point destroying all your hostages," Mason explains.

"True, they may be useful," agrees Budanov.

I'm trembling but trying not to show it. I ask him, "What do you need from me?"

He takes me aside and responds, "Oh I like that—a women asking how she can please me. We're going to get along fabulously." I doubt that. He continues, "I have something for you." He takes out an opulent necklace with huge gems, places it around my neck, grins and says, "Befitting my fiancé. You will marry me, Cami." I'm screaming on the inside that he must be mad. He continues, "Cami, Cami, I intercepted your wonderful reports on the valuable composition of this exoplanet. No one's bothered with it after the wormhole collapsed. There was not enough land to make it worth settling and the place is full of methane. After your reports, I filed mining claims and started drilling, messy business here, with all the methane pockets underground, just before the exoplanet was to be declared an undisturbed nature preserve. A nature preserve, can you believe that! I already have a buyer, but I have an issue about rights and can't sell without a clear title. Anyway, UNBI, discovered your messages, too, and they babble on that you are alive and have first claim. You cannot just disappear, your being famous. And I fancy the idea of being married to the famous Captain Cami. I want you and your friends to convince UNBI that we are engaged and all of us are one big happy family. What do you say?"

I would like to scream that he is completely out of his mind and a delusional psychopath, but I don't think that would go unpunished. Instead I say, "I'm stunned."

He continues, "Yes, it must be a lot to take in, marrying the soon to be richest man in the universe, but I always get what I want, always have, always will. I must prepare. Cami, I will take you to your cabin to dress properly for our call with UNBI."

With a guard and his huskies, he takes me down a hall to a large, luxurious bedroom, decorated in red velvet, with gilded ceiling, plush king-size bed, large gold vanity and ornate mirrors. After he leaves, I throw the hideous necklace on the floor and cry uncontrollably on the red silk sheets.

A few hours later, he returns with an armed guard and picks up the necklace. He complains menacingly, "Dollface, you look like shit! I told you to get dressed!"

I say, "I can't."

He hands me a wipe and orders, "Here, this will clear the red from your eyes." He says impatiently, "True, you are not familiar with the ship's artificial intelligence. Ida, recognize the guest Cami–zero security clearance," as he takes my hand and places my fingers face up on the vanity. He says to me, "Look in the mirror." After a minute, he explains, "Now the AI has recorded your print and retina. It will allow you to replicate clothes and do make-up, whatever. Ida, allow Cami to order clothes, access cosmetology functions and use the powder room. Ida, take full measurements and store in file. Cami, say something."

"I can't think of anything to say."

He responds, "Good enough for voice recognition. Ida, analyze compatibility and show the women's dress catalog." A 3D image of an elaborate red dress appears. He nods and explains, "We don't have time now, but if you do not like a dress, just shake your head or say 'no' and another will appear. Ida, select and replicate matching shoes." A long tomato dress with gold trim and matching shoes appear in the windowed closet. He takes them and says, "Here, go in the powder room and put them on." I was told red is my color, but

I hate this outlandish dress. Still I go put it on without complaint. When I return, Budanov continues, "Sit in the chair with your hands there." Again, I do as he instructs. "Ida, do hair, nails and make-up." I sit still at the vanity's salon-style chair as a hood comes over my head and brushes on a heavy amount of face make-up. The chair's hood curls my hair and applies auburn highlights. Budanov places my hands in a device that paints my nails gold. When done, I look like a circus clown. He puts the necklace back on me and strokes my hair saying, "Hurry. Your friends are waiting."

Budanov guides me back to the conference room, where my friends are gathered. He announces, "I am about to start the quantum resonator set for a direct link to UNBI. You know what that is, right?"

"Yes," says Aurora. The rest of us look confused.

An older, distinguished-looking man appears in detail as a holograph above a credenza with a slender, younger man behind him.

The older man speaks, "I am Director Khalil Fayed of the United Nations Bureau of Investigation, and this is Special Agent Lieutenant Vincent Foxx. I'm here to ask you a few questions. Please state your names." Director Fayed seems stern, but Lieutenant Foxx seems friendly.

"Vladimir Budanov."

I provide my name and my friends do too.

Despite the stressful situation, I notice that Emma and the young agent are making eye contact. Everyone else seems too preoccupied to notice.

"Mr. Budanov, we are investigating a possible infringement on the claim of this Ms. Tremblay. Ms. Tremblay, do you understand that as the first person to report the metals on Ross 128 b, you have a legitimate claim to whatever is mined there? Your name was on the report transmitted five months ago."

Speaking softly, I say "I understand."

He continues, "Mr. Budanov filed a claim over four months ago. He claims that you are aware and consent."

I can see the weapons pointed at my friends and respond, "Yes, I do." Emma checks the guards to see they are distracted and ever so slightly shakes her head no.

"He further asserts that you consented because you have been in a relationship since you landed, and you are to be married."

I answer, "Yes, that is true." Emma shakes her head again.

He continues, "You will be allowed to mine as you wish once the life scans come back negative for intelligent life on the exoplanet. Mr. Budanov, as you know, it is illegal to mine, as you have been without the scans performed by a neutral party. The scans you submitted are signed by an officer of your subsidiary and are invalid. You are to cease all activity until then."

Lieutenant Foxx interjects, "And we will have to do a DNA test on Ms. Tremblay." This time Emma nods.

Budanov frowns. "Yes, sir."

Director Fayed concludes, "That's all we need from you. I'll be sending Lieutenant Foxx with special agents Pavlov and Kumalo to run the DNA tests. I'd like to talk privately with Ms. Tremblay." Budanov leaves with his guards directing my friends out.

Fayed says, "Miss, I've researched your background. It seems you may be naïve regarding your fiancé. I feel I should warn you. Do you mind if I speak frankly?"

"No, please do." I know Budanov is probably watching but I want intel.

"We've been studying him a long time—he knows this. The child Vladimir Budanov was raised by his mother but later reunited with an abusive father. Vladimir's father died young, and Vladimir took over the family gold mining business. Then he acquired other mining operations, many after mysterious mishaps–explosions, death of owner, disappearances. We suspect he masterminded competitors engaging in predatory pricing to drive them into bankruptcy. None of these activities were ever linked to him. We've had a lot of suspicions but could never get an arrest to stick due to whatever— lack of evidence, judges who won't act, or missing witnesses. He consolidated almost all metal mining operations, clearly violating anti-monopoly laws, but no investigation. Now he sells essential metals at exorbitant prices and is one of the world's filthy rich. Can't believe what he's asking for the Ross load."

"Thank you, sir," I say.

"Also, from what we can tell, most of his crew come from the Russian maximum-security prison except the one ex-police officer with a record of violence. Be careful."

"Yes sir, I will. Is that all?"

"Yes, our agents will see you soon."

"I'm looking forward to it."

The conference room door opens. I look for my friends, but they are gone. Budanov tells his guards, "Screw that. Learn what you can about that intelligent life. Come dollface, let's celebrate. You did great. And yes, I know all that. No evidence–he's just trying to make a name for his pathetic self. I take all the risks in this business and they still complain. I give people a second chance and UNBI gets paranoid."

He takes me to a cozy dining room with a table covered with white hemp linen fabric and a wall-size cupboard of white shadow kuzbas marble displaying polished silver dining sets. He orders his huskies to wait in the doorway while he and two guards walk in with me. Looking around, I see on another wall, two large paintings, one of a Kodiak bear catching a fish, and on another of a harbor town in a blizzard. On the fourth wall is a large round window. He and I sit at a dinner table, set romantically, with elaborate silver dinner ware and luscious food and wine. I barely touch any. He keeps insisting that I eat, so I swallow a few nibbles. He chatters constantly though I don't want to listen or talk. I flinch every time he calls me dollface or Cami.

He orders, "Talk to me. I like sweet nothings."

I'm dumbfounded. All I can think of saying is, "Are we in space?"

"Sure, I will take you. Ida, fly *Polyus* to orbit six hundred kilometers. We have gravitons now, so you won't feel it, not like you would with that antique wheel."

"It was innovative then."

"So, you are aware time has passed?"

"Yes." There is an awkward moment of silence. I continue, "You intercepted all of our transmissions? Even our distress call?"

"Yes, thinking of going out there, but then you transmitted that all was fine." I remember that this transmission was sent many hours after Arla sent the distress call and wonder how someone could be so callous. Changing the subject, he says, "You can see almost the entire northern continent in the window. It's lovely, no?"

"It is. Why am I famous?" I ask.

"Dollface, you're the first person to ever go through a wormhole, to try out the fusion engine. You radioed letting everyone know it was safe. Too bad yours was *really* unstable. It disintegrated after a second ship went through. Of course, we can make our own wormholes now and go anywhere. It takes a tremendous amount of energy to make traversable wormholes for superluminal travel. So, we're powered by antiproton nuclear fusion and can travel wherever we want . . . Look at the stars, Cami, aren't they lovely?"

"*Si*, I do not deserve the credit."

"No matter. History is like that. Only the leader is remembered."

I'm thinking it matters! Zoë, who designed the fusion reactor and died for us, deserves to be remembered. Harper, who tried to protect us, deserves to be remembered. My sacrifice is insignificant next to theirs. I ask, "Would it be possible to have a burial ceremony for Harper?"

"Maybe. Excuse me for a moment." He walks over to his head guard, talks softly with him, and returns. "Yes, we can do that, anything in particular you need?"

"An open plain, a horse—?"

"Sure, she can be buried just below the tundra, tomorrow. Today, I'd like to spend time with just you." I wince and feel a knot tightening in my stomach.

He continues, "Now, do you want to watch your show? I loved this when I was a kid. Ida, show screen." A screen appears over the table with 3D images. He starts a show of an artificially brave, but ignorant, Captain Cami with a crew of thirteen females, none of whom resemble any one of my friends: One is an obnoxious, petty teenager; another a silly, stupid rhesus monkey always messing things up. It is a super silly slapstick comedy, and I couldn't understand why anyone would watch this. It is appalling to watch my character act so stupidly, but at least Budanov isn't talking, and I don't have to think of anything to say. I can't get Ava and Harper out of my mind. I'm too worried about the others to risk saying anything to offend him. As he laughs hysterically at all the jokes on the show, I pretend to like it so as not to provoke him.

When it's over, he asks, "Do you want to watch an adult version?" Before I can say anything, a naked, artificially voluptuous, fluffy-haired female calling herself Cami comes on the screen. She is bathing in greasy worms, which have big eyes on antennae. She is rubbing her body erotically all over the worms while beckoning and making orgasmic noises. I'm disgusted. I can feel my stomach getting heavier; it feels like a brick. "The film is about five years old. I had her then," brags Budanov. I imagine the loathsome, homicidal Budanov putting his body on mine and am overcome with nausea. I feel the brick moving up. I shoot up, desperately looking for a bathroom, but am unable to find one in the dining room. I run out and vomit around a corner.

Budanov says in a fake, pitiful voice, "What's wrong? Not like my show?"

"I'm sick . . . I'm tired."

Not caring or not believing it, Budanov licks my forehead and asks, "You no want to play?"

Appalled, I wince, but say as sweetly as possible, "Oh, I became very religious, raised by nuns, saving myself—"

"Sure, dollface. You like the chase, I will chase—Nasty. I will get someone to clean that up."

As we pass through the bridge, Budanov says to his guards, "I just remember. We need to get the doctor. Ida, display infrared image of the *Athena*." He looks at the image and then says, "No body heat.

She's not really necessary." He looks at me, "She must have wandered off. Enough for today."

He returns me to my cabin and leaves after licking my forehead again. After giving him time to walk away, I try the door but cannot figure out how to open it. It seems locked.

twenty-three

Hide-out

Arla and Tal are not the only ones to witness the scene in the air.
On Crusoe Island, after sunrise, Marquis wakes and sees the *Chidiya*
take flight and assumes it is looking for Arla. He watches it as Jean
wakes up and joins him. They see the dreaded spacecraft appear and
swallow the *Chidiya*.

"No!" screams Marquis.

Then, they watch the *Polyus* hover over the *Athena*, fire on it,
and capture the ladies. Marquis rushes down to help, being careful
to stay hidden. Jean follows him shouting "Slow down! The crater
is mined!" As they enter it, the *Polyus* disappears.

With Jean helping Marquis maneuver around the landmines,
they approach the *Athena*. They enter, hear someone groaning and
find a perspiring Ava face down on the floor near medical. The
ceiling had fallen on her, pinning her leg. Marquis and Jean rush to
remove the heavy metal ceiling.

"Lift, Jean!" shouts Marquis.

"Stop!" shouts Ava and motions for a communicator, which
Marquis hands her. "I think there's a puncture wound in the back
of my lower thigh. Marquis, you need to apply pressure to stop the
bleeding when Jean lifts the metal. First, wash your hands with soap
and then pick up the gauze and tube from the drawer. Put some
antibiotic from the tube around the wound."

214

Marquis attempts to do so. "It this it?"

"Yes, but put on the blue gloves. Also, you should be ready to apply a tourniquet—get that thing over there." Marquis brings it close. Jean lifts the metal, while Marquis pulls Ava out while applying pressure on the wound. They move her to the isolation bed face down and raise her legs.

Jean says to Marquis, "You stay here. I'll check for others. I know where the traps are. You're safe in here."

"Good idea," agrees Marquis. He washes the wound and then applies pressure for ten minutes, but the blood is still pouring from the wound through the gauze. Ava shows him how to use the tourniquet and hemostatic dressings.

"I didn't see any scraps. Does it hurt?" asks Marquis

"No, it's numb."

"That's not good either."

With her guidance, he also soothes the first- and second-degree burns caused by the hot metal.

After a half hour, she asks him, "Remove the tourniquet and try applying pressure again."

He does as she instructs. I few minutes later he says, "OK, the bleeding is stopping."

"Good, you'll have to stitch up the wound."

"You're kidding. No, you're not kidding."

She explains how and he does so carefully.

Jean returns. "I didn't find anyone else. I released the enclosed animals so they can fend for themselves."

"Makes sense. We need to leave. They could come back," says Marquis. Marquis and Jean hurry out, carrying Ava on a stretcher, with medical and food supplies in packs.

On the way up to their cave, Ava says, "Thank you both. I couldn't have gotten out of there alone and would have bled to death."

"Just happy you survived," says Marquis.

Jean and Marquis take turns keeping watch while Ava heals. They hunt the rabbits to provide her with the red meat needed after her blood loss. Jean is very talkative, telling Ava about their childhood.

Stranded on Crusoe Island, they have time to think and talk. Marquis finds it easy to confide in Ava too. Her calming influence helps him relax.

Ava asks, "What does it take to be a marquis?"

"Birth and training. I was raised to defend our people and had to learn our ancient texts. I studied the entire *Encyclopédie* and other translated philosophers–Plato, Socrates, Locke, Sun Tzu– and literature under the tutelage of my uncle, the king. He taught Confucian style, with lots of questions. Then I took the knight's oath to uphold justice, to protect our people from all harm, and to obey the king."

"So, you're a philosopher?"

"I guess so. Reading is fine. Though I prefer action. I learned how to wrestle and shoot—won competitions. I like exploring. I travelled all over the northern continent."

"And you protect your people?"

"Sure, it's my duty. I hunt down the felis who wander north. I've rescued stranded families after hurricanes. It was dangerous, but I always succeeded. I felt proud. I was a hero."

"Was?" asks Ava.

"Now, I'm hostile, aggressive, barbaric, insane. I don't want to be feared. I don't want Camille to look at me like I'm a monster."

"When did you change?"

"After the massacre."

"What happened?"

"About fifteen weeks ago, my family and I had gone to a market at an outpost. I remember it was a beautiful day. I don't like shopping, picking out fabrics, colors, fruit, and such. I looked at a few swords. Then got bored, so I took my nephew, Étienne, hunting on the mountain side. Both Étienne and I saw the ship. When I saw it, I decided to hide, and to hide him, because I had heard they kidnapped men for labor, destroying them. Then I heard the massacre. They killed everyone there. I saw them kill my family. They never had a chance."

"That's terrifying."

"I've been too ashamed to talk about it. I hid like a coward and failed my own family," he confesses.

"Could you really have done anything but get killed yourself?"

"If I had stayed with them, maybe. Thérèse always complained about my wandering off. Truthfully, we didn't have much in common." He stops and stares blankly. Ava urges him to continue. "Still I should have been there, have died instead. It isn't fair. They were so young. God, I miss them. I should have been able to help them," he says tearfully.

She gives him time to regain himself and then asks, "But was there *really* anything you could do? You were far. It's not reasonable to always be near them. How could you have known they would be attacked. I assume the market was a safe place before?"

"Yes, of course, before. I didn't think anyone would ever kill unarmed women and children for no reason. Now I'm more vigilant. I see the massacre all the time replaying in my head. I dream about it. It won't go away. I see threats everywhere. I'm on edge all the time. I know I'm crazy!" Hard as it was for Marquis to initially disclose his fears and failure, it was a tremendous release.

"No, not crazy—normal under the circumstances, but let's talk about being vigilant and seeing massacres *all* the time," starts Ava.

Jean enters the inner room and interrupts them, "It's dinner time!"

Over dinner, Marquis and Ava find that they share many common values and are enjoying each other's company.

"You would make a great partner for someone," Marquis tells her.

Jean gets angry and says to Marquis, "What, have you forgotten *her* already?"

"Who? Thérèse?" asks Marquis.

"No, you know I didn't like Thérèse much, sorry. She was too uppity. I mean your marchioness, Camille!"

"Of course not."

"Why are you talking secretly with Ava?"

"We're just talking, nothing more."

"Not what it looks like to me," says Jean accusingly.

"It's not what you're thinking," defends Ava.

"I wonder what is happening up there," says Marquis. He walks out of the cave to the edge of a cliff overlooking the ocean. He stares at the endless expanse and then looks up to pray, "Dear Lord, is Camille still alive? Please, please keep them safe. Use me however you want. Do whatever you want to me. Just keep her safe."

twenty-four

Female Riding Horse

After a fitful night on the *Polyus*, I wake up and decide to obtain more intel on this ship and crew in order to help my friends. I need to put aside my disgust and play his abominable game.

All the gadgetry in my cabin is so new to me. When I touch a few buttons, I see a glowing light in the mirror. I feel a draft of cold air think, I screwed something up.

I walk into the bathroom and fumble with the fixtures. I take the silly red dress off and try to figure out the shower. I give up. "Ida, can I have warm water in the shower?" Water pours out.

After I shower and dry off, I say, "Ida, show me an orange prison outfit."

Ida responds, "Mr. Budanov has preselected wedding dresses. Please choose from one of the following."

"I am not getting married! What is it with this planet." The selection does not change. I view dozens and decide on a short tight light-blue dress.

"Ida, easy on the hairstyle and make-up." After Ida is done, I put on the dress and his gaudy necklace.

"Ida, I need shoes." I get light-blue high heels. I try them. "Ida, I can't walk in heels this high. Lower them."

"Mr. Budanov requested the height." Frustrated, I practice walking in them. I hate this—feel like a whore. I know the outfit looks good. I feel he wants another piece of art, a famous trophy for his ship.

I'm startled by Budanov, who with two bodyguards, enters my cabin. With body language and whistles, he compliments me on my taste.

"I see you can become accustomed to being with one of the wealthiest men in the universe. Bravo. Join me."

In order to have any chance to rescue my friends, I learn all I can about the *Polyus*, Budanov, and its crew members—how many there are, where their stations are, what they do and when. He stops at the bridge and I observe intensely.

He orders, "Locate the Neanderthals on the surface. Force them back into the caves. I don't care how. I want them out of sight before they scan. There's a reward for each one found. Top six get a visit with one of our guests."

I protest, "You cannot—"

"What can't I do?" he says menacingly. "Follow me." He directs me to the conference room.

I ask, "May I please see my friends?" He obliges me by showing me live images of them in the cell.

"We should be married before UNBI arrives."

I try bargaining. "When this is all done, will you bring us all back *unharmed* to the *Athena*?"

"I don't really need a bunch of unhappy passengers. That's the plan, unless you give me a reason not to," he threatens. Then he changes his tone, "I can get them other women. This needn't be unpleasant. Now where is the marriage program on here? Oh, there it is. All you need to do is say 'I do' and sign these forms, and *voilà*, it's done. You and I can be joined in eternal bliss, Cami. Sound nice, my dear? Look, here's a romantic view of the ocean to set the mood. This is one of my favorite spots. Just over the horizon is your *Athena*. Look, way out there, moving, it's a whale and a bunch of dolphins." I peer out and can barely distinguish the forms.

"Is there an alternative to marriage? I mean, I can sign whatever rights over."

"Not a valid contract without consideration."

"A donation."

"I doubt anyone would believe that I need charity, dollface." Sensing resistance, he adds menacingly, "Too bad your friends are too busy to witness. Ida, run marriage program."

I answer, almost inaudibly, affirmatively to the questions.

He then has me sign electronically, along with two guards as witnesses, and insert a thumb print. "Wonderful!" he says, "It's done. See, that was easy, Mrs. Budanov. Let me kiss the bride."

"No," I recoil from him and step away.

He grabs me by the waist. Then he gropes me, holds me against the wall, and presses his horrible self against me. I want to push him away but see the ceiling unit on yellow alert and lift my hands up in a surrender position. He grabs both in one hand and kisses my lips hard. Then moves one hand to lift my dress and thrusts at me as if to enter me. I notice there's just a pelvic bone and soft tissue—no penis. I realize he is just doing this for show. The other day, I had thought he relented due to a shred of decency. Now I understand that he cannot consummate a marriage. I'm relieved. I doubt he would take any refusal. After repeating the thrust several times and exhaling as if to release, the terrible embrace is over. I'm disgusted. I feel defenseless and dirty. Shaking, I turn and try to hide my face in my hands.

"That should satisfy UNBI. Everyone back to your stations. Ida, take *Polyus* to the plains, forty-eight degrees latitude north, by the western shore."

We arrive within an hour. He orders his men to help with the burial. They respectfully take the body out in a shroud. A dark-haired youth operates a small digging machine. As I exit, I notice six cranes, three on either side and bent in the middle, holding *Polyus* level on the uneven terrain. With the cranes and the dark, bulging, tinted glass of the windows, the *Polyus* looks even more like the giant multi-eyed beetle that Marquis had shown me.

The air is as cold as Budanov and the wind moans. We are on a high cliff overlooking the wild glistening ocean to the west and surrounded by vast grassy plains of reddish-green grass to the horizon in the northeast and mountains in the distance to the south. I can picture Harper running free with a herd of wild mustangs.

"Good place, ma'am?" asks the head guard.

"I am sure she would have loved it."

The guards escort my friends outside. I hug them. "I asked for a funeral for Harper." As we huddle, I say "I still can't believe she's gone."

"I know. How could that happen?" questions Lucy.

"One minute she was alive and then, poof," says Lilian.

"She was a really great help with the yeast research. Without her, I'm sure it would have taken a lot longer. I owe her a lot," I say.

"I still remember her with the little bunnies," says Lucy sadly.

"She sure loved her animals," says Vivian.

"She was doing so much better," adds Emma.

"Good-bye Harper," Riya whispers as the guards quietly place her body in the ground and bury her. They pull out a life size replica of Dali's abstract "Female Riding Horse" in bronze and cement it onto a wide headstone.

"May you rest in peace beside the still waters," I say.

"May you ride free in the next world," says Aurora.

Then I clasp my hands together and suggest, "Let's have a moment of silence."

In a few minutes, everyone's, even tough Emma's, eyes water. "I could have . . . should have been nicer to her," she says.

Lucy stutters, "What's . . . what's going to happen to us?"

"He says he plans to let you go back to the *Athena* unharmed soon," I try to sound reassuring.

"In exchange for what?" asks Emma.

"For mining rights. We found the metals on this planet first. I signed them over," I say, then shudder. I whisper to Emma and Riya, who are closest to me, "He seems unstable, a psychopath. I do not trust him. You should escape if you can."

"No shit," whispers Emma.

"I will help, if I can. I'm trying to figure out how."

"How are you holding out?" asks Riya.

Thinking of the assault, I close my eyes and exhale hard and slowly. I don't want to talk about it.

Budanov yells out, "Girls, no whispering. I'm cold. Time for everyone to get back in the *Polyus*."

Just before I listlessly re-enter the *Polyus*, I see huge roaming beasts in the distance. I hope they don't destroy Harper's grave. I think how much Harper would enjoy seeing them roam. I bitterly watch my friends escorted back, while Budanov and I return to the bridge.

A couple hours later, Budanov takes me to the small dining room. He seems relaxed, sets the table, and pulls out my chair with exaggerated manners. Then he ominously closes the door to the bridge. We are alone for the first time without at least one of his guards or even his dogs. I notice there is no ceiling weapon device in this room, but he is fully armed. He intentionally stays far enough away from me to prevent me from quickly attacking him before he could pull a weapon. I wonder if I could overtake him, but then what? He has men just outside this room, and they are all armed. I wonder if he's bluffing about their loyalty and skills. He has no trouble lying.

Interrupting my thoughts, he says, "Sit down. Want breakfast?"

"I'm not hungry."

As I sit, he says, "Ida, secure guest, moderate." A seat belt fastens my waist to the chair. Cuffs attach my feet to its legs. I sigh.

He continues, "That's the problem with women. Never wanting to eat. Want coffee?"

"Yes, sweet with cream, please," I say afraid of his next move.

I watch as he waves his hand on a painting, which disappears revealing a control station. He presses buttons and pulls out two hot cups of coffee and a tray of tea cakes and pastry. Then he offers, "Apple sharlotka, try some."

"Thank you," I say, as I politely sip the coffee.

"I know all about you. What do you want to know about me?" he asks.

I know more than I want to know. I think Ava would find him an interesting study of a madman—provided he was locked up. "I don't know where to begin."

He puts one of each breakfast item on a small plate in front of me and says, "Eat. You had no supper. My company is not so revolting, no?" To avoid answering, I take a bite of the sharlotka, sense my stomach devouring it, and realize I'm very hungry.

He continues, "I'm sure you could tell that I'm missing a part. My father found me revolting. 'Not a real man,' he would say. Right after I was conceived, a terrorist group set off a nuclear bomb near my mother's town, and I was born without certain tissue. Though my father offered me his DNA to generate this tissue, it sickens me to have his part. I prefer the way I was born—no need for women, for anybody—no paternity suits, though some have tried." He chuckles. "Still, keep it to yourself," he adds seriously.

"Understood," I say.

"Some say it promotes true intimacy—bah, intimacy is a trap. Though I do enjoy having you here. Sure you wouldn't rather stay? *Polyus* is much more comfortable than your crammed old ship."

"Are you giving me a choice?"

He laughs. "No silly girl. I plan to keep you for insurance—make sure your friends *stay* quiet." He pauses and then continues, "Do you realize the opportunity you have? In every generation, there is a top one percent in wealth and power and fame. I am in that one per cent and, with this world and its resources, will be at the very top. Your fame allows you to join our echelon. I have allowed you in, as an equal, as my consort. I would not be with just anyone. No one else has a historically important beauty by his side. We are superior. The masses worship us. Keeps them feeling secure. These friends of yours, and all the others on this ship, and this world, billions on Earth, are peons. They serve us. They need us to guide them. Sure, some try biting our heels, like UNBI, but they're powerless. Real men have *power. I have power.*"

"I do not see them as peons."

"But they are! You can do charity stuff, sit on a board, be a spokesperson—good for public relations, to be *seen* as compassionate— You play chess?"

"Ah, yes, a bit." He opens a cabinet, pulls out a board and sets it up. The board is of opal and black sapphire, with pieces cut ornately of deep lilac lepidolite stone and rose quartz.

"Ida, play Mussorgsky, low. I like classical music with a classic game. Ladies go first." I assume I should let him win. "I prefer a challenge. Don't patronize me."

During the game, I mention, "It seems you, and everyone from Earth, speak English."

"Yes, by the end of the twenty-first century, the entire world uses English for business, but some languages remain—most of my crew speak Russian. There's also Spanish, Chinese, Hindi, Arabic, Malay. The French, of course, kept their language—proud since the Renaissance."

We play a long, quiet, tough game and reach a stalemate.

"It's been a pleasure." He takes and kisses my hand. "But I have private work in my study. Ida, allow Cami to order drink, food. You can eat when hungry. You can wander around this floor. There is a gallery and art history library between the conference room and your cabin. Look at the paintings and art—but *stay on this floor.*"

As he steps out, he orders, "Ida, allow Cami restricted access on the bridge floor only. Ida, release Camille." My belts unfasten. I hear him order his men to leave me alone, but to watch me.

Stunned, I stay alone in the dining room, staring at the walls. Then I try out the food console and manage to get another coffee. After drinking it, I wander onto the bridge, quietly watching the security images in 3D over the security head's control station. He touches a spot and then seems to adjust the images with hand signals. I need to learn the lay-out of the *Polyus*. I try to look bored. The bridge crew ignores me, unless I approach an exit. By monitoring the images, I can see that there are four stories. The lowest floor consists of the extra high bay for equipment, where we first entered. The second is a high storage warehouse with robotics for moving commodities. There are several large storage containers and bins. The third floor, or the deck below us, has plain cabins for the crew and the prison cells. I can see everyone on these floors, including my friends. The fourth floor is the top deck. It has this spacious bridge and Budanov's more luxurious living and storage rooms. I notice they can monitor my cabin. I cannot see Budanov. He seems to be cloaked. I note that in addition to the elevator, there are two stairwells at opposite corners.

I watch the monitors and see three armed guards enter the hallway outside the cell of the gorillas. One mean-looking guard barks, "It's time to get back to work." Moving to the ladies' cell, he tells them, "I'm the supervisor. I'm told to bring Miss Karlsson and Miss Patel down too. The borer's stopped tunneling—electronic glitch. Prove your usefulness. Get it working again and you will be rewarded. Do something stupid and, well, Miss Kelly here will not be a hot sexy vixen anymore." The supervisor and the two guards take Lucy and Riya with them, along with the gorillas.

Later, I can see an image of three gorillas with Lucy and Riya, dressed in coveralls and miner's hard hats, on the surface, under guard. They appear to be at a mine site within a massive limestone cavern with unusually wide stalactites hanging from the ceiling and an opening the size of an industrial garage door. Lucy and Riya eye the huge excavator, drill and borer. The gorillas are told to work building tracks for the minecarts that will be used to remove large stones. The two guards dismantle the drill. There is also the young driver operating the excavator. The supervisor watches everyone. If the gorillas fail to perform as he tells them, he administers electric shocks to their wrists. At each shock, the gorillas stare and snarl angrily at the supervisor, but work harder.

Lucy and Riya are told to work on the borer, and they investigate it thoroughly. When Riya thinks no one can hear, she whispers softly to Lucy, "Do you know anything about this?"

Lucy responds, "I have no idea. I've never seen this type of circuitry before. Makes no sense to me."

Riya whispers, "Let's fake it until we can figure it out."

The supervisor bellows, "What are you whispering about?

Lucy picks up a tool and says, "Just looking for this." Then she pretends to use it.

Most often I watch my friends, but I also start to observe the roles and how many crew members Budanov has. All are armed. Three on the bridge seem to be monitoring navigation, engineering and communication. On the second floor, one is analyzing core samples, and a couple are controlling refining processes. There appear to be two mechanics on the first floor. Others guard the *Polyus* inside and out.

I watch as some rotate shifts, sitting at a couple control stations, doing a long-range search with infrared and other scanners. Fortunately, they do not find many. I assume this is because most of the French are in caves due to the flood and fear of the felis. When they find someone, his guards eliminate the target with lasers or scare him into hiding. I notice some are perverse, bragging about a hit, even cheering. I cringe at their coldness. Others, even the well-touted Mason, are quiet and miss their targets, allowing them to escape into caves.

I find it tiring to conceal my desire to scream at them to stop— that these targets are human beings. They could even be Guillaume or Claude, maybe Jean and Marquis. By evening time, I can't stomach any more and start toward my cabin.

As I'm about to leave the bridge, we notice sparks from the electrical circuits. Then the cavern goes completely dark. I return quickly to watch. "What's going on?"

We hear scuffling, banging and terrifying shrieks for at least five minutes.

"Oh, no! Riya, Lucy. Where are you?" I say fearfully.

Emergency lights come on. We can see a gorilla viciously destroying a guard. Riya grabs a petrified Lucy and they hide behind the borer.

A guard onboard the *Polyus* announces, "The gorillas revolted. The two guards, the sup, and two gorillas appear to be dead."

Budanov quickly storms onto the bridge, takes over the controls of the viewers, and then moves to a laser control station. He shouts, "Those idiot engineers just connected the borer to the main power source. Blew out all the circuits! Triggered the dumb beasts." Budanov blasts the entrance with lasers, causing an avalanche of rock. "That should do it. They can't get out of there."

I'm stunned. We can still monitor the mine site. Huge boulders land on the arm and bucket of the excavator, almost killing the driver. Much of the other equipment is broken beyond repair. The gorilla Seth is checking out the other gorillas, trying to revive them. They don't move. He wails, "Brothers dead."

Lucy hears him, approaches him, and on seeing why he is wailing, tears up too. When the dust settles, Lucy and Riya check the entrance, which is completely blocked with huge boulders. They are trapped inside with just emergency lighting.

They also notice the young driver still in the excavator cockpit, afraid to move. He did not have a big weapon, just a small pistol. Seth quickly climbs up the excavator. The driver tries to take out his pistol but is so nervous he drops it. Seth grabs the driver and throws him out. The driver is barely moving. Seth jumps down to pounce on the driver.

He begs, "Please don't. I know . . . I know where there's water. Don't let him kill me."

Lucy rushes to them and begs Seth, "No, don't hurt him! He's just a kid. Please don't!" Seth backs down.

Riya walks to the driver and questions, "How do you know?"

He stammers, "I was paying attention to the geologists' reports. I can show you a stream. It'd take you days to find water. You'd die of thirst."

"OK. We can grab what we need and set up camp there while we look for a way out," suggests Riya.

"Good idea. Let's go," says Lucy.

Seth asks, "To jungle?"

Lucy replies, "Hopefully. Maybe. To water now."

Riya and Lucy look over the human bodies. "No sign of life in the supervisor," says Riya.

"Or the other two men," says Lucy. "Should we bury them?"

"We should, but the ground's all stone," says Riya.

"You're right. It's impossible," agrees Lucy.

Keeping his distance from the bodies, the driver says, "Gross . . ." He looks pale and backs away. Then he exhales, looks around, and stutters, "Umm, there's food over there."

The others meet him by the supplies. Limping on one leg, he carries a box of snacks. Seth carries another small food box, as well as cleaners, a box of rope, hammers, chisels, pickaxes, shovels and the weapons. Riya finds a first aid kit, flashlights and batteries and carries them in a bucket. Lucy picks up four coats and small tools. "Maybe I can remove those bracelets from Seth's wrists."

"OK. We're ready to go," says Riya.

They are soon gone from the viewer on the bridge of the *Polyus*. I need to be alone. I am visibly upset. Budanov says, "There are casualties in this business, dollface. I can't have them disclosing the location of prime real estate."

I can't look at him.

While the crew discuss the situation, I walk quietly to my cabin. I can barely focus. I overhear the head guard mention the need for an experienced driver and the expense of costly new equipment, but Budanov is too angry at the driver for offering aid to the others and too stubborn to listen.

In my cabin, I scream, a loud primal scream. I can't imagine how he could barricade them in there, even his own driver! I keep repeating that thought in my head while pacing the floor for at least an hour, until I am completely drained, emotionally and physically. I pray for help. I think of Marquis shooting the felis and wish he was here, protecting us. I remember his warnings, his cooking, the fun in the rapids, smiling at our joke, his handsome face. I remember how I felt when he was teaching me archery and imagine him beside me, as I pass out on the bed.

twenty-five

Gossip

In another cave, the small community of Carcassonne is in turmoil from reports of violence. Because of attacks on the few hunters and farmers who ventured out, Comte Antoine has become even more concerned and has secretly doubled the number of recruits.

The vicious rumors against the newcomers have spread. Claude has been too absorbed in his new romance to notice the whisperings. However, Guillaume, always a part of any gathering, has been listening and talking with various people. In this community, not much can remain a secret. Nothing escapes conversation. Guillaume has heard things that may concern his close friend Claude and decides to visit him.

"Good morning," starts Guillaume as he enters Claude's shop.

"Good morning, how've you been? Want a coffee?"

"Sure, and good, busy helping hurricane victims and families afraid of the felis settle in. How is this new married life?" Guillaume teases.

Claude laughs, "Couldn't be better. Do you need any help?" He pours two cups and they sit at a small table.

"No, no, we've had plenty, thanks."

"Sorry, I've been so focused on accommodating Kiara and her friends—teaching them French too. Kiara says the communicators

230

won't last long outside their ship. You haven't been around your ladies."

"More to conquer, even the princess, maybe," whispers Guillaume.

"You're seducing *her*, a bit young, don't you think?"

"And her father would *kill* me! Makes the chase stimulating."

"Better to stay with adults," advises Claude.

"Well, everyone is talking about them, and you."

"Really? It seems there's no interest lately. Kiara was getting a lot of invitations the first couple days here, but none lately. Not sure what's up."

"Rumors, bad gossip. Women can be mean."

"What rumors? What could Kiara have done to offend anyone?"

"She didn't do anything. Some people are afraid of them—still believe some of Marquis' initial accusations. The ladies talk to me. Marguerite is feeding it, even after the dinner party when I overheard her uncle tell her to stop."

"Or do you *talk* to the ladies?" Claude teases, but then continues, "That's not good though, could it be dangerous?"

"Could be. I heard some recommend they be locked up, in solitary. Some are calling for much worse after the attacks on the hunters and farmers. People are getting nervous. A few of our friends have even been asked to join the royal guard for a possible invasion of their ship, which they complain is invading our sacred site," divulges Guillaume.

"And King François supports this?"

"Maybe he changed his position, because of the attacks. I'm not sure."

"I need to know. I'll ask for a private audience." They continue talking as Claude offers bread, sliced meat, and cheese. After breakfast, Claude heads for the castle.

twenty-six

The Mine

Beyond the view of the *Polyus*, **Lucy, Riya, Seth and the driver** walk through the passages in search of water. Lucy asks the young driver, "So, what's your name?"

He answers, "Thomas Mason, or just Tommy." Tommy leads them through a maze. It takes a couple hours until they arrive at a chamber with a large aquifer.

"Just like you promised," says Riya, "Let's set up camp by the spring, which seems to be here."

"Here's your sleeping bags," says Lucy handing them a coat, "Hate to say this but you guys stink."

"Yeah, really bad," adds Riya.

"There's a stream on the far side. I'll wash there." Tommy puts soap and a coat in the bucket and limps a long distance around a natural wall where the stream disappears into the ground. He had lost bodily functions when Seth attacked him and wants privacy to bathe and rinse his clothes. Later he returns, wearing just a coat. "Better?" he asks.

"Much. Let me look at those scrapes," says Lucy. She uses the bandages in the first aid kit to treat the scrapes from his fall. "Now rest and elevate your leg." He lies on a flat rock and she gets a stone to raise his swollen leg.

Then Lucy complains to Seth, "You stink. You are dirty and need a bath." He appears confused. Lucy grabs soap from their supplies, goes downstream, and gets in the water, saying, "Come on in Seth."

"No water. Water bad."

Lucy lifts her pant leg and goes in knee deep. "No, see. Water good. Come in."

He follows her. He soon discovers he is safe. "Good water." He starts splashing excitedly.

Lucy is completely drenched but determined to lather him with soap to clean him. Lucy is gentle, and Seth is loving being pet all over his back, arms, legs, head and belly.

When Lucy is done, she says, "OK, you're done. Come on out." She leaves the water.

He obeys, but then rolls in the dirt. He utters, "Seth dirty, need bath."

Lucy scolds, "No, this time you wash your own self!" Lucy takes off her wet work clothes and puts on an oversized coat too.

The animosity between Seth and Tommy subsides. Lucy says to Riya, "Tommy seems a bit less nervous now, still pretty fidgety."

A curious Riya asks Tommy. "So, what's your story?

"Umm, what do you mean?"

"Where are you from?"

"Mars. Lived with my brother."

"We stopped there. How is life on Mars?"

"Awful—what a terrible idea to live on a planet with no life, no heat, too little air, no water—nothing. They tried terraforming, but that was a fail—too massive a project they say. It's just an overcrowded hell hole."

"Why didn't you leave?" asks Riya.

"We're orphans, no money."

"How did you live?"

"Worked. Fighting. Danny was always fighting someone—gangs, thieves. He wouldn't let me though. He kept getting tougher, won a bunch of fighting competitions, shooting too. Anyway, he got a job with the Martian security police. He was nicer then—kidded a lot. He liked protecting people—saved a bunch of people during the Riker explosion—got a medal. But it paid nothing. He couldn't pay for nothing, like school. So, I got a job, drove a forklift—lied about my age."

"Why didn't he apply to something better?"

"He did. He applied for better positions on Earth, but his applications were always tied up. He'd gotten into trouble for me once, fighting off this bully. He was cleared, but . . .

"So how did you wind up out here?"

"Well, somehow Budanov noticed him, gave him this job, supposed to be big money. Danny couldn't leave me alone on Mars, so he had me come with him to work machinery. I like machinery, but all we do is work twelve, sometimes sixteen, hours a day. I had no idea Budanov would be so bad, but where could I go? No one would help me. Most of the crew are about as scary."

"Yeah, Budanov seems cold as Hell, and the crew real jerks," says Riya.

Lucy adds, "That's terrible, we work long hours too, when we need to, but it's not scary—well, except space walking."

"and Emma's driving."

"Hey, stay with us."

"Love to!"

"What did he do that was so bad?" asks Riya.

Tommy continues, "Lots. At first, Budanov had us drilling into methane. We wore masks but killed everything else, even some of the locals spying on us—they could have just been curious. Then Budanov was short on workers, so he forced the locals to work. They were too strong. Budanov was afraid of 'um, so he drugged 'um. I couldn't believe Danny was helping with that. He does whatever Budanov says. That drug killed 'um—we didn't know. About three months ago, the men wanted women so tried to kidnap some. They grabbed some swords. That ended up horrible. Danny and I had stayed inside to guard the bridge and cargo. I saw it on the monitors.

Danny jumped in to save Budanov. That was the worst. And now this . . ."

"That's horrible, and tragic," says Lucy.

"Yeah, it was. I'm afraid of 'um—even of my brother now. He's not the same."

"So, you don't think your brother would help us out of here?" asks Riya.

"No, not even if he wanted to. I'm surprised I got to see plans to the water. The geologist guy seems nice, likes to talk a lot—maybe he was hitting on me. Anyway, Budanov is super secretive. He wouldn't have told anybody, except the sup, the location of any mine."

"Looks like we have to find our own way out."

Working in pairs, they tie ropes to one person to explore a possible alternate passage to the outside without getting lost. After many attempts, they are still unable to find any signs of an exit.

While dozing off to sleep, Lucy sees the light flicker, feels a cold chill and wraps herself up tighter in her coat.

A startled Lucy stammers, "Riya, do you see the ghost? He said 'help'."

"I don't. You must be dreaming."

"It seemed so real. Did you see or hear something Tommy?"

"No, but my eyes were closed."

"Maybe I was dreaming, or just going crazy. I'm going to sleep."

"Good idea," says Riya.

Twenty-four hours after the cave-in, they are half out of food. Lucy and Seth are at camp while Tommy and Riya search. Lucy manages to remove the bracelets from Seth, which makes him excitably happy. He jumps around and spills the remaining box of food all over the ground.

Lucy scolds, "Calm down! We need that! Stay still!" He tries his best to clean up the mess.

Seth asks, "Lucy mad?"

"No, Seth, just be careful. I know it's dark with just this one lamp."

Seth puts his arm around her and squeezes her saying, "Friend, best friend."

"Seth is my friend too," says Lucy, "Ow, not so tight Seth."

"Hi guys," says Riya returning dejectedly.

"No luck?" Lucy asks.

"No," answers Tommy, "only dead-ends."

"And sudden drops," adds Riya, "We almost fell."

"Just killed two flashlights for nothing. Only two left. And my leg is hurting again," complains Tommy as he lies down and raises his leg.

"We'll need to stay still and conserve," says Riya.

"What are we going to do? Seth and I already went back to the main entrance to try to move the boulders. They won't budge," says Lucy.

"I know. It seems they would want to re-open the cavern, even if only because the ore is valuable," says Riya.

"I don't want to be rescued by him, stuck in that cell again—who knows what they'll do to us."

"We have to keep trying," says Riya.

"What if no one comes. We can't just die here," whines Tommy.

"Our friends won't give up. Wonder what's going on out there," says Lucy.

twenty-seven
The Investigation

In the *Polyus*, Budanov and his dogs enter my cabin while I'm still sleeping. "Wake up! Get ready. The UNBI agents will arrive in an hour."

I'm startled. Half asleep, I ask, "What?"

He orders, "Pull yourself together. Keep that temper in check and meet me in the conference room."

After he leaves, I get up, shower and use the computer to select something again. I know Riya and Lucy must still be alive. Maybe if I do everything he wants, I can convince him to re-open the barricaded cavern. I'm tempted by the long black dress and veil. Feeling that would irritate him, I decide otherwise. It seems Budanov likes red, so I select an attractive mid-length maroon dress with open mid drift and gold accents and matching heels instead.

With agent Kumalo at the controls of the UNBI space vehicle, the three agents arrive at the *Polyus*. The agents enter the conference room where Foxx greets Budanov coldly congratulating him on his marriage. Foxx takes a DNA sample from me and runs the test. He concludes, "The sample is consistent with the sample she gave years ago to NASA. I'd like to run the test on the other astronauts."

Budanov says, "Why? I don't know where they are."

"But they were just here."

Budanov says nonchalantly, "Yes, but gone now."

"They didn't want to celebrate after the marriage ceremony?"

"You can never predict women."

Realizing that cajoling isn't working, Foxx says, "We researched the astronauts thoroughly. We were able to locate signals from the nanobots injected into them before their flight. We are aware that there are four others on the *Polyus* on the deck below. I insist you take us to see them."

"You got me. They're hung-over from too much celebrating, but as you insist. Right this way," says Budanov.

Foxx whispers to me, "Stay close for your protection. We were stalling during our transmission to do a nanobot sweep. We know one just died here."

Budanov guides them opening the door to the prison hallway, where six guards ambush the agents pointing a weapon at their heads. Budanov orders, "Put down your weapons. We have others aimed at the *Athena* crew."

"This constitutes multiple felony charges," says Foxx as the guards remove the agents' weapons.

"Lock them up while I figure out what to do with them," orders Budanov. "Good work Mason, I'll see that you're rewarded." He sighs, "Damn, I'm going to have to pay a lot of expensive people." I try to see my friends, but Budanov grabs me leading me away.

The lights flicker, and I feel a cold chill as Budanov opens the door. We return upstairs where Budanov heads for his study as I hurry to watch the monitors.

Foxx peeks through the cell window and notices Emma. "Hi. How are you?"

"Hi, yourself," say Emma curling her hair. "We're fine, so far. But Riya and Lucy were forced to fix equipment on the surface, and we haven't seen them since."

"Our absences won't go unnoticed. Soon more UNBI agents will follow. We should be rescued soon." Then, he complains, "Augh, this place stinks."

"Yeah, you're roommates with three talking gorillas."

"Nasty. But we now have witnesses to at least seven counts of felony kidnapping and three animal cruelty misdemeanors. This will be hard for Budanov to wiggle out of."

Many hours later, on the bridge, Budanov, dismisses his crew and while petting his huskies, insists that I watch the sunset through the window of the bridge with him. The sunset means we have been held prisoner in the *Polyus* for over three Earth days. He is sitting comfortably in an armchair and seems less irritated now. As he seems calm, this could be a good time to talk to him about releasing Lucy and Riya. I've been studying his precious artwork in the gallery as a conversation starter.

"It's beautiful, isn't it?" he asks.

"Yes, picturesque, with the whale and dolphins."

"Have a seat." He motions to the armchair close to his. I sit down, expecting to be tied in again.

"No need to strap you in with the AI armed above. Have a glass with me." He nods toward the table with a bottle of vodka with two shot glasses and sliced Borodinsky bread with butter. He pours us both a shot.

I bring it to my lips. Because it smells of rubbing alcohol, I push it away. I say, "I have never tried the vodka—it's strong. I have not had any alcohol in about two years."

"I thought not. Ida, switch automatic security protocol for Cami to manual." To me, he says, "The AI does not tolerate intoxicated persons near me."

A voice says, "Please confirm command."

Budanov says, "Ida, confirmed." I sip the vodka. It is very bitter and clears my nostrils. I wince. He laughs and says, "That's not how to drink vodka," and downs his entire shot. "Go ahead."

I have not had any dinner and against my better judgement—so as not to offend—I drink mine in two gulps. I feel it burning my throat. He takes another and pours me another also. I leave it on the table, taking a slice of bread instead.

"I see you've been in the gallery today," he says.

"Yes."

"My studies were in art history. It's a lifetime passion. Do you find anything interesting?"

"Yes, lots. I was curious about the double moving images—where all the tall, thin men are marching. They look exactly the same, opposite all the tall, thin women, who are also marching and look the same. The men and women even resemble each other. The march goes on endlessly. Does it relate to a war?"

"No—though there have been wars—it's a commentary on genetic improvements based on preferred characteristics," he explains. "We started manipulating genes over a hundred years ago—first eliminating life-threatening genetic defects, then improving eyesight, hearing, attention spans. For the past seventy-five years, parents can order taller, slender, more intelligent, well-behaved offspring. So now, with everyone perfect, it's boring. No one is unique—like you."

We discuss more of the artwork from the gallery. After about twenty minutes, I start to feel warm and light-headed from the alcohol.

Then, he pauses and asks, "How old do you think I am?" He hands me my second shot and pours himself another.

I drink it down slowly and say, "About twenty-five years."

He laughs, "Thank you, but no, about seventy. About eighty years ago, we discovered the gene that causes aging. My parents had the funds to eliminate it. It's not an eternal fountain of youth. We do start to age after seventy and haven't eliminated death. My life expectancy is about one hundred forty years."

"But longevity is only for the wealthy?" I ask.

"To prevent overpopulation."

Feeling braver, I say, "I was wondering if you would reconsider opening the mine. You will need to eventually, right? And Lucy and Riya did not intentionally participate in the revolt. They cannot possibly know its location."

"They obviously haven't a clue what they're doing."

"Technology has advanced so much."

"What are you offering me, to reconsider?"

"What do you mean? I have nothing."

"Maybe. I will be aging soon. As I said, my life is not infinitely long. I want a son to carry on my name, even prepared my DNA, enhanced with all tissue. But we have not been able to replicate the women's womb. I need a surrogate."

"No! You cannot be serious. I will not carry your clone! Find a cow or something—It's hot in here."

"Not a clone. I don't want just any *something* to carry *my* son. I want to share DNA with someone unique, different. *My* son will be distinctive. I have the program for artificial insemination here—just need your permission to have the AI initiate."

"I will *not* give it."

"Then you have nothing to offer."

"I hate you."

"Irrelevant, isn't it?"

"I cannot. What about the effects of my exposure to cosmic radiation?"

He finds a hand scanner and runs it on me. "You're perfectly healthy."

"That's an invasion of privacy."

"You have a little time to decide. After three days without water, they will die, probably pretty thirsty now."

"I know, but they mentioned some there and they will find it— *You are merciless.*"

He smirks. "Maybe. But I *can* wait. Your Riya and Lucy *cannot.*" He displays, just in front of my seat, a holographic image of the dimly lit mine site and then pans outside the cavern to the huge boulders blocking it. I refuse to talk to him, stand up, and stare out into the sunset. He stands behind me like a dark shadow. He puts each of his large hands around each of my upper arms, squeezing so tight it hurts. Smiling menacingly, he says, "You cannot win. This stalemate breaks tomorrow."

After a minute, he says "But for now, we need dinner." He lets me go, and I see bruises where he touched me.

He walks into his dining room and soon comes out with more finger foods for the table. I can only stomach bread and water. He talks incessantly on how this is an honor for me and about the rewards of motherhood. I barely listen, but after an hour of his ceaseless chatter, I become sober and realize he was trying to ply my permission with alcohol.

After dinner, he says, "Excuse me, Mason is off duty tonight. Ida, run security check on all floors." After a quiet ten minutes, "Ida, explain why the prison hall is blank?"

I fear I may have been too blunt and beg, "Please don't—"

"Error in command," says Ida.

"What! Ida, find Mason," orders Budanov angrily.

"Cannot locate Mason," responds Ida.

"Why not? . . . Because he did this! What the hell is he up to? Ida, override Mason commands for the past hour. Ida, show me the prison hall from the time Mason disabled the viewer."

Ida shows the events in the hall from a few moments earlier. We see Mason enter the hall. Vivian sees him hurry past their cell. Her eyes widen and her mouth opens wide. The others look to see what frightened her.

Talking quickly to Foxx, Mason says, "We don't have much time. I'm sick of this crazy bastard Budanov. He just dropped an avalanche of rocks, nearly killing my kid brother. Don't think you'll live long enough for a rescue. If you promise to help me find my brother, I'll help you out and testify against Budanov."

"Yes, yes of course. If you help the ladies out too."

"Please, take us" begs Lilian.

Mason looks at her, unlocks both prison doors with a code and says, "Quick, follow me. I know where the sensors work and where they don't." The prisoners all run out after him, except Vivian who freezes. Emma grabs Vivian's hand pulling her. Then Mason opens the prison hallway doors.

Budanov, red with anger, sounds the alarm. Guards arrive on the bridge. Three check the cell, but everyone is gone. "Ida, show me Mason. That traitor!"

All the monitors come on. The escapees have disappeared. A minute later, they can be seen entering the cargo bay. Mason explains, "Now the tricky part. I disabled the tractor beam, but we can be seen on monitors in here. You must move very fast. I'll open the bay doors. You ladies can pile into that craft of yours. The rest can use the UNBI vehicle parked next to it." He grabs Lilian's hand and runs.

"OK, hurry," says Foxx. Emma pulls Vivian again.

They are just outside the vehicles as the bay doors open. Budanov orders, "Damn! He knows too much. Tip the *Polyus* to the ocean and dump them!" His guards promptly obey. All the equipment, including the *Chidiya*, fall into the ocean. The escapees barely miss getting hit as they plunge deep into the ocean.

On the bridge, Budanov orders his guards, "Kill anyone who surfaces."

I yell, "No! Don't!"

Budanov glares at me. He does not change the command. No one listens to me. Desperate, I apply a front snap kick, dropping the weapon from the hand of the surprised guard next to me. I dive and grab the weapon. I hold it the way I had observed them holding it, in a ready position.

I aim at the guards and shout, "Stop, hands up! I will shoot anyone who fires a laser!"

They lift their hands up. I watch them intensely.

In a minute, I am hit hard from behind and drop the weapon. I am taken to a furious Budanov. While I'm still dizzy, he grabs and angrily slaps me several times before releasing me, saying "Don't you ever . . ."

My cheeks sting and eyes water. I want to strike back but fear he would activate his AI.

He returns to his monitors. The equipment quickly sinks, except the amphibious *Chidiya*. Budanov and the guards look for survivors. They see none. He sneers. "It's done. *Bon apetit* whale."

"No, no, no, no. Please don't, don't let them die."

Ignoring my pleas, he says coldly, "Lucky thing I like you, dollface, or you'd be swimming with the fishes too. You're just as valuable to me dead as alive. I'd inherit all your rights to this world's resources, everything you have. I will tolerate no more outbursts." Budanov barks to his crew, "Keep a closer eye on her."

I whimper breathing heavily. I think about them and my other friends, Harper, Ava, all dead. My stomach starts to tremble. Sobbing, I hide my face in my hands. Then I look at him, begging, "Please help them."

He raises his cheeks, curls his upper lips, and jerks his head backwards. "Ugh," he utters while shaking his heads side-to-side, like my friends are meaningless. Then he turns to watch the monitors.

With that look, completely devoid of any compassion, all my muscles tighten up. Everything looks blurry. My face is flush. I crave to strangle his scrawny neck with my bare hands. All I want now is to kill Budanov and his murderous crew. They're all responsible for so many deaths. I'm screaming inside, ready to explode, but I know I need to restrain myself. I breathe deeply. Using all my martial arts training, I focus on tightening my fists to regain self-control. I hold back, telling myself I need to wait for the right moment.

Budanov complains, "Damn, just lost all my mining equipment. I will have to get more funds. All mine are tied up in assets. I don't have a license yet to sell what I have. I know, I will sell the *Chidiya* and the *Athena* for a fortune. 'Finders keepers' for objects over a hundred and fifty years old on unowned real estate. Ida, set the tractor beam and pull in the *Chidiya*."

Ida responds, "Tractor beam disabled".

Budanov orders, "Damn him! Get out there and bring it in manually!"

In fifteen minutes, a crew member on the bridge confirms, "It's in."

"Ida, head for the *Athena* now," orders Budanov.

twenty-eight

The Whale

In the ocean, when the sea people and whale see the people being dumped, they instantly rush in. The escapees fall deep, too deep to be seen from above. They manage to avoid the falling equipment and aim for the surface. Instead of helping the escapees to the surface, the sea people drag the escapees deeper under water. Frightened, they struggle to get free. The sea people pull the escapees under a giant auburn whale. Desperately needing air, the escapees panic. As the sea people touch them lip to lip, the escapees sense that the sea people are trying to help. Strangely, the kiss makes them feel at peace. They cease struggling. They open their months to allow the sea people to breathe in air.

When the *Polyus* leaves, the whale slaps its tail. The sea people allow the escapees to surface. Then all, but one of the sea people, swim away.

Lilian surfaces beside Mason. She squeals, "I can't swim!" He wraps one of his immense arms around her thin body and swims a back stroke with the other. "Thank you. Do you swim often?"

"My pleasure. No, only once on Earth at the academy."

"The whale seems friendly." Mason helps her onto its long wing-like fin and climbs up himself.

Then the others struggle to board the slippery fin too.

Foxx surmises, "Looks like everyone survived."

"Hard to believe," says Emma.

"That was incredible!" says Vivian, "Real mermen!"

"Truly amazing," says agent Pavlov who is beside her, "I've never encountered an alien up close."

"Me neither, that was surreal," says agent Kumalo.

"It was magical. I would normally be terrified of the water, but I felt calm, at peace," says Lilian.

"Indeed. But I don't see any land," says Foxx moving close to Emma.

"I'd say we are to the south and close to Crusoe Island," says Aurora. She almost falls but agent Kumalo catches her.

Lilian holds out a hand to Mason. "So, you seem to be a security systems expert. I work with computers too. I'm Lilian Jones. What's your name again?"

"Daniel Mason, most just call me Mason."

"Can I call you Daniel?"

"*You* can." He says smiling to Lilian. The others introduce themselves. Then he asks, "What do we do now?"

The remaining sea person seems to guide the whale to the north. The escapees shiver as the whale swims fast, causing a cold wind to blow on its wet passengers. They huddle close for warmth, the men, each preferring a woman to huddle with. Because of the wind, they can only talk to the closest person. Lilian starts to talk to the usually taciturn Mason about computer systems. Aurora and Kumalo talk about improvements in interstellar navigation. Vivian and Pavlov talk about changes in forensic science. Soon the topics become more personal. Foxx and Emma sit especially close together, appreciating the beauty of the ocean and the rising stars.

"Why did you save us?" asks Lilian.

Mason tells Lilian, "For my brother. And . . . I was just supposed to be his bodyguard and secure shipments. It was a great salary, with part of the cargo as bonus. But things turned ugly. I want nothing to do with killing innocent people and abusing women. I've already done enough terrible things to protect Budanov. It sickens me. I stopped believing any of his promises. My brother and I wanted out but were constantly watched."

"What will happen to Camille?"

"I don't know. I am sorry I couldn't do anything to help her. Budanov was always too close."

"I'm worried about her."

"She's resourceful, constantly watching everything. I'm sure she'll figure a way out," concludes Mason.

The four couples arrive near Arla's island, as she swims to greet them. She easily gets on the gentle whale, completely calm, naked and unabashed.

"Well, hello," says Pavlov.

"Arla, you're OK!" shouts Emma. The ladies warmly greet each other.

"How did you get here?" asks Lilian.

"Tal, a member of an advanced aquatic species, rescued me and brought me here. He's close. He, well his people, have been watching us and the *Polyus*. He orchestrated your rescue from the ocean and teleported to see my, our friends. We don't have much time. The *Polyus* is headed straight for the *Athena*. Camille is in grave danger. Lucy and Riya are alive but trapped in a complex cave system with two others and have no way out. They need your help too. *He* can't get to them first."

"Where is the cave?" asks Mason.

"I don't know. In the southeastern mountains. Tal cannot tell us the location more precisely because his teleportations are inter-dimensional, based more on emotional energy than our science."

"The southeastern mountains cover a really big area," complains Mason.

"First, you need to get to the *Polyus* quickly and silently," says Arla.

"You're coming with us?" asks Emma.

"I can't. Tal can't. I'm bonded to Tal. His people want to help you but there will be violence. Their empathy is too strong to endure

killings. It would destroy him, my being too close. Be very careful."
Then, she jumps in the ocean and unites with him.

"Thank you!" shouts Foxx waving, along with the others.
Tal feels Arla's immense gratitude at him saving her friends from
drowning and is in bliss.

On seeing them intertwined, Emma exclaims, "Go Arla!"

Foxx asks if he can kiss Emma, and she says, "You better," and
draws him closer.

He embraces her tightly in his arms. They press together with
slightly open lips, breathing each other in, in a long, slow, passionate
kiss. The whale moves on, gaining speed, forcing them to break the
kiss. They all hold on tight.

twenty-nine

The Battle, Part I

Budanov lands the *Polyus* on the inside edge of the crater. "We're here. Let's look at the famous *Athena* up close. I want to experience her. Too bad she's too wide to fit whole in the bay of the *Polyus*." Budanov orders six of his crew to dismantle her. I calculate this to be half of his entire remaining crew. Ignoring my mood, he says, "Come, Captain. I want the captain of the *Athena* by my side for the occasion." We disembark with six workers holding tools.

Budanov orders two of them, "Go in the hole we blasted and take out the body—don't want to see that."

They enter and come back, "We can't find it, sir."

"One of you, search the area. She has to be here somewhere." Then he turns to me, "There were fourteen of you. You never told me what happened to the other members of—"

We hear a loud blast and see his worker on the ground. Budanov glares at me and shouts, "What the hell was that?"

I answer, "Probably fuel from the booster rockets. It leaks—highly explosive. I have first aid training and can check on him." I'm too angry to care what happened to his worker but maybe I can escape or acquire his weapon.

"Hold on." He grabs my arm. To his men, Budanov bellows, "Forget the search, get to work on the ship!" He radios, "Sweep the area. Find the missing doctor." To me, he orders, "Follow me."

Budanov reaches the panicked sweaty man first and removes his weapon. "Go ahead."

The man's lower legs are blown off just below the knees. He is bleeding profusely. "I need to make a tourniquet, quick. I can cut off the bottom of this dress. May I have your knife?" He hands me his and steps back, pointing the man's weapon at me. I cut the dress and make two tourniquets as the man vomits. I see his blue lips, enlarged pupils and bump on his head. I turn him on his side. I take his pulse and shake my head. Looking at Budanov, I say, "He has a rapid pulse. See the bruises. He is bleeding internally and is going into hypovolemic shock. We need to get him to medical."

"Will he make it?"

The man winces in severe pain and holds his heart.

I respond, "Seems to be having a heart attack—probably not."

Budanov shoots the man in the head. "I *can* be merciful. Give me back the knife. Place it on the rock, back away, and let's go."

Placing the knife on the rock, I say, "That was a shock. Give me a minute." I need to take a few deep breaths. Budanov walks back to the *Athena*, unscathed.

He orders his five crew members to continue getting equipment from storage and to begin dismantling the *Athena*. As Budanov goes near the dimly lit main opening, I hope that Marquis is still on the island. If he's here, the sight of the *Polyus* and that explosion, would have alerted him that someone is here. I remember that the external airlock of the main entrance is wired and could be ignited. We had given a trigger to Marquis.

I pretend to be interested in rescuing a stray bunny as an excuse to get behind a rock for cover and to delay getting to the entrance. Budanov rolls his eyes and folds his arms, but then decides to enter the historic *Athena* alone. I hear a blast. I turn to see Budanov's mutilated body on the ground near the demolished airlock. His limbs have been completely severed. With a surge of energy, I rush to grab his weapons and see that his neck is broken. "I can be merciful too, you bastard," I say dryly, as I shoot him in the head with each of his weapons to test them.

My senses are on high alert. My only thought is to rid the world of these murderers. I hear the running footsteps of two men and hide behind the detached airlock door. Looking out, I take careful aim and then shoot one directly in the heart. Before the second can react, I shoot him in the stomach. Both drop within seconds. Using the *Athena* and a boulder for cover, I rush to check the kills. They appear to be dead, but I shoot them in the head to be sure.

Looking around, I see the three other workers rush back into the *Polyus*. I kick off my heels to pursue. Once in the bay, Ida recognizes me and orders me to the bridge. I hope this does not alert anyone that I am here. I had been watching their security images and know where to stay out of sight. The rest of the crew are busy preparing to pillage the *Athena*. They are barely on guard for such an attack.

Marquis and Jean sneak down into the crater quickly, and in a couple minutes, follow me into the bay of the *Polyus* with bow and spears. They are spotted. Two men rush to attack them, but Marquis hears footsteps and acts faster, shooting one straight in the heart. I hear them also, and as the other aims at Marquis, I see and shoot that guard. Marquis and Jean confirm the kills by slitting the throats of the two. I make eye contact with Marquis and Jean and then use hand motions to tell them to come with me.

When they get to me, I say quickly, "Thank you guys for still being here. I'm so, so glad to see you!"

"Me too!" says Marquis.

"Same. Any more here?" asks Jean.

"There are seven more, but I can't tell where they went. Follow me."

I take Marquis and Jean with me up the elevator to take control of the bridge. As I approach the elevator, the doors open with Ida again ordering me to the bridge.

Marquis asks, "Where is she?"

"Who? Oh, you mean the voice. It's the ship, like the communicators. It's OK."

"The ship opens doors and talks?"

"Yes. It's OK. It's supposed to."

"No, it's not supposed to."

"You look as spooked as I was in the swamp. It's just science, technology. Stay behind me." As the elevator door opens a crack, I immediately shoot the ceiling device, destroying it. I peek at the bridge and say, "I can't believe no one is here."

"Why did you shoot the ceiling?" asks Jean

"Those ceiling devices shoot lasers. One killed Harper."

Jean is visibly upset, "She's dead?"

"Yes, she was shot in the room there."

"Bastards!" he says sitting down.

I pat his shoulder, "And he just dropped four of my friends in the ocean. I . . . I can't focus on that now." I expel air to drive out any emotion.

"I'm so sorry. That's, that's horrible, beyond words," says Marquis.

"Yes," I say with a long exhale, trying not to fall apart. "Can you guys watch the stairway doors there? I'll take out weapons."

"Of course." I point to the doors.

"These shoot lasers that kill your people," I say as I demolish the laser control stations. I continue to fire long after they are destroyed. Then I peek into the conference room and take out that ceiling device. When done, I keep close watch on the elevator doors. I try to operate the security monitor. "Ida, show me the interior of the *Polyus* and all crew members."

"You do not have security clearance for that operation."

Then, we silently listen for any sounds of approach. All is quiet. After a couple hours, we start to relax our watch.

Jean says, "I wonder if they fled."

"Maybe, but where would they go?" I ask.

Jean is closest and I give him a big hug.

Then I hurry to Marquis, who says, "I'm so glad you're alive, I thought you were lost."

I confess, "I missed you!" For a moment, we just stare at each other. As the adrenalin leaves, I feel light-headed and start trembling. "Hold me." He holds me tightly. I ask myself why I should deny this impulse to be with him. I need him. I ache to be held, for more, to forget.

To avoid staring at us, Jean looks out the window. "Look! It's them! They're here!" Then he passes out.

"Oh, I feel faint." Marquis and I can barely break our fall.

thirty

The Battle, Part II

The whale continues to follow the *Polyus* from a safe distance. The ladies recognize Crusoe Island and see the top of the *Polyus*. They and their companions sneak up and into the crater. They see no one. They quickly slip into the *Athena* and grab the tranquilizer guns and a few explosive devices.

Emma says, "Look for Ava and Camille. Careful." The three ladies rush through the ship, being careful of their traps. They meet back with Emma.

"Didn't find anyone," says Lilian.

"No one near the lake either," reports Aurora.

"Where are they?" asks Vivian.

"Probably in the *Polyus*," suggest Emma, "Let's go."

The agents find and pick up the weapons dropped by the slain workers. The *Polyus* is still there, but the large hatch to the bay doors has been closed.

"No sign of Camille or Ava," Emma tells the agents.

Mason says, "I should be able to open a side door." The eight move quickly in that direction.

"Good, you and us three agents will go in. Ladies, can you secure the exits?" asks Foxx.

"I'm going in too. Camille and Ava might be in there," asserts Emma.

"No, it's too dangerous for a civilian," counters Foxx.

"I can defend myself. I'm a trained Air Force officer and going in."

"And so, you're needed out here."

"Lilian can handle guarding the exits. I'm needed in there."

"I'd rather you—"

"We don't have time to argue," interrupts Mason.

The four men enter with Emma, who brings a tranquilizer gun. Lilian, with Aurora and Vivian, stay behind to watch the exits. Lilian holds a tranquilizer gun and the others, the explosives.

"Duck behind these rocks. We can see the side door and bay from here," says Lilian.

"Makes sense," says Aurora as she crunches down and does not move.

Lilian hears Vivian breathing heavy and asks, "You OK?"

"Yes, I'm sweating and have goosebumps, but OK," she stammers.

"Me too," says Lilian.

The others enter the *Polyus* undisturbed. Mason says, "Hopefully, Budanov neglected to remove my security clearance. Ida, disarm and ignore all guests." He picks up a portable monitor and finds the seven guards. "Yes, it works," he says, "Oh, not good. Camille and two men, not Budanov's men, just passed out on the bridge."

Foxx looks and then asks, "Where *are* Budanov's men?"

"On the second deck. They're meeting at the other end. Quiet so we can hear what they're saying," says Mason.

"They're speaking Russian. I can translate," offers Pavlov. "One said, they will be completely out cold in a minute... They can get rid of them... Take over... Another agrees... Have everyone they need to run the operation ourselves... One called Budanov a tyrant... They are threatening to abuse her. We better move fast."

"Let's ambush them," suggests Foxx.

"You can get there unseen by crawling up the ventilation shaft. You and Emma are thin enough to get through. We'll circle around and meet you," says Mason.

Foxx and Emma crawl through the vents to the location. By the time they arrive, most of the guards have moved away, leaving only the geologist. Foxx shakes his head in disappointment. He and Emma quietly exit the vent with the geologist unaware. The other agents join them from another side and easily surround him.

Foxx orders, "United Nations Bureau of Investigation, stop and put your hands up."

"OK, I give up. I'm not violent, just a geologist," he says.

Mason says, "Damn. He triggered an alarm."

Foxx arrests him while the other two agents disarm him. "We'll put him in prison," says Kumalo.

Then Mason says, "Here's the code. He's tricky. Guard him."

As Pavlov and Kumalo take the geologist, Pavlov says, "I'll be right back."

Emma, Foxx and Mason proceed through the second-floor warehouse meandering around containers. They try to capture the next guard, but he aims his weapon at them. Foxx, Mason and Emma instantly back away around a container. Emma slips between containers and circles around. Two other guards sneak up on Mason and Foxx from behind, weapons ready.

Emma notices the guards just in time to quickly kick the weapon from one of their hands. She grabs his arm in a half Nelson and uses him as shield. The scuffle alerts the others. They jump for cover. She recognizes her captive and says, "A few of you can't hold me down," as she kicks him hard in the butt and shoots him with her tranquilizer.

As Foxx and Mason take cover behind a wall, the other guard shoots Mason, wounding him in the arm. "Damn, that hurt," complains Mason, "and it's my shooting arm."

The two remaining guards meet and move toward Foxx and Mason who retreat. "We're penned in," says Foxx. Shots are quickly exchanged. "Argh, I ran out of power."

"Mine's low too," says Mason.

The two guards approach. The returning Pavlov sneaks in, shooting them, fatally wounding them. They look for Emma and find her with her unconscious captive.

Foxx says, "We shouldn't separate." Mason finds rope and they tie up her captive.

"There are three more," says Mason, "The two ore processors and the navigator."

"I'm pumped," says Emma, "Let's go."

"Hold on, tigress. I don't see them anymore. They were heading that way, which leads to the third deck where there're only a few places they could hide," says Mason.

"I'd bet they can see and hear us," warns Foxx.

"Probably, we'll need to be careful," says Pavlov.

"Follow me," directs Mason. They make a careful search in the warehouse, but do not find the guards. Then Mason directs the agents and Emma to the stairs to the crew members' living quarters. They carefully search each separate cabin and finally find the three crew members. They are hiding and trembling. All three beg for mercy and are taken to the prison cell also.

thirty-one

Search for the Miners

Hours after the battle, I wake up and slowly realize that I'm in medical on the *Athena*. I'm in the insolation bed, and the brothers, Jean and Marquis, are in the other beds. Jean is tallest, and his feet are sticking out the end. I see Dr. Ava Campbell.

"Ava! You are alive."

And you too!" says Ava.

"Oh, it's so good to see you!"

"You guys have been out cold from the odorless sleeping gas BZ. It must have come in through the vents." Then Ava tells me about the attack and how grateful she is that Marquis and Jean rushed to help her. She shows me her wound. "See how well it's healing."

"I'm impressed. I have not seen Marquis show tenderness toward us."

"I think he's mellowing."

Emma enters with a tranquilizer gun, and I can hardly contain myself.

I hug her until she complains, "OK, OK that hurts."

"You are not dead!"

"We survived—me, Aurora, Vivian and Lilian, and even Arla— are very much alive."

"How?" She describes their miraculous escape and relays Arla's information.

"We could move in secretly, thanks to you guys distracting them. We secured the ship and I helped—captured one jerk myself." Then she gives me a play-by-play.

"Wait, Mason was with you. He is one of *them*."

"Was. Anyway, Vivian, Aurora and I have been dismantling the land mines and booby traps while you were playing Sleeping Beauty. Lilian is working with Mason and the UNBI agents to find those trapped in the cavern by searching the AI files."

"That's great!"

"Not so good. Budanov apparently was a mastermind, also an expert in geology and navigation, and had been very secretive. He hid or protected the location files for all his promising mine sites. So far, they've not had any luck in breaking through the firewalls."

"Wish I could help."

"You're not getting up," orders Ava.

"Why the gun Emma? I think we're safe now," I say.

"Are you sure?" asks Emma.

"Yes," say both me and Ava.

"If you're sure. We still have more work to dismantle all the mines." Emma sees Marquis moaning. "I'll leave it with you, just in case. See you later."

"I'm going in the lab to run some blood tests. You stay put," orders Ava.

After she leaves, I get up to talk to Marquis, who is also just waking up. "How are you?"

"Ahh, head hurts."

"Mine too."

"But I guess I'm fine," he says yawning.

"Thank you for taking good care of Ava. She told me all about how you saved her. That was really brave."

"Your doctor is remarkable. I learned a lot from her. She's a really smart lady." He confides in me about their private talks and concludes, "I'm trying to change. I don't want you people afraid of me. I need to settle down, think first—not *everyone* is a threat."

I'm moved and say "Marquis, I want to apologize."

"For what?"

"Lots. Because we scared you—used you as a study specimen. It seems our radio broadcast brought Budanov here. Then we considered you a lunatic when you were just trying to defend yourself and save your people. We were rude. I was. I heard about what happened to your family, but I was too angry to think about the pain you went through. I can understand it now—the rage against those who kill the people you love. I was so angry. I killed three people, and caused the deaths of more. I would definitely have dragged one off and demanded his death."

He reaches over and gently kisses me on the forehead and smiles. "Thank you. I hold nothing against you. Budanov's actions are on him. What you did, how you acted, was understandable too. And everyone thinks I'm a lunatic."

I sigh and whisper, "I cannot believe I killed people."

"You did what you had to do. Any one of these greedy bastards could have continued slaughtering our people. I *want* people like them afraid."

"You're right. They were horrible." I continue to tell Marquis how we were imprisoned, and how I was forced to marry Budanov.

He looks at me scowling. "You cannot stay here with me. If my people learn you were unfaithful, no matter the circumstance, they would persecute you. The sentence is death. For your protection, you need to return to your own world. How could you even consider marrying him, being intimate with him?"

"We were not intimate!"

"That's hard to believe."

"It's impossible. Budanov doesn't have a penis. Check him."

"I need two witnesses."

Marquis and I walk out to the mutilated body. He sees Vivian and Aurora and asks them to act as witnesses. "For real? No, that's so beyond gross," says Vivian.

"I'd rather not," says Aurora.

"Please, it's important," I beg. "We'll cover everything else."

"OK, but only for you," says Vivian.

"Here goes," warns Marquis. He strips the body and grins.

"After all we've been through, I thought you might trust me," I say.

"I'm sorry I doubted you. It's just that you have every reason to hate me and go. Do . . . Do you want to stay?"

"I don't know. I know it hurt when you told me that I had to leave. Though a week ago, I never wanted to see you again."

He responds tenderly, "I was a brute to take you, Camille. I was completely in the wrong. I'm ashamed. I've never done anything like that before and never intend to again. When I realized I was wrong, I chose marriage, thinking I could make it right by you. I thought the marquis was a prize and you'd be happy, after a while. I was just being arrogant."

"Not totally unjustified—I was interested in you when I first saw you. I'm sorry, but just before we were knocked out, I wanted to use you just to satisfy my own needs."

"Are you apologizing for that?" he asks quizzically and then leans closer and smiles. I feel flush.

Regaining my composure, I ask, "Do you think we can ever stop hurting each other?"

Just then, Lilian interrupts us, "There you are! Glad you're awake. We need to talk to you about Riya and Lucy."

"Lilian!" I give her a big hug.

"C'mon!" she says.

Marquis and I follow Lilian into the *Polyus* where we are called into a meeting to discuss how to find the mine site. First, Marquis is introduced to the agents and their new assistant, Mason.

I recognize Mason and ask, "Why is he *here* and not in prison with the others?"

"I remember him too," says Marquis glowering, "He was at the market protecting Budanov."

"But he's been working with us to find his brother," says Lilian, "He saved us, and me from drowning."

"I saw that he was dumped in the ocean too. He was one Budanov criticized for not shooting anyone, but I still don't want him with us."

"He doesn't belong here," insists Marquis.

Foxx argues "Mason has been acting for us, even wounded for us. We need him. His knowledge of the *Polyus* is critical to finding Lucy and Riya. We can't find them otherwise. Nanobot signals are too weak to transmit through rocks. We interrogated the prisoners, but the prisoners don't know where the mine site is located, or won't tell us."

Lilian offers, "I'll watch him."

"OK," I say.

Marquis nods but watches Mason suspiciously.

Lillian tell us, "We've been unsuccessful in breaking the file protection protocols."

Foxx asks me, "Did Budanov give you any indication where the site might be?"

"No, not at all. I only saw the images at the security station on the bridge like everyone else. And the one time by the window."

Masan says, "The files are only secure at this station. Those files, I may be able to retrieve. It'll still take time."

"Why?" I ask accusingly.

"Listen, I want to find that site as much as you do. My kid brother is in there."

"The young machine operator?"

"Yes." After an hour, he finds and restores the deleted file and replays it for clues. On the image, we can see the mine site inside the cavern and the avalanche.

Marquis says, "I recognize those. The stalactites are unusually flat. See here. But that massif is more than a two-weeks march south of here and then we'd have to search for the exact site."

"We can fly there much faster," offers Mason. "Draw us a map." Marquis does. Looking at Lilian, Mason says, "With some help, I can fly the *Polyus* there."

"We can help, of course," offers Foxx.

"I'd love to learn this new technology," says Lilian.

"Me too," says Emma.

"I need to stay here. Ava is barely hobbling around," says Aurora.

"Jean hasn't woken up yet either. He was closest to the gas vent. Also, we need to repair the *Athena* from potential water damage from the demolition," says Vivian.

"It looks like rain is coming," adds Aurora.

"Aurora and Vivian, you should stay here," I say. "There is no more mining equipment. It all fell in the ocean. How do we remove the avalanche of boulders blocking the entrance?"

"It'll take weeks to get equipment like that from Earth," says Foxx.

"My people could move the boulders with levers, ropes, and brute force," suggests Marquis, "But they fear the *Polyus*. The ship would only scare them into hiding."

"Could you talk them into helping us?" I ask. "Your people respect you."

"It would be better if you came with me," he says.

"I could bring you two to Carcassonne in the *Chidiya*," suggests Emma.

"You could take us to the entrance," says Marquis.

"OK, let's do it," I say.

"Let me check in on Jean," says Marquis. He and I walk to medical.

With her arms crossed, Ava asks us, "Where have you been? I told you to rest."

"Sorry, we could not," I say.

Marquis asks Ava, "How's he doing?"

"He's recovering and should be fine soon," assures Ava.

"We should go. Vivian and Aurora are staying here with you."

Marquis and I head immediately for the *Chidiya*, still in hospital gowns and bathrobes. He looks at it and takes a deep breath before entering.

As we're flying, I notice Emma wearing a taser and sitting beside a gun. I turn to Marquis and see the tension in his face and body. "Are you OK?"

"I'm good . . . Quite a view."

"You are safe. Emma's an awesome pilot. That is the river we followed before, right?"

He nods. "Looks so small from here."

"Can you show us a dry entrance to Carcassonne?"

"Yes, it's over there."

After we land, Emma stays behind to guide the *Polyus*. Marquis takes me through the long, secret entrance to the living room of his uncle, King François V. "I apologize to rush in unannounced," says Marquis.

"No need. You're a welcome surprise!" he says. "We've been worried." We exchange hugs and *bisous*.

"We defeated them Uncle! Even commandeered their ship. I rode in the belly of the dragon to get here!"

"I'd love to see that."

"You can."

"So, tell me everything." Marquis proceeds with the highlights after Guillaume and Claude left, being very brief about my relationship with Budanov. "So, she knocked out two felis and captured a ship! Extraordinary!"

"Thank you, sir," I say.

"Yes, but now she needs help rescuing her friends," says Marquis.

"Bad timing. Through Claude, I learned that Marguerite, in direct disobedience of my order, kept up with her gossip, poisoned Antoine and others against them. She advocated launching an attack."

"When? If they had left Carcassonne, all would have been killed. It would have been horrible, better to stay hidden," says Marquis.

"I stopped it, put Antoine in prison until he reconsiders. Many men may still resist, even elect to march against them. I approved Marguerite's marriage to Henri yesterday. I had him take her and Étienne through the tunnel under the mountains. It may have been too late to prevent damage. The people are starting to doubt my decisions. It was all I could do to keep them from imprisoning the ladies here."

"I think I should speak in the courtyard."

"I couldn't agree with you more. I'll call an emergency public meeting while you two get dressed properly." He calls out, "Francine, help her get dressed."

The young Francine, who was eavesdropping, gently takes my hand out to the hallway. She says, "Wait here until I get you the proper attire to wear."

As I wait quietly, I can barely hear Marquis and the king talking about the recent events.

The king asks, "You know, I never got her birth name?"

"It's Camille."

"She looks a lot better now. Lovely wouldn't you say?"

"Yes, she looks beautiful, enchanting—in a good way."

"And so, the marriage between you is good?"

"Well, I'm the only one married, but we're talking."

"Hm, this is a delicate issue. If she refuses to acknowledge you as her husband, it will seriously jeopardize your credibility, and later your ascension to the throne, and make me look like a fool or a liar, not good."

"I know, but I'm not going to force her—I need to hurry to get ready."

Francine comes back to me with a bundle, brings me to the hot spring as before. There, she happily helps me bathe, combs my hair, and helps me put on an elegant but simple long dress. "You are healing well."

"Your potion helped a lot, thank you."

She shows me a matching cape. "It's beautiful, no? It's your proper cape, the symbol of the marchioness," She shows me an emblem in the middle. "Take it." I hesitate, not sure if I can wear it.

I protest, "It is wrong that the men alone decide that women are married. Women should be able to decide for themselves."

"I hadn't thought of it like that. My dad introduces me to guys at dinners and parties. I know he watches to see who I like."

"But you don't really choose, I mean if he didn't like someone, and you did?"

"True, but that doesn't really happen. Like right now, I'm checking out Guillaume, Philip and Gerard—*He's so cute*! I told my dad I like Gerard best, and my dad likes him too."

"Sweet."

"Your women choose themselves? And everyone lives happily ever after?"

"Well, not always," I admit. "We should go. I think they want us for the meeting right away." As we leave the springs, I grab the cape.

The meeting was called quickly. King François V and Marquis are ready to preside over a boisterous crowd gathered in the courtyard. As Francine and I arrive behind them, I see scowling faces and can hear an angry murmur.

"Where has he been while we were being attacked?" asks one farmer.

"Some say he went crazy," says his friend.

"I'd never follow someone who'd abuse a woman," says a young man to his wife.

"You're right about that," says his wife.

The crowd hushes as I step toward Marquis. When Marquis sees me in the dress and cape, he beams with pride. I blush as he squeezes my hand and kisses my cheek. I kiss him back and whisper quietly in his ear, "Tough crowd. We can work on rights later."

I hear voices in the crowd. "Guess the abuse rumors are exaggerations."

"She seems happy."

"Seems sudden. I don't trust them," warns Nanette.

As the king steps forward, the crowd hushes. He smiles at me and opens the meeting. He informs the people, "You are safe now. The marquis and his party, along with our new allies, the Amazon women, were able to defeat the others. Many thanks to the new marchioness, who herself destroyed the sky weapons." He continues with more details. The news was a relief to all, and the crowd cheers.

The king motions for the crowd to be quiet and then announces, "The marquis has a challenge for you."

Then, Marquis makes a convincing speech explaining the need to travel in the *Polyus* to rescue their allies trapped in the cavern and that these strangers may still be endangered by remnants of the others. He appeals to their sense of gratitude, hospitality and ingenuity. He concludes, "Who will come with us?"

Kiara and Claude attend hand-in-hand. Claude is first to say, "I'll go." However, no one else steps forward.

The king states, "There is nothing to fear, and I myself will go."

An opposition leader counters, "How could you suggest going in *that* ship? Our friends, family were killed by that ship!"

The crowd starts to stir angrily. "We don't know them."

"They could just all be possessed. See how the king volunteers right away," adds Nanette.

"It's a trap!"

"Where is Comte Jean-Louis?"

"Did they kidnap him?"

"Must have!"

"Is he still alive?"

"They killed Comte Jean-Louis."

"They won't get away with this!"

"Let's destroy the ship."

Someone starts a chant. "Attack the ship. Attack the ship. Attack the ship . . ."

The mob looks angry enough to attack the royal party. Marquis and the king put their hands on their swords, ready to draw.

Suddenly, Claudine, who was standing in front with a few friends, jumps on a rock to face the mob, and shrieks, "Have you all gone crazy! If the others are on that ship, attacking it would be the stupidest thing you've ever done. You all know Kiara and her friends! They've done us no harm! Is this how we treat guests in our lands? You savage ungrateful cowards!"

Guillaume adds, "She's right! How many times has the marquis saved you? He was out there risking his life for you! He wouldn't lead us into a trap. He certainly would never allow any harm to come to Jean. I'm going too!" The sentiment becomes contagious.

The divided people argue until the opposition leader acquiesces, "If you must go, do what you want you fools."

Marquis motions for quiet and states, "I assure you that Jean is fine. If you are coming, raise your hand!" In all, thirty of the strongest individuals raise their hand. "Great, thank you. Please gather up strong levers, rope, climbing gear. Bring your personal gear, and a weapon and meet outside the cave." As the crowd disperses, I'm excited to see Evelyn, Bella and Kiara.

"*Bonjour*!" says Evelyn. We all hug and exchange *bisous*.

"How have you been?"

"Good, we have a real bedroom with fireplace. Love their hot springs," says Bella. "I'll show you our room. We're right in front of it."

As we walk, Evelyn opens a door and says, "We're meeting new friends, learning French, drinking tea. I'm helping to make an animal themed quilt for the children of a widow." In their room, she holds up a quilt square. "Here's mine."

"That looks like a worm," I say trying to hide my disgust.

"It is! No one else guessed it."

I see Bella's rose butterfly appliqué, "This is lovely. You have a talent."

"Thanks," says Bella.

"And I have an art studio downstairs," says Kiara. "Everyone seems really nice, except for just now. I'm sorry we couldn't get canoes out. The king said it was too dangerous with the hurricane and flooding."

"We heard many farmers and hunters were getting killed," said Bella.

I start, "We stopped—"

We hear a knock and Bella says, "Come in."

Claude and Marquis open the door and wait outside the doorframe. Marquis says, "Sorry to interrupt. We should get moving."

"We want to help too," says Kiara.

"We can gather food and handle meals," offers Bella.

"OK," says Claude, "I'll go with you ladies to our surplus supplies. We'll hurry, Marquis." The ladies gather food supplies. The volunteers bring their stock outside the cave to the plateau. Mason lands the *Polyus*, and the thirty volunteers follow Marquis in nervously. As we fly to the massif, I show my friends my cabin. We talk about all that happened after they left the *Athena*. I also make myself tougher gray camouflage clothes and hiking boots in order to aid in the search.

In the *Polyus*, Marquis, the king, and new bridge crew scan the massif. After several hours, they find the avalanche and land. Mason, the agents, Lilian and Emma scan the surrounding area outside the mountain.

The king helps to coordinate logistics. Claude and the other ladies help prepare meals. Marquis and his volunteers work non-stop to remove the rocks. The volunteers push stone away with levers. They also tie rope to a fulcrum and pull down other stones.

I climb the precarious pile. "Marquis, can they move faster?"

"No, not and work safely. This is dangerous work. You shouldn't be up here."

"I'll be quiet and stay out of your way."

After a few hours, the men are finally able to pull away enough stones to create a small opening. I rush to look and quickly grab rappelling gear. I start down before Marquis can object.

Marquis and I are inside first, followed by some of his volunteers. They are armed with swords, and I with a *Polyus* weapon, should there still be any hostiles. I also have a backpack with water, snacks and a first aid kit.

"Here grab this," says Marquis giving me a torch.

"What a mess!" I say walking around.

"Eek, gross!" says one man. "I found a dead body. What is that hairy thing?"

"Found one too! Eish!" says another.

"They are gorillas, used as workers—the poor beasts." I say, looking at them and swallowing hard. "You'll find three human corpses too."

"Come away. It stinks here," says Marquis.

"What if Riya and Lucy are dead too?" I say.

"Stay here. Let us look around," offers Marquis.

After ten agonizing minutes, Marquis and his volunteers confirm three more dead bodies and that none are women for which I am very relieved.

Marquis directs some of the volunteers, "Remove and bury the carcasses. You four continue to remove the debris and look through it for any possible survivors."

"Lucy! Riya!" I shout but hear no answer.

"Hey, I found small footprints along with a large animal print and another man-size boot print leading deeper into the caves," announces Marquis.

"They must belong to them and the third gorilla and the young driver," I say.

"Could they be dangerous?"

"I don't know."

"I guess there's no point in telling you that this is dangerous, and you should be in the *Polyus* helping the women."

"There is absolutely no point."

"Let's follow these," Marquis says to me and a few men. "We may need to split up later if they disappear. We need to work quietly to not alert a possible assailant."

I attach a long rope to him from the entrance of the cavern. Many times, he loses sight of the footprints in the bare rock. There are many different passages. We try each one. Other two-person crews search the diverging passages. Most lead to dead ends. We must move slowly, watching for cavities and wet slippery stones. For deep fissures, Marquis directs volunteers to investigate the bottoms in case of accident, as he and I continue to search deeper into the cave. I almost fall a few times. Even Marquis loses his footing and scrapes his shin on a rock. We crawl through numerous crevices with no luck. A couple were too narrow for Marquis to fit through. Marquis and I cooperate, working quietly and diligently, but there seem to be never-ending series of dead ends. Seeing my discouragement, he kisses my dirty cheek and encourages me to move on.

After over ten hours, we are completely exhausted and filthy. We reluctantly decide that we need to turn back to rest for the day. I can't stand the thought of not finding them. As we head back, I miss a small crevice in the floor, twist my ankle, and walk holding onto Marquis' shoulder. Still, I find letting go of the hope of finding them today very hard. My stomach aches knowing they are somewhere in here, probably without water, light or food.

Tired and with our light dimming, we take a wrong turn going back. Suddenly, Marquis hears a faint sound and follows it. After sneaking around a corner, he meets an angry hairy beast.

Seth charges on all fours. He howls a frightening threat. Then he bounces off the rock near Marquis, who backs away and draws his sword. I limp toward the noise.

Seth charges again standing on two legs, raising both arms and showing his teeth. Marquis lifts his sword ready to strike.

Lucy recognizes me in my dim light. She shouts, "No, Seth, friend!"

Taking her cue, I say, "Stand down!"

Marquis steps back. "Why?"

Seth submits. "Friend?"

"Yes, definitely," says Lucy smiling and running to us. "You came for us!" Hugging Marquis, who is closer, she says, "Oh thank God. I completely forgive you."

"Thanks, I am very sorry," says Marquis.

Riya touches Seth and says, "He's been helping us. He and this boy Tommy were prisoners too."

In seconds, we all happily greet each other. I'm tearing up. We excitedly tell each other what has been happening on the way back.

As we leave the cave and all the search crews return to the *Polyus*, the survivors and I thank Marquis and his people for volunteering and for all their incredible hard work. The Mason brothers hug. Then Mason offers the third-floor cabins where they can wash as Marquis and I continue to manage the returning volunteers.

Soon, we celebrate in the bay with fine wines, foods from the ship's stores and hearty local foods. Marquis and I join them, extremely hungry and still filthy. The aroma of the foods makes our stomach rumble. While we eat voraciously, all get acquainted. Foxx and Marquis discuss mining rights.

When Mason returns, Lilian says to him, "I appreciate you showing me the *Polyus*, but you didn't seem to *need* any help."

"Umm, true, just wanted your company—no women where I'm going," he confesses.

"So, this is your last night of freedom."

"Afraid so. I have a lot to answer for."

"I'll always see you as my hero."

"Thanks, means a lot."

Evelyn rushes in. "Mason, quick help me prepare a playlist of fun, peppy songs."

Soon it is done, and some start dancing. I can only watch because my foot still hurts. When all the ladies are back from showering, Evelyn insists that we dance to "We are Family" by the Sisters Sledge with all of us—Kiara, Evelyn, Bella, Riya, Lucy, Emma and Lillian—lining up, arm in arm, to do the Cancan in honor of our French rescuers. Evelyn insists that I join them. I try, standing with my one good leg and kicking with the other. We are all laughing. Seth joins in the Cancan near Lucy. We look ridiculous. I see Marquis laughing and smile back at him.

After our silly dance, Marquis whispers to me, "That was funny. In answer to your question, yes, I think we could stop hurting each other."

"I'd like that. I think we can do better. I really appreciate your help, proves you care. I also like that you listened to me when Seth attacked. That took restraint. I can forgive you, for everything. I'm not angry anymore."

"I'm so glad to hear that. You know I love you Camille."

"You're amazing, the bravest, most compassionate man I know. I love you too. I want to stay with you."

Then, I add, "I know where *we* can shower." We sneak away to my cabin on the *Polyus*, where I say "Ida, play soft, romantic music, French, twenty-first century, low. Ida, dim the lights too."

Marquis looks at me confused until the music starts and the lights dim. "Nice trick."

"And Mason, if you are watching, stop."

We take off each other's clothes and head for the shower, running the warm, refreshing water on our dirty bodies. We soap and lather each other and start kissing. Showing off, I lift my sprained foot to his shoulder and flick his ear. We press together. I feel his hardness. It feels so perfect. I feel him release. Then, he complains that it was too quick and takes me to bed.

Lying in bed, he asks, "You had lost me, when you whispered about rights at Carcassonne, what did you mean?"

"I meant my rights to my body, you need my permission for anything, like touching me."

He adoringly caresses my skin and teases, "Can I touch here? What about here? And here? And here? And—"

"You're teasing me. Will you stop asking?"

"No, I have to get this right," and he finishes by asking about my toes and tickles my feet until I giggle.

We look in each other's eyes. I massage behind his ears, pulling his head toward mine. We kiss softly and are ready to start again, slowly this time. Afterward, we relax into the soft mattress, with my head on his chest, and fall into a blissful sleep.

thirty-two

Agreements

After Marquis and I awaken, we choose brand new clothes and go for breakfast in the conference room of the *Polyus*, still in our new private paradise. Marquis has his arm around me as he checks out the artwork. He stares at "Black Square" and asks, "Did someone peel off the painting?"

"No, it's not supposed to depict reality. It was revolutionary some three hundred years ago," I say.

"It seems to depict a phant trudging in the dark. See, it's protecting a little one underneath."

"What's a phant?"

"A large beast, a third the size of this room. Very gentle. The people on the plains ride them."

"I would like to ride one."

"You can soon. My older sister is getting married there."

"She didn't seem to like me, but we can wish her happiness."

He smiles, "Of course, she doesn't like people she can't control. She'll have seven little ones to control, and Étienne of course."

"She agreed to this?"

"I don't have the details. She's been arranging a marriage between our families."

"*She* arranged it? There's hope for you yet."

He looks around and says, "I like these round things."

"They're Fabergé eggs."

"What's that?"

"They're jeweled shapes, very rare, also over three hundred years old."

"Nice."

The first to greet us are Lieutenant Foxx and Emma, each happily carrying trays; one with a large tray of coffee cups, and the other with a large tray of various sweet breads for breakfast. They are soon joined by the king and a tired Lilian and Mason, to whom Marquis and I remain cordial.

"Good morning," says Marquis in French.

"I like you better on our side," I say to Mason.

"Me too." He gives Marquis and the king each a soft globular crystal and says, "Sirs, put this in your ear. It will translate for you," while making hand gestures on how to install it.

Marquis is reluctant. Foxx says, "It's OK, I have one. See." Foxx shows him the crystal in his ear, and Marquis inserts his.

"Can you understand me?" asks Emma.

"Yes," answers Marquis.

"Yes, I do. Thank you," says the king.

"Good. I wanted to let you know that while you guys were *occupied*, we dropped off the volunteers and moved to Crusoe Island," states Emma. "The *Athena* crew and your brother should be joining us."

Ava walks in and greets everyone. She sits beside the king and talks to him about his nephew Jean's recovery. He talks about his wife's ailment and asks if Ava can help.

Foxx states that he still needs to take Mason into custody, but Mason seems more relaxed than ever. The rest of the *Athena* crew and Jean mosey in for breakfast.

Arla arrives clothed and with her two seals. "Hi! Nice to see all of you."

"Hi. It's wonderful to see you too," I say as we hug.

"Tal is here too. He has a message for you," says Arla.

"Tell him we are so very grateful," I say.

"He was happy to help. Do you see him?"

"No."

"I see him. He teleported. He's the fuzzy white cloud," says Arla.

"Oh, I see him now, over the table."

"I'll give his message after the UNBI meeting."

"Who's with you?" asks Lucy referring to the seals in Arla arms.

"My pets, Brittany and Setter. They keep me company when Tal's away. We have different sleep schedules. These little guys hate being alone."

"They're so cute!" declares Lucy petting them.

"Precious," says Kiara, as she walks in with Claude.

"Are you happy?" I ask Arla.

"Yes, very," says Arla smiling. "I'll tell you all about him, us, later. Looks like they are ready. We can go on with our meeting with UNBI."

Foxx speaks, "I'm connecting us to Director Fayed of UNBI in order to settle outstanding issues. On the agenda are rights to mining and Camille's marital status."

Fayed is visible and speaks, "Yes, that's right. First, I am happy to meet your majesties."

"Same here. We are happy and grateful for your help in removing Budanov from our world," speaks the king.

Fayed continues, "You are welcome, but I understand all the people in that room deserve the credit. Good work. Let's get to our business. According to our laws, Ms. Tremblay was legally married to Budanov. We cannot recognize her previous non-consensual marriage to Marquis. Therefore, she inherits the *Polyus*, and everything owned by Budanov."

"What? That's blasphemous. What do they mean, her married to Budanov?" asks the king to Marquis.

Marquis whispers to him, "Not really. No cardinal. They didn't consummate. It was a paper deal only. He forced Camille to agree to give him her mining rights, by threatening her friends."

"What rights? I'm not happy with this," he whispers back.

"It's complicated. We'll explain later," whispers Marquis.

Fayed speaks, "If you're done, I'll continue. Because she hadn't infringed any rights, all that he mined can be hers, and I hope she'll sell it at a reasonable price to the United Nations. We desperately need heavy metals. In exchange, the marquis informed agent Foxx that Carcassonne could grant a license to allow a reasonable amount of additional mining, provided that it does not jeopardize anyone's safety."

"If his majesty approves," says Marquis.

"I will allow Marquis to oversee this. It's time he took on a government role. I'll name him ambassador, plenipotentiary to Earth," pronounces the king.

Fayed announces, "Then it's agreed. It is illegal to kill humans of course. Though we should take the marquis and Ms. Tremblay into custody, I received permission, due to unusual circumstances, to allow them to be tried by the local Ross court."

"Of course, we'll be happy to provide them with just consequences," says the king smiling. This time, I'm not worried about the outcome.

"Mr. Daniel Mason and the remaining members of the *Polyus* crew will come with us. That concludes my segment," states Fayed.

"We can provide just consequences to them too," offers the king.

Mason looks concerned. Fayed states, "We have rules. Now, I believe the sea life has some comments."

The cloud merges into Arla. "Yes, that sea life is an advanced species who call themselves the Serafim. They send you their greetings and best wishes."

"Same here," says Fayed. "I apologize for any offense."

"However, they ask that humans stay out of the oceans and that no further humans settle their world. They have seen the devastation of wars and pollution on Earth and want to avoid that here. Your aggressiveness is harmful to them."

"We can agree to that," states the king, "We were not planning to move into the ocean."

Fayed says, "There is a group on Earth calling to preserve this world as is."

"The Serafim are aware," states Arla.

"I promise to lobby for that," I say.

"Thank you," says Arla, "Also, the felis on this world are a vicious and primitive species. An advanced genetic branch moved into space in ages past. They are far more powerful. You need to avoid them. In exchange for preserving this world, the Serafim can provide warnings if you get too close."

"Good to know," says Foxx.

"Thank you," states Fayed, "We hope for a mutually beneficial relationship."

Foxx asks, "Anything else?"

"Yes, he wants Marquis to know he remembers him well and is happy to help him anytime."

"I remember you well too, and thanks," says Marquis.

Later, an UNBI vehicle arrives to pick up its agents and their prisoners. Daniel Mason is arrested and granted a lenient sentence for his help with freeing the prisoners, bringing in the crew of the *Polyus*, and finding the miners. The sentence is suspended for his testimony against the *Polyus* crew. His teenage brother, Thomas Mason, is found innocent of any charges.

The Court of Carcassonne declares it best to give us a victory parade and celebration. With the proceeds from the metals, I decide to set up a trust to preserve Ross, to allow anyone to return to Earth and to start over, to establish a fund for Martian orphans, and to allow Seth to return to the jungle. Lucy, Bella, and Evelyn decide to stay on Crusoe Island to develop more food varieties for the people of Ross. The *Athena* becomes the center of a small horticultural college. Arla stays on Ross, too. She learns to communicate with us wherever we go, as Marquis and I explore the universe with our friends.